NIGHTS OF NO MOON

BY STEVE DUFFY

YOU ALWAYS KNOW A BAD HOUSE WHEN YOU SEE IT. The road has led you through some one-horse Midwest town, past the stoplight that swings in the prairie wind, past the bars and bowling alleys and tractor dealerships downtown, on past the cemetery into nothing at all, and just when you think you're into the long, lonely country again there's one more house by the roadside, and straight away you know it for what it is.

Imagine some old mansard place, clapboards warped from many winters, dirty lace curtains like cataracts in the staring sightless windows, a bare tree in the yard, leaves blown across the dead-grass lawn, a porch seat askew on a broken chain that creaks monotonously in the wind. It stands too high for its surroundings, this house, too remote from things, incongruous and unsettling. Driving on this lonely road, it feels as if everything you've passed has been like that humble country cemetery with its rows of modest gravestones, only now you're out into unconsecrated land, and here's some sort of mausoleum rearing up from the plains.

This house has known sadness—known madness, even. It's known fear and repression, thwarted ambitions and close harbored resentments, forty thousand nights of smoking lampblack and guttering candles and the high storms of winter rattling the window frames like a madman testing the bars of his cell. It's known sleepless nights, or else fitful dreams of death and what comes after. It's known black crepe and open coffins on trestles in the parlor. It's known blood-soaked towels in bowls of cracked porcelain, the blank demented vigilance of mirrors in empty rooms. Overwhelmingly, it's known the boredom bred of hopelessness, the melancholy of acceptance, the everyday demon of despair. And then there's the worst thing, the worst of all things: the thing that wears a new face each time it comes upon us, and so remains the best-kept secret of them all.

The dead weight of this knowledge has borne down on the house through the generations, lain on it like the impossible gravity of dead planets, pushed it down towards the black and sodden soil. And in that soil there are dark roots growing, reaching down among the bones of dead things, sucking something eternal from the deep places of the earth: the evil that was here before men gave this place a name, before the first peoples walked these plains, the cruelty that lies beneath all things, undying and indifferent. It comes up through the cellar walls like damp rot, it leaves its stains on the bricks and planks, and on the inhabitants too.

You drive past the house, and almost unconsciously you push down on the gas, wanting it gone from your rear view and from your consciousness as well. But not everyone can escape the bad things by driving faster and putting the good miles between themselves and the place that made them. You know that there will always be some who have no choice, the ones who'll live and die on the outskirts of everything, in these bad, bad houses. Linger here awhile. Come inside their dreams.

HE WAS LOOKING OUT of his attic bedroom window in the top of the house, a pale thin face in a room full of shadows. The last sliver of a waning moon was rising above the October fields, and he sensed straight away that tonight would be a bad one. Sure enough, once it got full dark he heard her. One time it sounded like she was right inside the house, screaming his name, but he kept silent and after a while her voice died away. The door to his room was locked, of course. *Keep out of her way, Ben,* his father had told him. *When she's like this you just keep out of her way.* He had very quickly learned to take that advice.

He thought he heard the sound of the Victrola from downstairs, warped and fluctuating as if it had barely been wound up, but when he pressed his ear against the door there was nothing; maybe it had been the wind in the chimneys. In the summertime she used to take the Victrola out on the porch to play phonograph records of Chopin's étude while she sat in the rocker and stitched, and the shade beneath the tree on the front lawn was cool and green, and the music sounded like the shade felt. He missed those times.

But this was autumn, and there was a gale stirring up from off the prairie, stripping the last of the leaves from the trees, shriveling the unharvested pumpkins with frost. It slashed razor-edged against the house, finding every crack, every weak place, and it carried on it the desolate smell of woodsmoke and decay. And on that wind came his mother's voice.

IT HURT TO THINK of the day when everything changed, that last good summer of his youth; still, Ben couldn't help but remember. He'd been over to town to see if the library had new books, and was almost home when he spotted some kind of ruckus in the fields behind the house, near the little stand of trees around the fishing hole. Running to see what it was, he saw his elder brothers, the twins George and Harold, arms linked to form a seat, hoisting someone between them back towards the house. Alongside them ran his father. His little sister Sally was following after, her wails carrying across the field in the still summer afternoon. Old Mose, the family dog, was barking from the kennel where he was tethered.

When Ben got close enough he could see it was his mother they were carrying. Her clothing was torn and disarrayed, and her head was lolling back. "What's wrong," he shouted, "what happened to Ma?" but nobody answered, they just kept on going and paid him no mind. "Get out of the way, Benjamin," his father told him, not bothering to look at him. Ben grabbed Sally and asked her what was the matter, but all she could tell him through her tears was "Something happened. I don't know."

Flavia the cook was standing at the back kitchen door. The men barreled straight past her, on into the house. Flavia intercepted both the younger children and told them to stay in the kitchen with her and not to bother the grown-ups. Their mama had had a mishap—those were the words she used, he remembered them so clearly—but everything would be all right. She made them syrup sandwiches as a treat, but his throat was all closed up with worry and he couldn't swallow. Sally was sniffling quietly, holding on to Flavia as she rocked her.

That evening it was Flavia who put them to bed, with their father a shadow in the dark hallway. Mother was all right, he said, choosing his words carefully; she'd had a mishap—again that phrase—and they'd need to be very quiet and good around the house till she got better. Later that night, Ben heard the noises for the first time. At first he'd thought it was Mose, that he'd gotten himself caught in some hunter's trap out in the woods. He went to the window and pushed

DEAR ABBEY

$\mathbf{M}$Y DEAR ABBEY, how I love your shuttered windows and darkened chambers, your winding corridors and cobwebbed ceilings, your hidden rooms and secret passages. But, my dear Abbey, how you *do* test my resolve.

Pardon me for grumbling, but maintaining the rambling haunts of Nightmare Abbey is a mission not without its share of headaches. For instance, those meddling neighbors are complaining once again about the condition of the grounds. They say they're not at all happy with the weeds surrounding the Abbey. So, I had all the weeds pulled, and planted fresh ones. I think the new ragweed and sagebrush look rather nice, but wouldn't you know it? The neighbors are still complaining.

That's trivial, of course, compared to this latest complication: I received a truly nasty, threatening letter from the local Health Department, stating I have until the end of the month to take care of the rats infesting the Abbey. Haven't I enough to do without having to feed and care for these creatures too? Nevertheless, I'm now placing large chunks of cheddar cheese in a corner of each room; and I've hired a groomer to come twice a week to bathe and brush the little fellows.

Here I go again, referring to Nightmare Abbey as though it were some ancient and storied structure made of crumbling brick and mortar. But I like to think of this old pile (of paper, ink, and glue) as a *home,* where good friends meet to share spooky stories, or to discuss a classic horror movie.

What's that? Can words and lines on a printed page frame a suitable dwelling for writers of the weird? Can fiction fabricate a home for readers seeking shelter from the storms of life? (My, how lyrical your questions, my friend.)

Now, I'm well aware, to paraphrase an old English proverb, a house does not necessarily make a home. Perhaps the novelist Jim Butcher, creator of *The Dresden Files*, said it best: "When the place has got history, family, emotions, worries, joys worked into the wood, that's when it gets a solid threshold." Nightmare Abbey is well furnished with such things, memorably supplied by a band of creative people who continue to faithfully submit to these pages. These creators continue to write the history and lay the bricks that give Nightmare Abbey the "solid threshold" that welcomes readers *home* with each new volume.

So, *please*, do come in. We'll never ask you to remove your shoes—or to even wipe your feet. We doubt your tired dogs would leave prints on our dusty floors anyway; and besides, we'd rather not be exposed to your fragrant tootsies. Beyond that, make yourself at home. We hope you'll find the accommodations…exceedingly uncomfortable.

Currently occupying our guest chambers are returning writers David Surface,

Helen Grant, Steve Duffy, Gary Fry, James Dorr, Matt Cowan, Gregory L. Norris, and John Llewellyn Probert, as well as our new visitors Ian Rogers and Ray Cluley. We've also dug up Maurice Level, E.F. Benson, and Perceval Landon to help raise the chill factor. After all, what's a spirited celebration without a few ghostly chaperones?

For that matter, what would an abbey be without a resident saint? We do have one, friends. In the acknowledgements section of my mammoth, 2008 anthology *Bound for Evil: Curious Tales of Books Gone Bad,* I described prolific illustrator Allen Koszowski as "a patron saint of the small press, whose artwork so beautifully embellishes many of my books." That descriptor is even more appropriate today, as Allen helps make the Abbey a hideous showplace worthy of the cover of *Haunted House & Garden.* Thanks, Allen!

Now, let's get back to that Jim Butcher quote. "When the place has got history, family, emotions, worries, joys worked into the wood, that's when it gets a solid threshold." That's probably when it gets a reputation for being haunted, as well.

Nightmare Abbey 3 is haunted.

Yes, this volume's stories are *haunting,* but the magazine itself is *haunted.* Allow me to explain.

When I started *Nightmare Abbey,* I was determined it would remain a non-themed publication. I state this because I have edited numerous books with themes. For instance, *Black Infinity,* Abbey's sci-fi sister, features a different theme in each volume, such as "Deadly Planets," "Strange Dimensions," and "Renegade Robots." (I'm currently sweating over volume 10: *Creature Features.*) But I felt that was the wrong approach for *Nightmare Abbey.* In fact, I shuddered at the idea. Too restrictive for writers, too monotonous for readers, too much work for me! (I'm not lazy, but I do enjoy getting an ocassional hour or two of shut-eye.) Which is why I solicit a wide variety of tales for the Abbey, stipulating only that the stories be *chilling.*

And what do I receive? Five outstanding stories featuring spooky houses. Four tales with tormented souls. Three featuring the creeping unknown. Two genuine ghosts—

And a partridge in a pear tree.

I certainly didn't mind, though. All the tales are excellent, with each writer putting a novel spin on the material. But then Matt Cowan turned in this volume's installment of his Horror Delve column, listing his favorite *haunted house* stories! I realized Abbey was trying to tell me something, so I threw in a couple more tales highlighting the hangouts of haints—including Perceval Landon's 1908 classic "Thurnley Abbey."

Note the cover blurb: Haunted Houses, Tormented Souls, and the Creeping Unknown. I know when I'm licked; but don't expect a theme in the next volume. Ain't gonna happen. At least, I don't *think* it's going to happen. Abbey?

By the way, *Nightmare Abbey 2* received a nice tip of the hat from *The Washington Post,* in Pulitzer Prize-winning author and critic Michael Dirda's article, "9 Strangely Wonderful Books Beyond the Bestseller List." We're exceedingly grateful for Mr. Dirda's kind words of praise:

Nightmare Abbey…isn't just an illustrated magazine, it's a showcase for essays on the horror genre and "chilling tales of terror," both old and new. In its just-published second issue, Gary Gerani reflects on the TV show Thriller, *inimitably hosted by Boris Karloff, while [Tom] English traces the influence of Theodore Sturgeon's novella "It" on swamp-monster comics. There are also excellent new stories by Helen Grant, Steve Duffy and many others, as well as the older, too-little-known tour de force "By One, by Two, and by Three," written by Adrian Ross, a Cambridge friend of ghost-story master M.R. James.*

(February 24, 2023; https://shorturl.at/hNQW0)

And with this last paragraph, I conclude yet another chapter in the life of my dear Abbey. I greatly enjoy hanging out with you, but the hour is late, and already there's a faint glow on the eastern horizon. The security of the coffin is calling. Ah, quiet repose and the sweet touch of cool silk. Do be a pal, and lower the lid for me.

Tom English
New Kent, VA

NIGHTMARE ABBEY

3

HAUNTED HOUSES • TORMENTED SOULS
AND THE CREEPING UNKNOWN

DEAR ABBEY .... TOM ENGLISH   3

SPECIAL FEATURES

HOME IS WHERE YOU'RE HAUNTED .... MATT COWAN   61

HORROR FLYING HIGH:
REVISITING *NIGHT OF THE EAGLE* .... JOHN LLEWELLYN PROBERT   108

STORIES

NIGHTS OF NO MOON .... STEVE DUFFY   5

THE GREAT MAN .... JAMES DORR   18

SEEING IS BELIEVING .... HELEN GRANT   25

THE ONE THAT GOT AWAY .... GARY FRY   37

THE TEST: CONFRONTATION .... MAURICE LEVEL   47

NIGHTLIGHT .... IAN ROGERS   50

CATERPILLARS .... E. F. BENSON   70

THAT MADDENING HEAT .... RAY CLULEY   75

STORE IN A COOL, DARK PLACE .... GREGORY L. NORRIS   85

AN ABSENCE OF MALICE .... JOHN LLEWELLYN PROBERT   91

THE PIONEERS OF PIKE'S PEAK .... BASIL TOZER   101

CLIMBING .... DARRELL SCHWEITZER   123

THURNLEY ABBEY .... PERCEVAL LANDON   129

LOST RIVER BOYS .... DAVID SURFACE   139

COVER AND INTERIOR ILLUSTRATIONS: ALLEN KOSZOWSKI
PHOTO ART: NATU SHABBEY
EDITOR AND PUBLISHER: TOM ENGLISH

www.DeadLetterPress.com   ISBN-13: 979-8-9862307-4-0

up the sash. The noises continued, only now it was clear they were coming from inside the house. What was worse, he recognized the voice.

BEN BECAME FAMILIAR with the cycle of his mother's madness, how it came with the moon's dying, and waned when nights were brightest. At dark of moon it was very bad indeed. Sleep was impossible, and Ben would imagine the rest of the family sitting up like him and listening behind their locked doors, in rooms that had become adjacent cells in an asylum. Only with the coming of dawn would it quiet down.

His mother never did get better. She hardly spoke; she never went out anymore, and soon enough no one came to visit her. She could stare at her family for minutes at a time with no hint of recognition. Questions they asked her would go unanswered. Nothing could hold her interest, and nothing could prompt her to react. Where once she'd been busy all day around the house with chores and cleaning, now she seemed to have lost all energy—more than that, all interest in everything and everybody. Instead she'd wander from room to room, looking for something she'd lost without knowing what it really was. If anybody spoke to her or laid a hand on her arm she'd look at them thoughtfully but quizzically, doing her best to place them from some long-ago encounter, then after a second or two she'd discard them as an irrelevance and carry on with her fruitless search.

When it came dusk she'd generally be found by one or other of the windows on the western side of the house, where she could see the sun go down behind the trees that fringed the pond. She'd press her forehead against the glass, at the spot where a white streak had appeared overnight in her hairline, and watch the starlings rise in a great flock, a thick twisting cluster in the shape of a bad dream.

That was the hour when Father would take her to her room, sit with her for a minute while she drank her draught, then kiss her on the forehead and lock the door behind him as he left. What happened next had everything to do with the moon, and in the months and years to come they came to fear its phases.

"WHAT'S HAPPENED TO MA?" Sally used to ask their father. He'd shake his head and tell her, "She's not well, sweetheart, she had a bad shock that made her ill. You must be quiet and good, and not bother her." At first she couldn't accept it, and she spent a long time trailing after her mother and crying, but after a while she no longer wanted to be in the room with her. "Is it really Ma?" she once asked, and Ben hadn't known how to answer her.

For Ben's part, those questions went too close to the bone. He didn't want to believe that something like this could happen to someone he loved. If his mother could suddenly become so hopelessly dislocated, who could say what else might change in a world that had once seemed unchanging? What if the same thing happened to him; what if he became a pale sort of ghost, haunting a house he no longer recognized? Suppose he were to fall asleep one night, and wake up screaming in the moonless dark? Better, he thought, not to have a mother than to have one in name only. Better to withdraw from her as she'd withdrawn from them. And so he told his sister, "I don't know, Sal. She had a mishap."

His older brothers took it badly too, of course. They spent most of their time either closeted away in their attic room or out of the house altogether. They were dutiful: they never missed a turn taking care of Mother, but outside of that they steered clear of her whenever they could, wary perhaps of the way she would behave around them, which since the mishap was not the behavior of a normal loving mother toward her sons. There were times she would stare at them too deliberately, for too long, and the expression on her face would set their skin to crawling in ways they didn't like to contemplate.

Neither George nor Harold seemed to have much use for their father anymore. From time to time Ben would hear raised voices in the study where Father went to hide away from the new reality. These altercations would usually end with one or other of the boys storming out and slamming the door behind them before stomping off upstairs. And so Ben was left to deal with day-to-day matters pretty much by himself, with only Flavia to provide any comfort or any help. And even she would lock herself away on nights of no moon.

As for Mose, the old lurcher, he'd vanished not long after Mother's mishap. Ben supposed he'd run away, and added Mose's betrayal to the list of things that had changed in this dismal new reality. One afternoon, though, he saw his brothers digging out near the trees. When he went over to investigate, they were placing a bundle wrapped in bloody rags into the ground. By the side of the hole lay a cross made of planking with the name of Mose carved into it. Ben asked them what had happened, but they just shook their heads. "Can't be helped, Benny," George had said. "He was a good old feller, wasn't he?" Trailing back towards the house he saw his mother's face at the back parlor window. The low sun was glinting off the glass and struck into his watering eyes, but he believed that she was smiling.

"DOGS AND WOLVES, they howl at a full moon," Ben's father told him, soon after the mishap. "Birds, they tend to get spooked. Hares and rabbits, they run and run, no one knows why. Doodlebugs get crazy. But when the moon wanes, now, when it dwindles: the animals are smart, they hide away. They know it's no time to be abroad, and they stay inside their houses. And we need to be smart as well, Benjamin." Leaving unspoken the corollary; that his mother was one with the animals now.

Those nights were hard on him. He'd watch the sickle moon slide over the open fields and see monsters in every cloud that sailed across its blade. It was a relief to see it disappear from the eastern attic window, but he also knew what would be happening by the time it was showing through the window on the west. Sleep was impossible: he'd sit with his knees drawn up beneath his chin and wait for the screaming to start.

His father would add an extra shot of the special medicine to her evening draught at that time of the month, and he'd always make sure the door to Mother's room was locked by sunset. The room had been filled with framed photographs in former days, and on the walls were samplers she'd sewn herself. Ben remembered one that showed a woman kneeling by a tree-lined pond holding a mirror to her face: *Prudence*, it said, and around the edges, *When this you see, remember me.* Another showed the same woman standing in front of a house that was clearly meant to be their own, and that one said *What is paradise, but a garden in the summertime?* Before long, photographs and samplers alike had been removed for safekeeping, or else smashed all to pieces. In some places even the paper had been scraped off the wall, clawed down to the lath and plaster as if by some caged beast grown ferocious.

The noises she made would rise in pitch and volume as the moon climbed to its highest point, its influence on her madness at its strongest in that hour. At first it would be just a broken sort of gabbling, as if the room was filled with a dozen people all chattering at once, in voices both low and high. From there it would rise to shrieks and bellows, and occasionally you could make out words, terrible words, that Ben scarcely knew the meaning of, and would have been ashamed to ask about. As the dying moon sank towards the trees out back, the cottonwoods that fringed the pond, her howls turned into a dreadful sort of low moaning, a mixture of desire and despair it seemed, and this would be the sound that haunted him as he wrapped himself in the coverlet and tried to sleep.

ONE JANUARY MORNING at the breakfast table George and Harold announced that they were enlisting, that they wanted to join the army to go fight the Kaiser over in France. Before their father could respond, their mother said, very distinctly, "You won't go to France. You'll die here. You'll go into the American dirt." And no one spoke. Ben guessed it was an honorable means of escape. He didn't grudge them, though it left only him and Pa to deal with things. It felt to Ben like there was no getting around it, unless another war should come along to free him too. So the brothers signed up, and

Ben inherited their room in the attic, as far away in the house as a person could get from Mother's room. But they never saw a war: both the boys died of the Spanish influenza that spring, at Camp Funston in Kansas.

The telegram boy came pedaling up to the house with the news, racing a huge black roil of cumulus piling up in the south. Mother was out on the porch sitting in the rocker, humming the same fragment of a tune over and over to herself. The sullen sound of thunder was coming closer, and the first forks of lightning were arcing from the storm clouds.

Stepping slowly as though sleepwalking, Mother came down into the yard to meet the boy, Sarah Ekstrom's eldest. With a squeal of brakes, he skidded to a halt and leaned his bike against the fence. There was a smile on her face as he handed her the envelope, and the first heavy raindrops began to pound down upon the dust. Father found her there maybe an hour later, soaked to the skin, smiling still, clutching the telegram unopened at her breast.

ON A HOT AFTERNOON of busy flies and silence, Ben and Sally were in the backyard, the house being intolerably stifling on such days. After a little while Mother came out to them, a thing that was so unusual that they gaped at her in surprise. "Come with me, children," she said, with an animation she hadn't shown since the day of her mishap, and rarely beforehand. It was more disturbing than it was reassuring. "I've got something to show you. Come with me into the trees." She took their hands, urging them towards the stand of cottonwoods.

They hung back, as they would have done if a stranger had bid them follow her. "Come along," she said, and her fingers closed around their hands with painful force. Sally began to whimper no, pulling back against her, digging her heels in the dirt. "Hush now," Mother said, "don't be afraid. There's something you have to see. Something's waiting for you by the pond." Sally began to scream. Mother took no notice, kept dragging them both towards the trees. By now Ben was yelling too.

Flavia the cook must have heard the ruckus, for here she was running all ungainly after them, elbows out, her full, aproned bosom shimmying side to side. She caught up with them when they were maybe halfway to the cottonwoods, and snatched at the children so that they were jerked hard in a tug-of-war between her and their mother. "You come on back to the house, children," she said urgently. "Missus Bella, stop now, you don't want to go there."

"Leave them alone," hissed their mother, in a voice they would not have recognized a year ago. "Damn you, you leave them alone." She called Flavia a foul name, one they'd never heard from any woman's lips.

Flavia didn't back down. "Missus," she said, "you've no call to say such a thing." And she redoubled her grip on the young ones. By now Father was hurrying towards them from the house, and Mother must have seen him, because she let go of the children. While Flavia was gathering them to her, Mother hauled off and hit her in the face as hard as she could. Flavia went stumbling backwards, landing in a heap with the children, and if their father hadn't separated the two women Mother would have struck her again.

Father grabbed at her arm, twisted it behind her before she could land the blow. Using all his strength he took hold of his wife by both elbows and pulled her away. Shakily, Flavia got to her feet. There was blood all down the front of her white apron.

"Mr. Holmsted, I'm leaving," she said. It sounded like her nose was broken. "Sir, you need to do something, for your children's sake as well as for hers." She seemed about to say something more, but she looked at Ben and Sally and bit her tongue. Holding her apron up to stem the blood, she turned and went back to the house.

Mother was no longer struggling. She relaxed into her husband's grip as a girl might swoon into the playful embrace of a beau, blinking as if suddenly aware of the bright sun overhead. "What a pleasant afternoon," she said, in something like her normal voice. "Why, Chester, we should have a picnic, don't you think? I'll ask Flavia to make us a pitcher of lemonade."

By suppertime Flavia was packed and gone. From then on a slow, sullen girl came from town twice each day to cook breakfast and an early evening meal. The times of her visits were calibrated to the changing seasons, and she contrived never to be in the house before the sun rose or after it had set. More than once Father offered her better pay and a live-in position, but each time she refused.

ABOUT THE SPECIAL MEDICINE: soon after his mother's mishap a new bottle had appeared on the top shelf in the pantry. The label on it said "Papine" in flowery writing alongside a drawing of a poppy, and informed the reader that the preparation was made in London for Battle & Co of St Louis. The small print said: "'Papine' is the anodyne or pain-relieving principle of opium, the narcotic or convulsive elements being eliminated. 'Papine' contains one grain of morphine to each fluid ounce." Then some complicated medical business, and after that "Dose: one half to one drachm, repeated as may be necessary."

Ben didn't know what a drachm was, but on evenings of the dark moon he'd watch his father add a spoonful or two of the Papine to the draught of nerve tonic Mother took before retiring. "It's mother's medicine, son," his father said when he asked him what it was. "Leave it alone now, don't you touch it." With a finger that had recently begun to tremble just a little, he traced the words on the label. "Papine," he mused. "From the Latin *papaver*, or poppy. *Papaver somniferum*, bringer of sleep."

After Father went blind the duty of preparing the draught passed to Ben. He was careful not to waste the precious medicine: two good spoonfuls, no more, and only when the moon was all but swallowed up. Once it was on the wane, one would be enough: this would hold her until the next cycle. His instinct was always to up the dose, but he didn't dare.

When the bottle was near empty, he took it into town and asked the druggist for some more. The old man seemed dubious, but he sold him another bottle anyway. "You got no business with that stuff, son," he observed.

"No sir," he said, "it's for my mother. My pa gives it to her." A white lie, it didn't matter. "He's indisposed, can't come into town, so he sent me."

The druggist grunted, and pursed his purpled lips. "Well, you be sure to tell your pa that's dangerous medicine, you hear? Stuff like this—" he held the bottle up to the window, so the light shone redly through— "it don't need much to be a fatal dose, understand? Fatal," and he looked over his half-moon glasses into Ben's wide eyes.

"Oh gosh, we'll be careful, sir," he promised. "Dad will. I mean, we all of us will." But the druggist didn't break his gaze.

"It might only need three, four times the stated dose," he said, very deliberately, stepping it out with a fingertip on the side of the glass. "It might be that easy to go wrong. It's been known to happen, son, many a time."

All at once he realized what the druggist was really telling him. In panic he snatched at the bottle, but the druggist caught at his hand and held it clenched in his own, until something he saw in Ben's face satisfied him and he relinquished his grip.

All the way home Ben held the bottle away from him, the way he might have held some small yet venomous creature. Back at the house he stored it away on its shelf, and went to tell his father he'd carried out his chores. "Thank you, Benjamin," he said, his lined and troubled face turned towards the warmth of the sun as it shone through the window. "You're a good boy." Ben thought again of what the druggist had told him, and decided to say nothing to his father.

HIS FATHER HAD GONE blind soon after the boys died. One morning Ben was woken by his mother's banging on the locked door of her room. He went looking for his father, who kept the key and normally released her well before breakfast. He found him sitting on the side of his bed. He was still in his nightgown, hair wild from the pillow, staring into space with eyes that seemed to have gone pale as pond ice overnight. "Is that you, son?" he asked, not even turning his head, and Ben realized that another prop had been knocked away from his defenses.

The doctor came to the house and certified it, said there was nothing to be done. Weirdly, Father seemed content to hear it, as if the diagnosis had given him permission to abstain from his duties as head of the house. Before long he was dressing himself and coming down unaided to his study each morning, where he'd spend the rest of the day at his desk. Ben wondered if there was a physical cause behind it, an illness or something hereditary. It seemed to him that it ought to be possible to wish yourself blind, to voluntarily turn your back on the vision of an imperfect world. He imagined himself in his father's place, so overwhelmed with sorrow that even the four walls of his own room became unendurable, because they reminded him of another, happier time. To be so sad that to look in the mirror was more than you could bear.

When Ben went into the study, he'd sometimes crouch directly in front of his father, staring into his aimless eyes, wondering if he could still remember how his last remaining son looked, thinking how it would be to forget his own face. Experimenting, he found that he could find his way around the house perfectly well with his own eyes closed. With lids tight shut, he would try to read the contours of his own face through his fingertips, but it made no sense to him: it could have been anyone. When he opened his eyes again, he was almost startled to find his own familiar face staring back at him in the mirror.

IN THE MONTHS that followed, life became increasingly lonely for Ben. If he struggled to adapt to the family's self-imposed banishment from the outside world, he tried not to let it show. It was something he'd taken for granted, their social erasure, and this in itself was puzzling to him. There were times when he wondered if Mother's mishap had been some sort of a judgement on them, that this was no more than they deserved. Maybe that was how the town saw it, too. At first it had felt uncomfortable when people stopped calling by the house, or when former friends would cross the street to avoid him. *But then*, he asked himself, *what would you do?* Probably they were just as embarrassed

as he was. He'd sooner avoid people than even try to explain to them what had happened.

When school had reopened that first summer after the mishap, he'd been told by his father that both he and Sally had been withdrawn, that they would be schooled at home as children often had been in his father's generation. And yet no books were given to them, no lessons, no structure imposed on their day. After Father went blind, of course, even this pretence of home-schooling came to an end. Directionless, Ben found himself gravitating to his old favorites, rereading them over and over, searching for the comfort of familiarity.

He knew Sally didn't have his resources, that she was too young to rescue anything, Crusoe-style, from the wreck of their childhood. He did his best to distract her by reading aloud to her, or thinking up new games they could play outside. But he didn't know any of the games girls liked to play, and when he read from *Tarzan of the Apes* or *The Rover Boys* he could sense her attention faltering. It had been different when Flavia was still around: she'd been able to take Sally out of herself, to stand in place of a mother who had overnight turned into a sort of uninvited guest, a ghost from ancient generations who just happened to haunt their house, having long forgotten why. He no longer saw much use in wishing for the old days to come back.

ONE TIME BEN WAS looking for his sister when he heard voices from the back drawing room. It was his mother, talking to Sally in a soft and loving tone, soothing her as she sobbed and sniffled. He crouched at the half-closed door and peered through the crack at its hinge. Sitting in the rocking chair was his mother, creak-creak back and forth on the polished boards, ever so gently. She was holding Sally in her lap, humming tender nonsense to her. The sight took him unawares: it knocked down all of his defenses, caught him up in an overwhelming rush of emotions. He was about to run into the room and join them, when he realized what his mother was actually doing.

With one hand she was gripping a wriggling Sally close against her, crooning a nonsense string of nursery consolations. In the other hand was a long hatpin, with which she was pricking at the exposed skin of his sister's leg with slow and gentle deliberation, murmuring a new endearment each time she stuck her with the pin and drew a little dot of blood.

He couldn't help it: he shoved the door open so it slammed against the wall. "No, Ma!" he yelled. "Stop it! Leave her be!" His mother jerked back in surprise, the chair lurched backward and Sally managed to squirm free. She pushed past him into the hall, crying inconsolably, running towards no comfort or succor but only some lonely hiding place. Ben was left to confront his mother. Who knows what he might have said or done? But he saw the way she was looking at him, that distorted travesty of a smile, and what he saw sent him running after his sister. That night, though the moon was not yet at its faintest, he lay awake for fear of dreaming, seeing in his mind's eye the way his mother's lips curled back from her teeth, her teeth that seemed more stained now than previously, longer, sharper.

AND THEN THERE CAME the day of the last and worst mishap, in the winter of his thirteenth year. Ben was walking home from town, just as he had been on the day of the first. The sun had come out after a thick fall of snow the night before, and the glare off the snow-fields caused him to screw up his eyes when he spotted a figure in back of the house. It was coming from the direction of the bare-branch woods, the blackest stain on all that world of white, and he could see it was his mother, heading for the house. He flashed back to the summer's day when he'd seen the original mishap, or its aftermath, from this exact same spot on the road. He scrambled down into the snowed-up ditch by the roadside, floundered up through the drifts into the flat fields.

He ran to meet her, wondering what she was doing outdoors. She wasn't wearing a winter coat, just her indoors clothes, but the cold didn't seem to bother her. She beamed as he came near, and waved eagerly with both arms. "Benjamin!" she hailed him, and he could scarcely believe it. She hadn't called

his name in that way—in a normal way—in an age, it seemed. "Dear Ben! Goodness, there you are! Shouldn't you be in school?"

"It's not a school day, Ma," he said, not wanting to overburden her with details of the way things had changed. "Say, aren't you awful cold out here in the snow?"

"I must tell your father," she said, and she refocused her ecstatic smile on the house. "Come, come, come."

"Tell him what, Ma?" he asked uncertainly.

"Why, tell him where I've been," she said, sweeping past him, trailing a hand to beckon him follow. "Who I've met. Tell him all about Sally."

"Where is Sally?" Somewhere back in the cottonwoods, he supposed. "I told her she wasn't to go out there, was she wandering?"

"Oh Ben, don't fuss so," she said. "Come along. We'll go and see Father together, and we'll tell him everything." But Ben was looking at the smooth crusted snow, at the footprints that stretched between the trees and the house. A single line of prints trailed behind his mother, but there were two sets heading in the other direction. Two people had gone into the trees. One was his mother; the other person had been smaller, and in some places there were drag marks showing instead of footprints.

He turned back towards the house, and what he saw froze him worse than any winter could. The back of his mother's long silk skirt was stained with thick dark blood, soaked through the fabric so that it clung against her body as she strode away from him. Here and there he could see trickles and smears of red in her path. So much blood. Had she come upon some dead and butchered animal?

For what seemed a long time he simply couldn't move. When he was able, he ran after her as fast as he could, but by then she was already inside the house.

He found her in his father's study. She was kneeling in front of his chair, both his hands in hers, and she was talking in that same persuasive manner she'd been using outside. Now it seemed every bit as disconcerting as her wildest outbursts or her most profound silences. "It's a marvelous thing, dear," she was saying. "Just marvelous. You'll never guess."

Ben wanted to say something, to warn his father though he didn't know of what, but he couldn't. He just stood in the doorway and watched.

"Bella?" His father's filmy eyes were flicking back and forth, searching for her image, the lost likeness of his wife, a white ghost in a white snowfield. "Bella, you're... What's happened? Tell me what's happened. Are you all right?"

"You simply can't imagine," she said, and her voice became almost ecstatic. Whether from the cold of the snow or from her exertions, her cheeks were reddened. She looked more alive than ever she'd been since her mishap. "He was there, Chester. I met him."

"Met who?"

"Why, *him*," as if the very pronoun ought to suffice. "*Princeps corvorum, princeps lutum*. The ancient of days."

In the doorway Ben gasped. The family hadn't been to church since the mishap, but he knew that his father had prayed every Sunday until his blindness overcame him and he lost sight of God. Had the Lord managed to find his mother, in the unholy remoteness of her solitude?

"He asked for the thing that was dearest to me," his mother was saying. "He really wanted George and Harold, the ones I loved the best, but they were taken, they were stolen from me by the stupid flu and so how could I give them to him? But the master showed me favor, he was... he was merciful." There was a sigh and a tremble in her voice. "Oh, Chester, you wouldn't believe, he's so benevolent, he saw what little I could offer and he accepted it. The widow's mite."

Again that cold. It was clutching deep inside Ben's chest, shriveling him up with fear. *Two sets of tracks leading out to the trees.*

"I don't know what you mean." His father's words were breathless, carried on some trembling medium less substantial than air. "Bella, for God's sake, what did you *do*?"

"Why, I gave him Sally," she said happily. "A sacrifice was demanded, I offered him our daughter Sally, and my offering was accepted." She sighed again. "He was content."

His father's face was twisted all out of shape. It looked like he was trying to scream, but no sound could come out. Ben would come to understand that look in the years ahead. It was the look you wore when your heart had been broken, and the pieces kept on trying to beat as one.

"No, Ma!" Ben blurted. "You didn't! You couldn't have!"

His mother turned in surprise, and now he could see that all of her skirt was covered with blood, seeping through the pale green shantung, staining it deep crimson. "Look, Chester, Ben's here," she said. And still she was smiling. "I didn't offer him *Benjamin*. He wanted the thing I loved the most. He told me, you know—he told me so I understood," she said, turning back to his father. "The old one. The crowblack master." She lowered her voice, a secret that was only for her husband's ears. "He rutted on me, Chester. There, in the shade of the trees out by the pond. Rutted on me, like an animal. He was well pleased in me." And she lifted her bloody skirts before her husband's sightless eyes.

Ben ran screaming from the house. He was making for the trees at first, panting Sally's name over and over, but what remained of his courage failed him when he came near. He turned back across the field towards the road, towards town, towards the last chance of sanity and an end to things. Behind him, the house closed in on itself like time and space collapsing, its planks and bricks, its very atoms, unequal to the gravity of the horrors that lay inside.

IT WOULD BE a long time before Ben went back to the house. That afternoon he came staggering into Swinney's feed store, panted a few words and then collapsed, and Mrs. Swinney took him into the back parlor and gave him hot tea to drink. He sipped at it while he told the story, as much of it as he could make sense of or bear to tell, to Sheriff Rawlins and his deputy. The men went grim-faced up the road to the house, and they didn't come back until night was falling. By that time Ben was in bed running a temperature. The little they told him about what they'd found seemed hardly to penetrate it.

When he was up and about again, a week or so later, they explained to him that his mother was dead. He never saw the body, though: perhaps if he had, then things might have turned out differently. His father was ill, the sheriff said, a brain-fever, a breakdown, and he'd have to go to the hospital. This turned out to be a sanatorium in the state capital, which was where he stayed until his death some five years later.

Something had happened between his parents, was all they'd say about that day. Well, Ben could work that much out for himself. But when he asked about his sister Sally, the faces of the townsfolk grew grim and closed. She was dead as well, that's all they'd tell him, and they cut him off sharp when he asked them how it happened. This was how it was in those days: there were things a boy shouldn't have to know, and folks thought it a kindness to leave him in ignorance. It was left to the town crazy, Bill Tuttle, to offer up a version of the truth.

"She's dead," Bill Tuttle told him. This was in the alley behind the feed store where Bill would try to make himself useful, carrying sacks and smashing up crates for nickels and dimes. "Some bad thing got her." His face was slack and lumpy like a scarecrow left all seasons in the field. "She went out into them woods back of your old place, and she was just turned inside out, was all. I seen her, they don't know what I see, and I seen her, how 'bout that?"

"Were you there?" Ben asked him. "When it happened?"

"Me? No," shaking his head vehemently. "Old Bill, everybody knows where he was. I seen you running, yes I did, standing right here and I seen you running past the boneyard crying and a-hollering. It was snow on the ground, winter of '18. No—" and here his voice became thick and secretive—"no, I seen her alright, but I seen it at night, out in the trees. He showed me."

"Who showed you?" Ben was aghast to think that his sister had been the subject of scrutiny, that people like Bill Tuttle might have stood around her and pointed at her corpse.

"The big boss." It seemed to Ben that the simpleton had surprised himself with what came out of his mouth. Bill held both hands to his face, peeked around the edges as if he couldn't hide the truth even if he tried, couldn't help but tell someone his grand and awful secret. Did he mean the sheriff, Ben asked?

Bill Tuttle snorted. "Sheriff Rawlins? Hell no. The night-time guy. Night-time's when he comes, 'cause he's the boss of everything that's dark. *Him*, you know. Ain't you seen him? Your mama seen him, your sister too, I reckon." Hissing now, spraying spittle on Ben's face: "You'd sure 'nough know him if you seen him. The crowblack boss." And with that, having said too much already, he turned and ran off down the alley.

IN THE END it all came down to Ben, the last surviving member of the family. All this time he'd been living with the Swinneys; they'd lost their boy to the influenza the year before, and they were more than willing to take Ben in, make sure he went back to school and caught up on the education he'd missed. He was grateful to them, and he tried to be a part of their family, but maybe he'd been apart from all of that for too long. The day-to-day life of the town went on around him: behind his back folks would talk about "that Holmsted boy," tapping their heads conspiratorially. "It's a bad strain in the family," they'd tell each other, "don't reckon he'll ever be right again." None of it was real to him, that was the trouble, and the sight of a sickle moon still made him feel uneasy.

Sometimes he wondered if the kindly Swinneys might be feeding him Papine on the sly. Everything came to him through a sort of slow muffled haze, and nothing seemed real except the road out of town, its long slow bend heading north past the graveyard towards the family house. That and the ache in his heart, which was forever and always real. He didn't want to think about it, would go out of his way to avoid it most days, but sometimes it was the only mooring point he could find in the fog.

He would go to the house in his dreams, some nights. He'd be walking beneath vast scraped swathes of cloud through fields entirely flat and featureless, mile after mile, till up ahead he'd see the house, and beyond it the bare black trees, their silhouettes the cracked edge of the great skybowl overhead. And then, with no intervening passage of time or space, he was inside the house, which was all rooms and corridors, impossibly complex, a labyrinth from which there was no hope of escape. No matter which room he walked into, the same thing was there to greet him: a vision of his mother as he'd seen her that last time, silk and lace all sopping red, trailing little rills of blood along the corridors. Only in the last room, the one in which she'd turn around to face him, would he wake.

One winter they found poor Bill Tuttle dead in a snowdrift, back behind the feed store. Ben saw the smile on his face when they brushed the snow away, shards of ice like shattered spectacles around his staring vacant eyes, and deduced, rightly or wrongly, that he'd been both smiling and weeping at the moment of his death. The smile disturbed him; it brought back memories of the look he'd seen on his mother's face that last day at the house, the look he'd seen forever after in his dreams.

THERE WAS A LOT of talk in town as to what Ben might do with the old Holmsted place. Sell it, the smart folks reckoned: what would a boy of nineteen want with a big old dump like that? "And the memories," they added, not needing to elaborate. Others said they'd heard it had already been on the market all this time, that the old place was just going to rack and ruin because nobody would buy such a house of horrors. Both sides expected Ben to somehow wash his hands of the whole affair and light out for the cities.

As it happened, Ben had inherited everything, which meant what little money was left, together with the house and land, that whole stretch between the country road and the cottonwood trees. He thought long and hard about what to do, discussing the matter with no one, until one night he told the Swinneys he was beholden to them for their kindness, and he didn't intend to be a burden on their hospitality any longer. Mrs.

Swinney cried a little; the old man simply looked at Ben and said, "Son, don't feel you have to do anything you don't want. There's always a place for you here."

The way Ben saw it, he had no choice. It truly would be nigh on impossible to sell the house, what with recent history being so vivid in the communal memory. As for the acreage, there was no money on the land in the 1920s. All the farmers thereabouts were carrying debt already, and none of them could afford to go any further in the hole on fields that had never been under the plow. Over and above these practical considerations, part of him thought it was time to go back at long last, that five years was enough. It seemed to him he owed a debt to the memory of his lost ones, an obligation to try and lick the jinx that had come upon them. If he couldn't do that at the family home, he guessed he'd never do it.

And so he found himself waving goodbye to the Swinneys at the door of the feed store, the last five years of his life packed in the valise he carried at his side. Before him lay the road out of town, and at the end of it all the dark conundrums of his past, and possibly the answers that went with them. There were fresh spring flowers on the graves in the cemetery, where the various members of his family now lay in adjacent plots. In his dreams he'd walked this way many times since that last catastrophic day, trailing along for what seemed hours under dull grey clouds, but today the sky was a clean washed blue after light rain overnight, and no more than a mile of walking brought him to the house.

The clapboards were weatherworn and peeling, and some shingles had come off the roof where the eaves faced the prevailing wind. Several of the windows were holed and cracked; he guessed that was the weather as well. Boys from town did not come out here at Halloween to throw stones at the Holmsted place. He noted all these things, in part relieved that things did not look just exactly as they had when he'd seen them last. All around the house was overgrown, his mother's careful planting choked out with crabgrass and foxtail. A rough winter storm had split the fork of the front yard tree, bleached and splintered branches lying on the ground like bones on some old battle-field.

He walked up the creaking steps to the porch. The sheriff had given him the keys to the place, but it took a shoulder to get the front door open. Inside was a sour earthy smell of disuse, basements damp with groundwater and unfreshened by quick-lime. Everything seemed just slightly out of scale, that curious discrepancy we sense when revisiting as adults those places we've only known when we were young. Thick dust and cobwebs blurred the shape of once familiar things. In Ben's eyes they blurred the memories that went with those things, and he made no effort to brush them away.

ROOM AFTER ROOM, each holding a silent faded image of the past, old photographs in a scrapbook. It seemed to Ben that the passage of time had caused the air itself to atrophy, to solidify into thick fluff like the mildew that grows on dead plants. For the last five years of his dreaming, each of these rooms had been haunted by the image of his mother, and now he needed to check them one by one, to reassure himself that they'd been empty all along, probably.

There were still a few cans and jars in the pantry, one of them blown but long past reeking, just a black and crusted scab now. Up on the high shelf was a bottle, nearly full, of Papine. It had separated out to a chalky residue at the bottom and a thick reddish liquid at the top. The red stuff looked dangerous, the dark sticky sap of some poison plant growing in the woods. The white stuff, he thought, looked the way the air inside the house felt. He shook the bottle till its contents recombined to their natural consistency, looked at it for a moment, then took it over to the sink and poured it away.

He unpacked his valise in the room beneath the eaves that had once been his brothers', and later his own. The rest of the day he spent fixing up the broken windows, nailing boards across the frames until he could organize some glass and putty. When night began to fall he was up in the attic room, watching the moon's fragile crescent from the eastern window. When he was a child, he'd believed that a crescent moon was thin and brittle, whittled away to a shaving, but one night his brother George had shown it to him in a telescope, pointed out the rest of the dark disc, the shadow side. The thought of a dark planet at once fascinated and terrified him. He imagined it as the hardest blackest coal, or a cannon-ball of pig-iron shot across the sky. Now he wondered if that mass of black iron mightn't be a magnet for all the darkness in the world, all the madness that hides in the pit of the night.

He crossed to the opposite side of the room and gazed out towards the cottonwood trees and the pond. He'd expected it to be different now. Five years had passed, he was no longer a boy, and if death had stripped away his hopes, then surely it might also have stripped away his fears. What struck him instead as the failing moon rose high was a slow and halting apprehension that some things might be everlasting, sunk too deep for the efforts of men to uproot. What if the likes of him were insignificant, he thought, and left only passing traces on the earth? What if their houses were built on a kind of slow quicksand, that sucked you in and wouldn't ever release you? Suppose the only continuity was in suffering and horror?

We make our own gods, Ben. That's what Harold had suggested once, here in this very room; *they're the fairy tales we tell ourselves.* But what about the Bible, Ben objected, thrilled and alarmed in equal measure, and Harold just laughed and quoted that back to him, *God said, Let us make man in our image, after our likeness. You pays your money, kid,* he said cheer-fully, *and you takes your choice. Either way, it's all bunk, the game is rigged.* Back then Ben didn't know which one to believe, and he still wasn't sure. But in a world that seemed to be ruled by cruelty and happen-stance he couldn't help but ask himself: whichever version was true, whatever dogma you chose to follow, what manner of gods would you be serving?

After a while he fancied he could hear something, very faint, as if it was coming from a place beyond the trees, somewhere over the horizon, farther than the eye could see or the mind could imagine. Although it was so remote, he would still have known it anywhere. A boy will hardly forget the voice of his mother.

He listened, and now he knew it was inside the house, here with him, the way it had always been. The old song, screams and cries and whispers, the rising tide of madness that the dark moon drags across the earth, a voice that sang to him in the wind that shook the branches of the trees. Before long he understood that whatever thing was singing knew him too, and welcomed his return.

A WEEK OR SO LATER Ben paid a visit to the drugstore. The old man was feebler these days, hair thinned out to a white scrape across the mottled dome of his head, but he recognized Ben well enough. "Good day, sir," Ben said, "I was wondering could you sell me a bottle of the medicine I used to get for my mother, that Papine?"

"That stuff's off the market now," the druggist told him. "Stopped making it in nineteen and twenty, thereabouts. Why do you ask?"

"Is there any other like it? I haven't been sleeping too well these last few nights."

The druggist looked Ben up and down. "You mean it's for you this time?" He scratched his stubbled chin. "I'd say you're a tad young to be needing anything like that. It's not a thing you'd give to healthy people."

Ben just shrugged. The old druggist squinted at him as though he was something perplexing on a shelf. After a little while he said: "Heard you moved out of the Swinney place, that right? Moved back into the family home?" There were audible quote marks round the last two words.

"That's right, sir."

"Mm-hmm," he said. "Wait there one second." He disappeared behind the frosted-glass partition at the back of the store. When he returned, he was holding the familiar bottle. "Fact is, I ordered a fresh consignment, last time you bought it. It's been sitting in the storeroom all that time, what is it, five years now? I tell you what, it'd need

a damn good shake if someone was fixing to use it."

"I guess it would, sir," Ben agreed. *Papaver somniferum*, bringer of sleep.

"See here, where it's separated? This part is pure unadulterated morphine, son. Swallow enough of that straight off, why it could kill a man, understand?"

Again their eyes locked. "I recall you saying so, sir," Ben said levelly. "We had that conversation once before, didn't we?"

"We surely did," said the druggist. "I was hoping you'd remember." A few more seconds passed in silence, then he shrugged. "I'll put it on your account, son," he said, handing the medicine over to Ben. "Mind what I said. And don't go telling people about this arrangement of ours." Again the quote marks round "arrangement."

"I don't see people," Ben said, pocketing the bottle. "Not anymore."

AND SO WE END as we began, with a pale face staring from an attic window, a sharp crescent moon over autumn fields. In the night sky a billion ancient lights tremble on the threshold of extinction, while down below men shuffle through the rooms of their bad houses, and nothing ever really changes. Up ahead the road is country dark, and your headlamps are good for just a few dozen yards at a time. Drive on.

Steve Duffy lives and works in North Wales. His most recent collection of weird stories, The Faces At Your Shoulder, *was published by Sarob Press in 2023; he's already in the process of putting together his next. Steve was the winner of the International Horror Guild's award for Best Short Story 2000, and in 2015 he received the Shirley Jackson Award for Best Novelette.*

THE GREAT MAN

BY JAMES DORR

"YOU HAVE COME FROM THE EXECUTION, MONSIEUR?" a voice next to me asked.

"Eh, what?" I said, turning to gaze at an elderly man who had just sat beside me at the long table, a *pensionnaire* by the still-soldierly look to his clothing.

"The guillotining, my friend," he said. "The man who, this morning, kissed 'the Widow'—you went to see it?"

I shook my head, no. I had in fact been at pains to avoid it, no lover of capital punishment I, though I had seen the stark silhouette of the two upright poles, the gleam of dawn on the triangle between them, when I had hastened past the crowded town square that morning. But, no, it was business that brought me from England to this small town in the south of France and I hastened to say so, that it was no more than the thirst of my journey that had brought me here to this

dim-lit cafe for a quick glass of wine, adding only that, at least, the poor wretch on the scaffold had felt no pain.

"Ah," the old man said. "Yes, that is the theory. When Dr. Guillotin first proposed it to the Assembly in autumn of 1789, close after the storming of *la Bastille*, when Dr. Louis conceived the design of it—it had a curved blade at first, you know, more like that of an axe-head—and the German, Tobias Schmidt, constructed the first one, the hope had been that the blade would be so swift its victim would have had no time to suffer. Yet even then there were some who doubted—who said it was only the *shock* of the cutting that the knife's quick descent would suppress, while the trunk and head both still lived on for some moments. You know the story of Charlotte Corday?"

I nodded. I knew at least who she had been. "The one who killed Marat?"

The old man nodded. "The murderess of Jean-Paul Marat, yes. I was there when she was executed on 17 July 1793, only just old enough at the time to be one of the soldiers who stood guard below *la machine fatale*. A very young man, you see—not as I am now."

I couldn't help staring. He'd moved his left arm and I saw, for the first time, that his coat-sleeve hung empty from a point just above the elbow.

He smiled. "Not like now"—he raised his arm higher to be *sure* I saw it, even as he went on—"not yet with the *souvenir* your Viscount Wellington left me with in Spain in 1813, outside of Vitoria, even if it may have saved my life later. But I was a corporal then, even as the lieutenant commanding us in Paris in '93 had become a captain—Captain Sarbeau, who I'll speak more of later. Suffice it to say there was pain enough with *this* wound, when that best portion of my arm departed my body, and there was nothing of *its* surviving after its 'goodbye.' But I spoke of Corday...."

"Yes," I said, finding myself with a fascination in what he was saying, despite what I felt was my better judgment. I called to the *serveuse* to bring us a bottle as I bade him go on.

"One of the executioner's, Charles-Henri Sanson's, assistants was a carpenter named Le Gros, who had at the time been of Marat's faction. So after the blade fell—it falls with a double crash, you know, the second being the sound when it bounces back up from the hole the neck has been thrust through—it was he who held Corday's head up, gripping its hair in the fingers of his left hand, so everyone in the crowd could see it. But not content, his anger was so great, he opened the fingers of his other hand and slapped it in the face. Hard, with a *crack!*

"And everyone saw it. Even I saw it. The blood rushed to the cheek—to *both* her cheeks, Monsieur—turning them crimson even as her features twisted into a scowl, such was the indignity she was still able to feel at such treatment! And as for Le Gros, he was punished for this, for showing disrespect for the dead no matter how or why she came to be that way, but do you know what he said then in his defense? That she was *not* dead. That death does not come so soon. That even certain doctors have claimed it, among them the learned Pierre Gautier as early as 1767—even before the guillotine's time!—that a head might live on, maintaining its consciousness for as long as fifteen more seconds, provided only the blood still flows through the brain."

"Well, yes," I said, "but you do say yourself that that's only *opinion*, no matter how learned the doctors who've held it. And as for the grimace you say people saw, well that could be put down to the excitement of the crowd, could it not? People do fool themselves, thinking they've seen things they haven't really. And as for the crimson you saw on her cheeks, it could just have been blood from this Le Gros's fingers, which I dare say must have been stained with plenty."

The old man nodded. "Yes, it *could* have been that," he agreed. "Or just superstition. Do you know that in the years right after, during the time of the Directory, there were priests who wandered the countryside with thin red lines painted around their necks, claiming they, too, were the guillotine's victims? This was in support of the Royalists' cause, to show that, through God's grace, they had been resurrected—and many believed it. You see, we were all naive in those days.

"But then, after Napoleon came home from Egypt to become First Consul, when order returned to France, well, it's been science since then. Science, with experiments that can be proved—that's the answer these days, eh? Tell me, my friend, have you heard of Lavoisier?"

Once more I nodded. I was no scientist, but I did know of Antoine Lavoisier, claimed by some even to be the inventor of modern chemistry. "It was he, was it not," I replied, "who disproved the *phlogiston* theory—that there is some substance within burnable matter that disappears from it when it's set afire? Was it not he who, of course with our own English scientist Priestly, showed that, rather, oxygen is *added* to things when they are combusted? As I recall, he did this in part by studying the behaviors of animals in various mixtures of air, showing the heat their bodies produced to be similar to that of fire as well."

"Yes," the old man said. "He had his own theory, that there is an *element* of heat—he called it 'caloric'—that, when added with air to any material, will cause it to burn, whether rapidly as in flame, or more slowly as in rusting or decay. Or, as you say, in the motions of life itself—something that what I wish to tell you, to prove that which you seem not yet ready to accept, may touch again upon later. But for now, you know, do you not, that Lavoisier, as well, was a victim of *Sainte Guillotine*? That less than a year after Charlotte Corday, he, too, mounted the scaffold?"

"An abomination," I said. "Yes, I knew that. That such a man should be killed...."

"Yes, an abomination indeed, though there were what people thought then were good reasons. But as I say, we were all mad then, in our ways, naive and easily diverted from the truth. Lavoisier, though, was one who sought truth, as was another I shall mention shortly, a great man, too, in his way. One who was, some say, Lavoisier's student, some say who in time became a general who died at Waterloo, and yet whose body was never recovered. One who, some say, still lives—which is why I shall not mention his name to you, lest he still uses it, though it is more likely he would have changed it.

"But, as for Lavoisier," he continued, getting finally back onto the track of what he had been saying, "did you know he, too, when he knew he had no more hope of preventing his execution, proposed an experiment? I did not see this. By then Lieutenant Sarbeau and I had been mustered to war, to aid in retaking Belgium and Holland from the alliance, including your Britain, that had earlier in 1793 risen against us. But I did hear of it.

"This is what Lavoisier proposed: that as soon as the blade fell he would begin blinking. He would blink his eyes as many times as he could, even as his head was lifted to show the crowd, while one of Sanson's assistants would count the times. This I know well—the assistant was bribed, yes, to carry his part out—but there is no reason to doubt his honesty. And what he reported afterward was that the severed head of Lavoisier blinked no less than *eleven times*."

The old man paused then while I called for more wine. "This is still no more than hearsay," I protested, yet, as I say, I found I could not suppress a desire to hear more of this *pensionnaire*'s gruesome theory. And so I prompted: "But, if you have more proof...."

The old man nodded. "Yes," he said. "You know these were troubled times for France, and many things went on behind the scenes. Many machinations—some of which affected us in the army. In September 1795, the Directory was formed to replace the Committee of Public Safety, and so we marched back to Paris under a new command, that of Napoleon, to assure the fairness of these new elections. Then we went back to war, finally in Egypt where our commander, as I have said, having heard chaos had once more taken over in France, was forced to return to become First Consul. And still later, Emperor.

"And as for us, Lieutenant Sarbeau, like I, young and hale, then became a captain, and I, who had had some education, some time later received my own rating as well as a post as adjutant to Sarbeau. Thus, together, under the Emperor we fought first at Naples, then in Saxony, finally in the invasion of Portugal until, Napoleon himself in the north now, we fought the grinding series of battles we later called the Peninsular War...."

"And where you met Wellington," I interrupted. "And who you would meet again."

"Yes," the old man said. "Where we fought your Arthur Wellesley, still just Viscount Wellington then, and where, in time, I lost my arm, thus precluding my own meeting him again. But, as for my Captain Sarbeau, well, while what I have to say ends before Waterloo, as for *him* I will leave you to draw your own conclusion."

The old man paused then, sipping his wine slowly. Finally he went on. "Now the time comes to tell you of the man I will not name—I'll simply call him the 'Great Man' now. He was not then of the army, nor a politician, nor of the nobility either, I think, yet behind the scenes, as we were to discover, he wielded much power. He knew Napoleon, that much is sure, and may well have been one who had influence on that man's rise to power.

"Be that as it may, it was after I had lost my arm in the Peninsular War, after France had been driven from Spain, that I and my captain were convalescing in a village not far from here, I to recuperate from my wound, and as for Sarbeau, simply because there was no place to send him. France had fallen. The Emperor had been defeated in Russia, Paris was occupied, Louis XVIII had been placed on the throne, and the Emperor then sent in exile to Elba.

"And yet there were rumors. Rumors flew in all directions in that January of 1815, some that the Great Man himself had been killed, perhaps as early as twenty years before, some that the Emperor had plans to rise once again. And it was during *this* time of chaos that we met the Great Man.

"It was January, as I say, nearly the end of the month, when Captain Sarbeau and I received a summons to present ourselves at a certain chateau, one that had not been lived in, or so we had thought, since that earlier chaos of the Directory. Even for the south it was cold, with ice in the rivers, so we bundled ourselves in our winter clothing and rode that night to where we were told, I myself as best I could with just one arm,

and so presented ourselves as requested. At the gate we were met by servants with torches—servants as if we were still in the days of the *ancien régime*—and helped with our outer coats, then ushered into a room so heated that, had we been clothed in our summer uniforms from Spain, we would still have felt some amount of discomfort.

"And then we were left there, alone, in a room filled with apparatuses of all description, great casks and boilers—a steam engine of some kind—retorts and pipes from which one could hear bubblings, and, sitting before us in a huge, throne-like chair, covered from chin to toe with a thick blanket, a figure we both recognized as the Great Man.

"We didn't know what to do. First the captain, then I, saluted, although, as I said, the Great Man was no soldier, at least to our knowledge. Nor did he return the salutes we offered but simply bade us, in a harsh, rasping voice, to turn around, several times, then strip our jackets and waistcoats from us, I with my one arm and Captain Sarbeau, who was built like an ox then, and stand at our ease in our shirtsleeves and breeches while he explained why he had wanted to see us.

"And then he spoke to us of *la guillotine*...."

I must have looked puzzled then, because the old man paused. "Yes," he finally went on, "as I said, my tale will give proof of what I maintained before. Oh, the Great Man spoke of other things too, of France, of the Emperor and how the rumors one heard were correct, that the Emperor and others, with the Great Man's help manipulating affairs behind the scenes, sending a message to this one or that one, a summons to others, planting a new rumor here, a denial there, planned an escape from the prison of Elba in scarcely more than a month's time.

"But always he returned to that other rumor, that he had been executed himself during the confusion that swept the countryside at the time the Directory had ruled. He had fled Paris by then, you see—there were factions against him—to the southern part of France here, anticipating his own guillotining were he to stay longer. And yet, even here...."

"Well, he told us that even here he took precautions. He had studied the theories of Lavoisier and, having money, he bought this chateau in which we found him, and started the rumor that it was deserted. He brought in apparatus, some that we saw now, secretly by night. He hired assistants, bribing their silence as to his doings, and bribed officials too, including those who were the executioners. Or so he told us.

"You see, we were skeptics. Oh, we had seen Charlotte Corday with our own eyes, and heard of Lavoisier's proof as well, of the instant of life that still remained after one had been beheaded, but to carry it as far as *he* planned to—well, we were convinced that what he then told us could not have been true. That perhaps his reversals of fortune had driven him mad. The Great Man did not begrudge us our whisperings during the pauses in his conversation, and there were many, gaps of several minutes or more while the pipes behind him bubbled, while others hissed softly, as if he must catch his breath before he went on.

"But still he did go on, of how the baskets the heads of a guillotine's victims fell into were said to be found with their bottoms chewed by the gnashings of teeth. Of other theories, Gautier's and others later, including that of the German anatomist Sommering that if only some artificial lung be attached quickly enough to it, the guillotined head would even speak of how it endured. And that of our country's own Dr. Jean-Joseph Sue of how the body, too, its limbs and organs, must still feel sensation. At least for an instant.

"But after that instant, well, then it came back to Lavoisier, the Great Man told us, and to his theory of *caloric*, the element of heat which maintained life, but also, when life ceased, engendered decay. And so the Great Man began to take precautions. He had, as I said, bribed the town's executioners so, at last, when the moment he had so feared had come upon him, when he took the walk up the steps of the scaffold, his hands bound behind him, when he felt his body lashed to the trestle, his head thrust through the hole—'mounting Madame,' as we called it in those days—he looked down to see not the red-painted wicker basket sprinkled with bran to soak up the gore, as would have been usual, but an apparatus of his own devising. This was a bucket already filled to the brim with fresh blood—never mind where it came from—to keep his brain nourished, the bucket in turn placed within a barrel of ice and salt to draw the caloric out from his severed head, to cool it until it was nearly frozen, and thus slow the process of death itself until it could be returned to the chateau where other apparatus was waiting.

"Then, once more, he paused to take more breath while Captain Sarbeau and I whispered among ourselves, that even if such a thing could be, surely it would have driven one insane. Imagine the horror, even if one has assured one's survival, of having one's head *cut off!* And knowing when it was—feeling its separation from one's body. Feeling so helpless, knowing your body was dying while you still lived....

"That's when the blanket slipped. Just as we felt powerful hands laid upon us, those of the Great Man's silently returning servants, holding us immobile as we saw, not a body appear as the cloth fell from it, but rather a framework of tubing and uprights supporting a collar that held the head in place. And, as I say, from the head we saw piping, some branching off to a steam-powered pump to force fresh air through it—the artificial lung of Sommering, providing not just speech but oxygenation!—others to huge flasks of thick, red liquids, again from we knew not where, still others to the chamber's four walls, tapping the chimneys above its fireplaces to draw in caloric, to keep the brain heated to that which living blood would make it, combining with all the rest, inward, outward, fresh air, stale air, fresh blood and spent blood continually cycling for these nearly twenty years while all around it nations were tumbling, battles were won and lost, empires were rising and then, again, falling.

"And then, again, rising. The Great Man called halt to our whispered babbling while, within that grim head, his eyes rolled and swept about in their sockets, measuring us one last time as we stood there. Then with a scowl, as other servants wheeled in a great tub the size of a coffin and packed with salt and ice, as out the window I saw as the sun rose the shadow of a guillotine in the courtyard, the Great Man signaled for my dismissal, for *I* was not needed. I would be free to go, anywhere that I wished—no one, you understand, had I said at that time what I had seen there, would have believed me.

"But as for my captain, I saw, as the servants were ushering me from that dreadful chamber, the Great Man's gaze once again come to rest on his tall, strong form. I saw the Great Man smile then for the first time, a ghastly, mad smile, as he spoke again of his plans for Napoleon and his reinstatement, adding only this one thing more: that if he were now to aid France and her Emperor to the fullest, the time had come that he would require a body."

"The Great Man" first appeared in the Spring-Summer 1999 issue of The Strand Magazine.

James Dorr is a Bloomington, Indiana-based short story writer and poet specializing in dark fantasy and horror with forays into mystery and science fiction. His work includes more than five hundred individual publications in journals and anthologies, along with three collections (one of these, The Tears of Isis, *a 2013 Stoker Award® nominee), one "traditionally thin" poetry volume, and a mosaic novel from Elder Signs Press,* Tombs: A Chronicle of Latter-Day Times of Earth. *Dorr has been a technical writer, an editor on a regional magazine, a full time nonfiction freelancer, and a semi-professional musician. He currently harbors a Goth cat named Triana, and counts among his major influences Ray Bradbury, Edgar Allan Poe, Allen Ginsberg, and Bertolt Brecht.*

BLACK *Infinity* 6 INSIDIOUS INSECTS

RAMSEY CAMPBELL
ROBERT SHECKLEY
PHILIP K. DICK
JAMES DORR
TOM ENGLISH
KURT NEWTON
MURRAY LEINSTER
GREGORY L. NORRIS
MATT COWAN • VONNIE WINSLOW CRIST
JASON J. McCUISTON • ALLEN KOSZOWSKI
SPECIAL: GARY GERANI REMEMBERS THE OUTER LIMITS

BLACK *Infinity* STRANGE DIMENSIONS

ROCKET SCIENCE BOOK GROUP 4

STILL NOT 10¢

RHYS HUGHES
CLIFFORD D. SIMAK
MARC VUN KANNON
KURT NEWTON • STEVE DITKO • ALLEN NOURSE

PHILIP K. DICK
DOUGLAS SMITH
GREGORY L. NORRIS

WE ALSO LIKE CREEPY SCIENCE FICTION!
DON'T MISS BLACK INFINITY, NIGHTMARE ABBEY'S "SCI-FI SISTER"!

BLACK *Infinity* 5 DERELICTS

JAMES DORR
PHILIP K. DICK
DOUGLAS SMITH
STEWART C BAKER
GREGORY L. NORRIS
WILLIAM HOPE HODGSON
ALAN E. NOURSE • ANDRE NORTON
JACK WILLIAMSON • DAVID VonALLMEN

LOST IN SPACE REMEMBERED

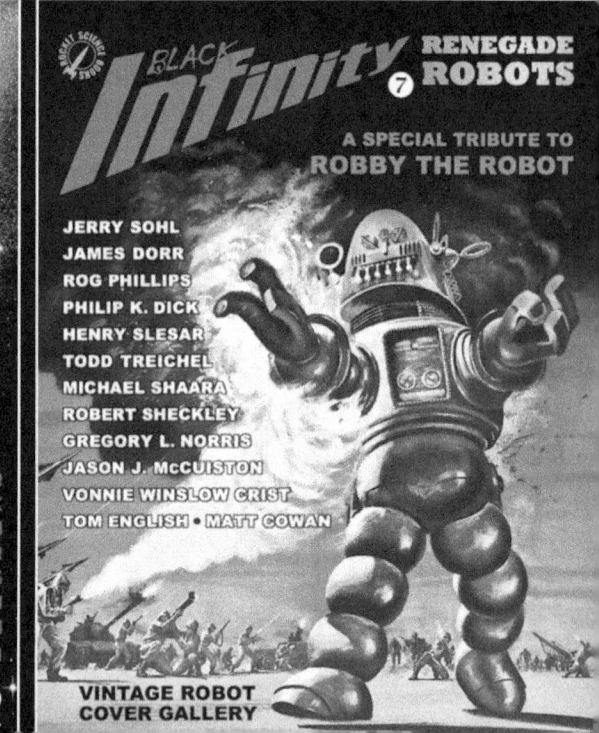

BLACK *Infinity* 7 RENEGADE ROBOTS

A SPECIAL TRIBUTE TO ROBBY THE ROBOT

JERRY SOHL
JAMES DORR
ROG PHILLIPS
PHILIP K. DICK
HENRY SLESAR
TODD TREICHEL
MICHAEL SHAARA
ROBERT SHECKLEY
GREGORY L. NORRIS
JASON J. McCUISTON
VONNIE WINSLOW CRIST
TOM ENGLISH • MATT COWAN

VINTAGE ROBOT COVER GALLERY

SEEING IS BELIEVING

By HELEN GRANT

*T**HANK GOD I NEVER TOLD HIM ABOUT AUNT DODO,* said Bethany to herself. She pressed herself into the corner, turning her face to the grimy window and willing people not to notice her. It was dark outside; she could just pick out distant lights, wavering with the rocking of the train. Inside, it was too cold, or else her khaki jacket was too thin. She kept shivering. Every so often she absently pushed her glasses up her nose. The tape was holding them together but they didn't fit like they had before.

Her bag was at her feet. She couldn't help it: she wanted to know that she could grab it and run at any moment if she needed to. After a bit she dragged it onto her lap and hugged it, feeling how tightly packed it was but knowing it wasn't enough; you couldn't shove a whole life into a bag and carry it away with you. All her other belongings—well, she didn't think she'd see them again. He'd have realized she was gone long since, and he'd be going through her stuff like a berserker. Bethany thought about him smashing her little pot of hyacinths and she grimaced into the cold glass. Then she thought about her small collection of Victorian fairy books, each saved for very carefully, and she actually sobbed.

The train clattered swiftly and dispassionately onwards into the dark, heading north. Bethany got off at a town she'd never visited before and sat for forty minutes by the heater in the brightly-lit waiting room. She ate a rather crushed Mars bar she'd put into the top pocket of her bag, and wished she had something to drink. Eventually another train came, and she climbed aboard that. Her whole body seemed infected with tiredness and yet she knew she couldn't sleep. No conductor came round, nor was there any catering. Eventually she went into the tiny toilet and in spite of the sign saying that the tap water was not potable she drank some from her cupped hands.

Later still, Bethany alighted at a country station that was little more than an up and a down platform; there wasn't even a ticket machine. Nobody else got off the train. She watched it clack quietly away. It occurred to her in a vague way that she ought to be afraid, a woman all alone in a strange place in the dark, but she wasn't. What she had left behind had used up every scrap of adrenaline.

She felt in her jacket pocket for her little torch and switched it on. The light it produced was disconcertingly feeble, and away from the station there was no other illumination. Bethany couldn't imagine staying where she was until morning though; she needed to keep moving or she'd freeze. The difficult thing was going to be finding Aunt Dodo's place; she'd never actually visited it before.

Bethany unzipped one of the side pockets of her bag and slid out a dogeared map. When she turned it over, meaning to unfold it, she saw that there was a price sticker on it, reading £1.50. She grimaced.

This map is ancient. *I hope they haven't built a bypass through here since then.*

She hoisted the bag onto her shoulders and ascended some very worn stone steps with an ornate metal handrail, the green paint peeling in places to reveal rust. At the top she found herself at the side of a narrow road which ran slightly downhill from right to left. Bethany set off downhill; the first part of the route followed the railway line, and as long as she didn't actually cross it, she couldn't go far wrong.

At the bottom of the hill she came to a fork in the road, checked the map, and took the right hand turning. There was a lot of grit on the road, washed down by the rain, and it crunched loudly under her feet. At no time did she see the lights of any building nor any vehicle, not even in the distance. She began to wonder why there was a railway station around here at all; who would use it?

She almost missed the track that led to Aunt Dodo's house. Framed by trees, it was heavily overgrown and nearly invisible in the dark; only the splintered remains of a white-painted mailbox caught her eye, a pale patch in the deep gloom. Bethany looked at the map again.

This must be it. She hesitated. *Probably.*

She waded through long grass and weeds and peered into the gap, directing the torch beam here and there to little effect. In the end there was nothing for it but to follow the track and hope she came to the house.

In the darkness mud squelched under her boots and brittle sticks snapped. There were other sounds too, of live things: light patterings, surreptitious scufflings. Bethany put out a hand, imagining branches at face level. How had Aunt Dodo managed to live here, at her age, alone? But she had, right to the end of her life.

She stumbled on. The bag seemed to have grown heavier as she grew more weary; the straps dragged at her shoulders. She was still too cold; her lower jaw was beginning to judder. When the faint light of the torch bounced back at her from a pane of glass she was briefly too stunned to realize what she was seeing.

A window.

Aunt Dodo's house.

The key on its loop of ribbon was at the bottom of her jeans pocket; she'd put it there for safekeeping, the moment she decided to run. Bethany fished it out. Her fingers were numb with cold and she half expected the lock to have rusted, but the key turned easily and then she was inside. Gratefully, she put the bag on the floor. Then she locked the door behind her. She stood there for a moment, leaning against the panels.

You know there's nobody out there, she told herself. Still, she felt happier knowing she was locked in.

After a little while she looked for the light switch but couldn't find it, perhaps because the room was so dark. There was a fat, half-burned candle on the worn wooden table though, alongside a half-full box of matches. Bethany struck a match, and then she froze. Over the tearing sound of the match scraping the side of the box she heard something move—a scurrying sound, definitely *inside* the house.

Mice? she thought, and then: *Rats?*

She hoped very much it *wasn't* rats; mice she thought she could stand, and after all, they were more of a nuisance than anything else, gnawing their way into packets of food and leaving their droppings everywhere, but *rats...* Couldn't rats actually *attack* you, or was that just in horror films? There was no going anywhere else though; even if she had had anywhere to go, she was too dog-tired to move on. Bethany decided the noise had been a mouse.

There was a battered-looking sofa pushed against the wall, so she went and sat on that, drawing her feet up off the floor. She unlaced her boots, and let them drop onto the boards. Then she leaned back onto the threadbare cushions, thinking that she would rest for a few minutes before she engaged with the business of finding a bathroom, a bedroom, clean bedlinen, all the rest of it... She relaxed and let her eyes slide shut, and when she opened them again it was morning.

BETHANY AWOKE WITH a stiff neck and the impression that something had roused her. A thud or snap. Voices, speaking very low.

She thought, *He's found me*, and she started up, looking wildly about her. The room was a blur; her glasses had fallen into her lap during the night, and now they slipped to the floor with a clatter. Panicking, Bethany groped for them, found them, jammed them onto her nose. They sat askew, the tape now barely holding, but at least she could see. The house was silent. In the sunlight slanting between the faded curtains dust motes moved lazily on the air.

Bethany exhaled. *A dream.* She rubbed her neck with her fingertips, wincing. She was aware of the urgent need to pee. But where was the bathroom?

The room she was in seemed to serve as both sitting room and dining area. She peeped through the two doors leading off it. One led to a neat bedroom: there was a bed with a crocheted counterpane, a

chest of drawers, a blanket box and an old-fashioned washstand with basin and jug.

The other door led into a kitchen equipped with a small iron range and a rectangular ceramic sink. There was a deal table and a lot of shelves housing cans and packets of food. But what caught Bethany's eye was the tin bath standing in a corner. She stared at it.

Surely not...?

Her head turned as she scanned the room for another door, one leading into the bathroom. There *was* a second door, but it looked very much as though it led outside. It was bolted on the inside, and there was a key sticking out of the lock. Bethany undid them both, and then she opened the door.

A stone path led away from the threshold, overhung with the dead remains of flowers. Her gaze followed it to the very end. There, amongst nettles that looked to be head height, was a wooden structure that was unmistakably an outside toilet.

"Oh God," breathed Bethany.

There really was nothing for it, though. She fetched her boots, because in no possible universe was she setting foot in that place in her socks, and then she made her way gingerly down the path. It was a relief to discover that Aunt Dodo had, at least, bought proper toilet paper, rather than hanging up sheets of old newspaper.

On the way back up the path, itching to wash her hands, she glanced at the open back door and she was *almost* sure she saw something move—something small and light colored. She pushed her glasses back up her nose with her knuckle and squinted at the doorway. It took her a split second to focus, and then she realized she had been looking at a patch of sunlight, a light spot that moved as the branches of a nearby tree swayed in the wind.

Bethany went back inside and washed her hands in cold water using a bar of soap that was as dry and hard as a pebble. It was beginning to dawn on her what she had done, coming to live in Aunt Dodo's house.

My house, she reminded herself. *It's my house now.*

There were letters to that effect in her backpack—letters she hadn't dared leave behind, even in the bin, in case *he* found them, and worked out where she'd gone. Aunt Dodo had left the place to Bethany, her only surviving relative. She was not really even *Aunt* Dodo; she was some kind of far more distant relation, and Dodo was short for something: Dorothea, Bethany thought. Bethany's mother had occasionally spoken of her, but Aunt Dodo had never come to their house and they had never visited her. Bethany supposed that was because Aunt Dodo lived so far away, and somewhere remote, too; it wasn't the sort of place you would ever just happen to be passing. She cast her mind back but she couldn't detect anything significant in what she remembered her mother saying about Aunt Dodo; no disapproval or distaste. Aunt Dodo just hadn't been part of their lives.

When she had found out that the house was hers, she had imagined all sorts of things: a listed stone cottage, a quaint little croft. She hadn't been able to find out very much about Aunt Dodo's house at all, because Aunt Dodo had lived in it pretty much her entire life. There were websites where you could check the value of a property, but that depended on there having been a recorded sale, and for Aunt Dodo's house there were none.

She told herself she was lucky to have somewhere to go; most people wouldn't have. But still she was dismayed when she renewed her search for the light switch and discovered that there weren't any. As well as having an outside toilet and a tin bath, Aunt Dodo's house relied on candles and a single hurricane lamp for light.

Bethany was dying for a cup of strong coffee, but she began to see that making one would not be a five-minute job. The range would have to be lit and she was pretty sure you couldn't heat anything immediately; it took a while for the heat to build. After some hunting about she found a basket, which she took outside to collect logs from the woodpile. She arranged them somewhat inexpertly and then had to search again, for kindling. After the fire was going she put a pan of water on top of the range, but she did not feel optimistic that it would heat up quickly. Then she went to look amongst the tins and packets for coffee, sugar, and, if she were really lucky, powdered milk.

These efforts were engrossing, and so it was some time before Bethany became aware that the house was alive with little noises: scratching, rustling, something that might have been muffled squeaking. She paused, her hands on a dusty box of arrowroot, and suddenly there was silence, as though something were holding its breath—watching.

She turned her head swiftly, thinking to catch whatever it was—a mouse, a rat, a bird—unawares. Her broken spectacles slid down her nose again and all she caught was a blurred movement down on the floor, by the tin bath. Bethany pushed them back up and saw the shadow of a branch outside the window moving gently back and forth on the floorboards.

"Jumpy," she said under her breath. She drew in air through her nostrils. "Get a grip," she said to herself.

Rather to her surprise, there *was* powdered milk, so she put that out, along with the coffee and sugar. The water was nowhere near boiling; it was barely tepid. While she waited for it she helped herself to some biscuits and wandered around the house, making a sort of mental inventory. Amongst other things, she found a workbox with a lot of different colored threads, a thimble, a darning mushroom and a pair of small sharp scissors. There was also a miniature of a young woman who might have been Aunt Dodo in her youth or someone else entirely; there was nothing to say. It was beautifully executed, with tiny details rendered with incredible precision. Bethany also discovered a single shelf of books, all of them in very old-fashioned bindings, a black umbrella with a duck's head handle, and a small pouch made of shabby turquoise velvet, with neat gold embroidery. This last item was on the table next to the bed. She picked it up and could feel that there was something inside, so she unbuttoned the top and drew out a pair of spectacles.

It was very obvious that these were not *modern* spectacles. Bethany's glasses had chunky plastic frames and large lenses which magnified her hazel eyes; these had delicate gold rims enclosing small ovals of glass which sparkled as she turned them over in her hands. On impulse, she took off her own spectacles and put Aunt Dodo's on.

If she'd thought about it she wouldn't have expected to see much, not without her own strong prescription lenses, and indeed for several seconds the room swam about her. Then suddenly it lurched into sharp focus. The turquoise velvet pouch seemed to throb with an intensity of color; the grain of the wooden cabinet stood out like the contours on a map; the soft pilling on every strand of wool in the crocheted counterpane was distinctly and clearly visible.

"Wow."

Bethany raised her gaze and between the vivid curtains she could see the gossamer tracery of a spider's web on the outside of the bedroom window, and tiny drops of water glittering on it, here and there.

Astounded, she turned her head this way and that, taking in all the details of the room—and then froze. There was something sitting on the blanket box at the end of the bed, looking at her.

Her first thought was: a *gigantic* moth. The multitude of slender, downy legs, the bulbous abdomen, the velvety wings in shades of ivory, ochre and brown: those things said *moth*. But the face was not an insect's. It looked like that of a very elderly human being—as faded and wrinkled as a withered apple. Its large yellow eyes peered at her myopically, and then the corners of the mouth twitched up into a faint and questioning smile.

Without knowing why she did it, Bethany snatched off Aunt Dodo's spectacles. Instantly the room was a blur. She fumbled for her own glasses, put them on, and looked again. The moth thing was not there. *Something* was there: the play of light and shade on the patterned lid of the blanket box. But not the creature she had just seen.

Bethany went over and put out a hand rather haltingly, touching the surface of the box. There was nothing there, but she thought she heard a tiny sound close by—something fluting and reproachful. She shut her eyes, swallowed, opened them again. Still nothing.

For a little while, Bethany stood there thinking. Mostly she wondered whether her own grip on reality had become tenuous. Eventually she put Aunt Dodo's spectacles on again.

The moth thing was no longer on the blanket box. Now it was sitting in the middle of the crocheted counterpane. It was still looking at her, in that slightly hopeful way. When it saw it had her attention, it opened its mouth and pointed inside with one of its fuzzy forelimbs.

Feed me.

Bethany swayed slightly on her feet, feeling lightheaded.

"I don't think you can really be there," she said to the thing.

Its face crumpled into a frown. Then it did the pointing action again, insistently.

"Alright," said Bethany in a faint voice, deciding to go along with the delusion, if that was what it was. She turned and went towards the kitchen, and as she did so she heard the droning sound of wings in the air following her.

Inside the kitchen she examined the shelves for anything that might tempt the appetite of a very large... Well, she wasn't sure what it was. As she was moving cans about the thing landed on her shoulder. She *felt* it. A wing brushed the side of her neck. She had to restrain a rather hysterical laugh. This could *not* be happening.

Bethany picked up a packet of dried onions and felt rather than saw the vehement shaking of the tiny head. Then she tried a can of condensed milk, and there was an immediate and enthusiastic flurry of wings. She put the can on the deal table, rummaged for a can opener, and began to open the can. The thing landed close to her hands, watching avidly. Bethany found a willow pattern saucer and poured some of the condensed milk into it. She was watching the moth thing drinking from it with obvious enjoyment when a second one landed softly on the table. Then she heard a rustle and guessed there were others coming.

She stepped back and sat down on one of Aunt Dodo's wheelbacked chairs. On the table the moth creatures moved back and forth, jostling each other for a turn at the saucer. Their trailing wings rustled.

Bethany put her hands up and slid Aunt Dodo's spectacles down to the end of her nose. When she looked over them, she could see nothing but dancing shadows, even at this close range. If she pushed them back up she could see the moth things perfectly.

"Aunt Dodo..." she whispered, but she couldn't frame a question—not one that would have had a sensible answer, anyway.

TWO DAYS LATER, Bethany left the house and walked to the nearest town big enough to have shops. She found it on the dog-eared map and reasoned that it was unlikely to have got *smaller* over time, only bigger. There was no other way of navigating her way about the area; she had left her phone behind when she ran, thinking that there were ways of tracking people through their smartphones.

She set off early in the day and reached the town in the late morning. There she used some of her store of cash to buy, amongst other things, more tins of condensed milk. As she loaded them into her backpack she reflected ruefully that they would probably feel like bricks when she had been carrying them for an hour. There was nothing for it, though; she couldn't see a supermarket home delivery forcing its way up the overgrown track to Aunt Dodo's house, even assuming she could find a way of putting in an order. She walked back again, more slowly, and whenever she heard a vehicle coming she did her best to step behind a tree or hedge. No point in advertising her presence.

As she walked, Bethany thought about the winged creatures in the house. In the shop, with its bright strip lighting and the beep of the scanner and the rows of colorful packets, the moth things felt unreal, impossible. Was it possible she was having some kind of hallucination, prompted by...what? She hadn't taken so much as an aspirin. Then she wondered whether the horrors she had left behind in London were the cause. Was that even possible? Moths with human heads were a strange thing to imagine, if that was what she had been doing. No explanation struck her as convincing. She

walked on, and when she finally came to the overgrown turning to Aunt Dodo's house she was none the wiser.

By now it was late afternoon. She unlocked the door and went inside. It was silent and seemingly empty; only shadows flitted to and fro as the afternoon sunshine filtered through the trees surrounding the house. Bethany put down the bag, took off her own glasses with some care, and put on Aunt Dodo's, which she had left by the door.

Four of the moth things were waiting for her.

She laughed, a little uneasily.

"Hi guys. It's alright; I bought more of that condensed milk you love so much."

She thought their reaction showed pleasure, and they certainly gathered very avidly as she opened one of the cans. Bethany left them to it, and went to unload the rest of the shopping onto the shelves.

As night fell she lit some candles and made herself some dinner on the range, which was properly warm now. After that she shut herself in the bedroom, taking care none of the moth things were inside with her, and had a sponge bath using the washstand. Then she settled down on the sofa with one of Aunt Dodo's books, which proved to be an old-fashioned adventure about orphans and smugglers. She was only a few pages in when she began to nod off.

Some time later, she jerked awake, Aunt Dodo's spectacles still on her nose.

What—?

She saw that the moth creatures—all of them, she thought—were clustering about her, three or four on surfaces close to her, and the others in the air, their wings a blur. Bethany sensed agitation coming from them and a wave of cold dread broke over her. Irrationally, she thought: *he's here—he's found me.*

Her gaze darted about the room. Instantly she saw that it was not *him* the moth things were anxious about.

In the corner of the room was something so tall that it had to stoop under the ceiling, something cloaked in dense darkness that bled into the shadows. It was fearfully gaunt, but its attenuated frame exuded a hideous suppressed strength. The head was a livid dome, pallid and gleaming like a great egg. Face it must have had, but Bethany dropped her gaze, horrified, and only retained the fleeting impression of *red*.

Her heart was thudding so hard she was afraid she would faint, but to be unconscious, defenceless, was unthinkable. Her mind groped for means of escape. The thought of fleeing out into the night with that cadaverous form in pursuit was appalling. With some irrational idea that being unable to perceive the thing would make it disappear, Bethany snatched off Aunt Dodo's spectacles, but when she looked towards the corner she knew that it was still there. It showed itself only as a long dark shadow and a single lighter patch at the corner of the ceiling but that was somehow worse. She put the glasses back on with fingers that trembled.

The moth creatures pressed closer, trying with increasing urgency to communicate something to her. Then one by one they fluttered down to the floor in front of her and bowed their heads, performing an obeisance towards the being in the corner.

Bethany stared at them, open mouthed. She understood, though. There seemed no option, so she slid off the sofa and prostrated herself on the floor. The boards were cool and solid under her hands and knees—else she would have thought she was dreaming.

She did not look up, but she felt the vibration of the boards, sensed the approach. Bethany closed her eyes, squeezing them tight. She felt something light, almost feathery, touch her wrist. A moment later there was a sharp pain. Opening her eyes, she saw with horror that one of the moth things had fastened itself to her arm and bitten her.

With an exclamation of disgust, she shook the thing off. Blood was oozing from the bite and running down onto her hand. She lifted the hand to examine the wound, but before she was able to do so, the candlelight was blotted out as a towering form crouched over her. A second later, something cold and wet moved across her skin, probing the bite.

Then Bethany *did* pass out.

• • • •

THE NEXT MORNING Bethany was weak and tired—and also angry.

When she got up from her bed, where she had staggered in the small hours after awakening on the floor, she put on her own glasses instead of Aunt Dodo's spectacles. She knew perfectly well that the moth creatures were still there; she could see the shifting patches of light and shade here and there. But she didn't feel like speaking to any of them, not at first. She made herself an enormous cup of coffee using the range, and ate half a packet of biscuits. She did not offer the biscuits around, nor did she open any cans of condensed milk. Arms folded, she gazed furiously out of the kitchen window and debated whether to leave.

Where to go, that was the problem. Not back to London, that was for certain. And then she had a reasonable amount of cash for daily living expenses, but it wouldn't last long if she went to a hotel. She had cards, but the minute she used those she would be advertising her whereabouts. If *he* had reported her as a missing person, she would pretty instantly be found. Even if he hadn't, the next bank statement would show where she'd gone.

She took a long swallow of coffee and examined her hand again. The bite seemed to have healed up pretty well already. Her ears detected a faint drone on the air, and —perhaps—a tiny squeak of sympathy or contrition.

With a sigh, Bethany took off her glasses and put on Aunt Dodo's. It was no surprise to find the moth creatures ranged around her on the deal table, looking at her. It was hard to judge them by human standards but she thought they looked rather shamefaced.

"What the hell?" she said to them. "You let that thing drink my blood."

A reaction ran through them. Then they began to bow down, the way they had the night before, offering obeisance.

"Okay, okay, I get it," Bethany said wearily. "You worship that thing, right?"

Half a dozen tiny heads shook vigorously.

"It's bigger than you, then?"

Nods this time. *Yes.*

"Well, I'm not being drained dry by

bloody Nosferatu, or whatever it was." She glared at them. "Is it coming back tonight?"

No.

"Is it ever coming back?"

Reluctantly the moth things nodded.

"Did it come when Aunt Dodo was here?" She saw the creatures looking at each other, confused. "You know, the old lady who lived here before? Dorothea?"

Yes.

"Well, what did *she* do? Don't tell me she fed it her blood whenever it showed up."

Bethany couldn't make head nor tail of the tiny sounds and enthusiastic pantomiming that followed. In the end, however, an idea struck her.

"If I got something from the butcher—some fresh meat, or—I don't know, blood sausage—would it have that?"

Yes, yes, yes!

Bethany picked up her coffee cup again. She felt in urgent need of caffeine.

"Look," she said at last, "If you tell me *before* it comes next time, I'll keep getting you that milk you like so much." She paused. "Otherwise, you can forget it. Do we have a deal?"

She looked at the moth things and saw that they did, indeed, have a deal.

Five days later, she walked to the town again. She bought half a dozen cans of condensed milk—the little supermarket had restocked, evidently seeing a thriving local market for the stuff. She also bought half a kilo of lamb's kidneys. If she had understood correctly, she and the moth creatures were due a visitor that evening.

When night fell, she found the grandest looking plate in the house—a Crown Derby dinner plate in scarlet, blue, and gold—and laid the lamb's kidneys out on it, raw and wet with red juices. The moth creatures nodded their approval.

Bethany had debated for a long time whether to wear Aunt Dodo's spectacles that evening or not, but in the end, she still felt it would be worse *not* to know—to see the shadows move and blend, and wonder whether she was alone or not. All the same, she was not sorry to bend her head and look at the floorboards, flanked on either side by cowering moth things. The vigorous smacking sounds, the sucking and slurping, the throaty sounds of pleasure made her feel nauseous. If she had actually watched, she thought, she would have thrown up.

When the tall creature had gone, she went into the kitchen, hunted until she found Aunt Dodo's cooking sherry, and poured herself a very large glass of it.

TIME DRIFTED PAST. Had it not been for her periodic visits to the town for provisions, she would have lost track of the date altogether. She knew autumn was sliding into winter, because the days were getting shorter and even colder. Keeping the range going was critical; she looked at the woodpile in a calculating way, and then went into the woods to look for branches which she could drag back and chop up, wielding the axe inexpertly.

How did Aunt Dodo manage all this? she wondered. The old woman had been over eighty when she died. Bethany thought she must have been very eccentric to live like this, and she also suspected that she herself was going the same way. The moth things no longer struck her as peculiar; she thought of them as something a little like pets. As for the other thing—the one which visited occasionally to accept the tribute of kidneys or liver or once, when she couldn't get anything else, black pudding—even *that* had become a distasteful routine, unpleasant but necessary, like cleaning out the drains or paying a regular bill.

Eventually there came a day when she did not have enough cash to settle the grocery bill. Bethany used her card instead, because there was no choice. Afterwards she went to a cash machine and got a balance and as much cash as she could, and then she walked home with unease gnawing at her. The money would not last much longer; then she would have to engage with officialdom in some way again, whether job hunting or signing up for benefits. Would *he* be able to trace her? She didn't know; it depended what story he had given out. There might be people looking out for her—or not.

And in fact, Bethany never did find out what gave her away—the use of her bank card, or some other thing, perhaps a further letter from the solicitor's about Aunt Dodo's estate. Late one afternoon she came home from the town as night was falling, hurrying because it was nearly too dark to see where she was going; she opened the door, put her bag on the floor and went to light a candle. As the flame flared up she shook the match out, looked up and there *he* was, standing in the kitchen doorway.

Bethany felt as if she had innocently stepped onto rotten ice and plunged into freezing dark water. She couldn't move, couldn't run; there was a crushing pressure on her chest. Every scrap of hard-worn confidence was draining out of her, whirling round and round, sucked away into the maelstrom of her fear.

"Mike," she whispered; the hated name, the one she'd sworn never to utter again, shivered out between frozen lips.

"Bethany," he answered, his tone reproving, a little mocking, and that made it even worse, because she knew that delicate control was the cork holding it all in.

"Please..." she said, and her voice trailed away as he stepped right into the room.

He made a play of looking about him, assessing the scene. Then his gaze shifted to her. "This is a dump, Bethany."

It's not, she wanted to say, but her throat was too dry; nothing would come out.

He kicked the door frame. "An absolute dump. And I have to wonder, Bethany, why you would choose to come and live in a place like this, when you had a home with *me*."

Bethany shook her head, but she made it a tiny motion.

"Why, Bethany?"

She shrugged, knowing he didn't care what she replied. It was just the cat playing with the mouse; the killing bite would come anyway, whatever she said, whatever she did.

"Nothing to say?" He folded his arms. "Well, let me tell you how I see it, then. You have a choice. You can pack up your things and come back to London with me right now. And on the way you can explain to me exactly why you thought it was acceptable to leave like that, without telling anyone where you were going. You could have been dead for all I knew, Bethany." He looked at her, dead-eyed. "I mean, if you died out here, who'd know?"

Bethany said nothing. There was a cold feeling in her gut.

"Yeah," he went on. "You can come home. Or—"

"I'll come home," said Bethany quickly. Her voice was hoarse. "I'll pack. It won't take long. And then I'll come home."

She knew he was studying her, looking for signs of sincerity, and she forced herself to meet his gaze.

"I will," she said.

There was a long pause—the time it takes a pendulum to swing to and fro, to and fro. Then Mike said, "Fine. Pack." After a moment he added, "Get a move on."

Bethany noticed he was still in front of the kitchen doorway. There was no escape that way. She was nearer to the front door than he was, but only by a few feet; it wasn't enough of a head start. She picked up her bag and went into the bedroom.

Mike watched her go. He didn't move.

Aunt Dodo's spectacles were on top of the chest of drawers in the bedroom. Bethany snatched off her own. In her haste she was rough and she felt the broken frames disintegrating in her hands. No matter. She unfolded Aunt Dodo's spectacles and slipped them onto her nose.

One of the moth things was sitting on top of the chest of drawers. Its tiny wrinkled face was puckered with concern.

"Help," whispered Bethany under her breath. She tilted her head towards the bedroom door, but she didn't dare stand around waiting to see if the thing understood. Instead she opened and closed drawers, making enough noise that Mike would hear. She upended her bag onto the bed, spilling cans of condensed milk, a bar of soap and some apples onto the counterpane.

Another of the moth things alighted on the bed and looked up into her face, its tiny eyes intense.

"Please—help," said Bethany in a voice barely louder than a breath. Her eyes slid sideways, trying to indicate the door through into the room where Mike was.

She kept moving, collecting up clothes, a hairbrush. The moth things rose into the air and she could hear from the drone of wings that all of them were in the room. They flew towards the door, and Bethany turned, following them with her gaze.

Mike was now standing in the middle of the living room, where he could watch her. As the moth things flew towards him, she had one moment of doubtful optimism: they might swarm all over him, or bite him, or just distract him for long enough that she could escape. But she saw them fly past him and realized they were leaving.

Mike couldn't see them, of course. But he saw Bethany looking.

"What are you staring at?"

"Nothing."

The front door was still ajar and the moth creatures vanished out into the night. Bethany turned away, sick at heart. She wondered whether Mike would really let her finish packing, and then they would leave Aunt Dodo's house together and walk calmly to a waiting car, or to the station, him close at her shoulder in case she made a break for it. She didn't really believe in that scenario.

He must know I could run again, she thought.

She kept moving about the bedroom trying to look busy, trying to buy herself time, though she wasn't sure for *what*. The desertion of the moth things was the last straw. Now she was simply delaying the inevitable.

"That's enough," said Mike from the doorway. "You don't need half that crap."

"Nearly finished…"

"No. Finished," he said. "You've had long enough."

Bethany glanced around the room. She had the sense that she was seeing it for the very last time. The feeling made her lightheaded, nauseous. She didn't want to walk towards Mike in the doorway; it would be walking to her doom. But there was nowhere else to go and she had to start moving. She picked up her bag, hugging it to her protectively. Unwillingly, hesitatingly, she stepped towards Mike.

"I told you," he said, "You don't need half that crap."

She could hear the coming storm vibrating in his voice. He reached out, making a grab for the bag. Bethany instinctively held onto it, and for several ludicrous moments they were struggling over it. Then Mike dragged it out of her arms—and promptly dropped it.

Things spilled out of it, rolling away across the floor. Bethany looked at Mike's face and saw—not indignation but a flash of gloating satisfaction. Bethany knew what was coming next: *Look what you made me do.*

Then her jaw dropped and she took a step back.

Mike smiled unpleasantly. He thought she was backing away from *him*. The smirk lasted for perhaps ten seconds before it began to falter. He couldn't help himself; the way she kept staring over his left shoulder with that stunned expression made him want to turn and look. In fact, he did start turning to look before he caught himself.

There was nothing there, of course—just long dark shadows which shifted with the dancing of the candle flame; just a lighter patch reflected onto the ceiling from some shiny object.

He turned back to Bethany. She was very pale.

"Mike," she said in a faint voice, "I think you should go. Right now."

Mike opened his mouth to ask her who the hell she thought she was. He never even got the first word out. The creature fell on him with terrifying swiftness, grasping his shoulders with wickedly long and curving talons. In one brutal movement the dirty white dome of its head thrust itself into the exposed flesh of his neck. There was a wet meaty sound and then a series of harsh grinding crunches as it began to eat its way through muscle and tendons.

With a choking sound Bethany snatched off Aunt Dodo's spectacles. It didn't really help. She couldn't see the thing battening on Mike's throat but she could see the progress it was making as it gnawed and tore, exposing anatomical structures she should never have been able to see. Scarlet oozed and sprayed, then vanished as the unseen creature pressed its mouth greedily to the source. Mike's body jerked and twitched and his head lolled back, unnaturally, the eyes rolling up to show the whites. He never made a sound though—not a scream, not so much as a groan. The thing had been too fast for him. His hands beat at the air, but it was only a reflex.

Bethany shut her eyes then, but she could still *hear* it. It fed with slobbering, grunting gluttony, but also with a luxuriating, lip-smacking pleasure that was somehow worse. After a little while the wet sounds gave way to cracking and splintering, and then a noisy sucking. She put her fingers in her ears and turned her back, hunching her shoulders. When that wasn't enough, she went to the far corner of the bedroom, under the window, and curled herself into a ball on the floorboards. She stayed there for a very long time.

WHEN SHE WAS becoming cold and stiff, Bethany took her fingers out of her ears, experimentally. Silence. She waited for perhaps a minute, and there was still nothing. No slurping, no crunching. She opened her eyes, and looked into blackness. The candle had burnt down and gone out. The thought of walking through the doorway and possibly treading on the remains of Mike was so awful that for a little while she didn't move at all. Then Bethany remembered that there was another candle by the bed, and matches too. She stood up, moving like an old woman because her joints ached, and felt her way to the bedside table. After a little hesitation she struck a match and lit the candle. She was going to have to know, sooner or later. She picked up the candle and turned.

There was nothing there. Where Mike had stood, there was simply an empty doorway, and bare boards.

Bethany saw something gleaming on the rug: Aunt Dodo's spectacles. Since her own were in pieces, she went over and picked them up. For a moment she held them in her hands. The house was so quiet that she could hear herself swallow. Then she put the spectacles on, and everything swam into very sharp focus.

To her great relief, the tall creature was nowhere in sight. Nor was Mike.

Bethany had been rather afraid there would be something unpleasant left to see:

bones with the marks of teeth still on them, or some other indigestible bits, like the scalp. But there was nothing. No—that was not quite right. There was a very small pool of dark liquid, congealing and almost turned from red to black. As she watched, down fluttered one of the little moth things, its eyes avid. It bent swiftly, like a bird; out came an extraordinarily long tongue and lapped up the liquid. In a second or two it was all gone. The moth thing looked at Bethany with an almost embarrassed expression. Then it flitted off into the shadows.

THE NEXT MORNING, when it was fully light, Bethany went all over Aunt Dodo's house. She found various broken and plundered things. Mike had found the cooking sherry, and finished it, and he had smashed a few of the Crown Derby plates. The lock was also hanging off the back door. There was, however, no sign of Mike himself. Bethany got down on her hands and knees and examined the floorboards by the bedroom door very carefully, but she could not see any mark or stain. It was almost possible to convince herself that Mike's appearance and all that had followed had been a dream, a hallucination. But someone *had* broken in.

She picked up her old glasses from the floor and sat at the kitchen table, examining them. While she was doing this, she was aware of the moth things settling on surfaces around the kitchen, their wings humming on the air. Bethany took no notice of them. She had asked them for help, she knew, and they had brought help, and there was no doubt that she felt safe now. Mike had been no ornament to the world either. But still she did not feel *quite* ready to look at them.

Her old glasses were beyond repair—that was obvious. All the tape in the world wouldn't have cobbled them back together. Unless—or until—she got some more, it would be Aunt Dodo's spectacles or nothing. Bethany wondered what would happen if she went out into the world wearing them—to the town, for example. She had only ever worn them in and around Aunt Dodo's house. What would she see, if she walked down the main street?

Maybe nothing, she said to herself. *Maybe the moth things and ... the other thing are kind of specific to here.*

She didn't really believe that, though.

After a while, she stood up and looked around her. She did not feel ready to say "thank you"; possibly that was never going to be the right thing to say.

Instead, she went to fetch a can of condensed milk, and an opener.

Helen Grant writes Gothic novels and short supernatural fiction. Her new novel Jump Cut, *about a notorious lost movie, will be published in autumn 2023 by Fledgling Press. Filmmaker and novelist Jack Jewers describes it as "phenomenally creepy." Helen's short stories have appeared in* Weird Tales, Supernatural Tales, All Hallows, *and anthologies including Egaeus Press's acclaimed* Crooked Houses, *Swan River Press's* Uncertainties 2, *and Black Shuck Books'* Ars Gratia Sanguis (Great British Horror 6). *Joyce Carol Oates has described her as "a brilliant chronicler of the uncanny as only those who dwell in places of dripping, graylit beauty can be." A lifelong fan of M. R. James, she has spoken at two M. R. James conferences.*

"Seeing is Believing" was inspired by the tweets about fairies by fellow ghost story writer, F. K. Young (Yellow Glass, Shades of Rome) *who has a particular interest in this topic.*

ALLEN K. '84

THE ONE THAT GOT AWAY

by Gary Fry

IT WAS BUSINESS RATHER THAN CHOICE THAT DREW ME BACK TO THE PLACE IN WHICH I'D GROWN UP. Bradford hadn't changed much in the last thirty years, its rundown city centre holding back even shabbier suburbs. I'd cringed as I'd driven into the area, fearing mood-changing recollections. All the same, once my meeting had ended—the kind of financial consultation that had begun to bore even me—I found myself with some time to spare and so headed off to my old childhood haunts.

Many of the city's satellite villages were embedded in countryside. To the north, chains of them intersected roads leading into the Yorkshire Dales. It was here, in one called Thornton, that I'd spent all my years before leaving for university down south.

I parked up the Merc, got out, and wandered up and down the high street. A few shops were open, serving customers looking as dour as the weather that autumnal day. Most of the architecture was forebodingly drab, cramped terraces made of the darkest stone. There was hardly anywhere to play, I recalled, just a small park with a pond populated by pigeons and ducks.

After getting back into my family saloon and driving on, I wondered whether physical territory had the power to determine one's character. I'd been a serious-minded

child, and then teen, and then young man. Cautious, methodical, a planner ahead, I'd done well at school and spent most of my spare time reading nonfiction. Still heading through this district, it wasn't hard to see how I'd become this way.

Before long, another somber village appeared, but just then I recollected a rare period of fun in my joyless youth. Good God, I thought: Jessica Bunton. I hadn't brought her to mind since I'd married, bought a house, had kids, developed my career, and all the rest of it. If things had started out grey for me, they'd grown a lot greyer lately. But that was unfair to my family. It was just that the daily grind of earning a living, coupled with advancing age—painful joints, failing eyesight, constant tiredness—had reorganized my priorities. Stuff I'd once considered important now felt trivial, and vice versa.

That was why the merest memory of a girl I'd dated for less than a month when I was sixteen forced me to slow my car, pull over into the kerbside, and simply hold the steering wheel.

Jessica Bunton. My God.

I drove on, trying to remember where in the village she'd lived. It was curious that I'd suffered no compulsion to return to my childhood home and yet now felt inspired to revisit hers. I turned up a side street, hoping this would be the right one, but none of the houses—rows of solemn terraces, cast into shadow by thick cloud that late afternoon—resembled the blocky semi she and her family had once occupied. I steered back and forth along more avenues and groves until at last, just when I'd been about to give up, I saw it: Jessica's old place.

Its front door and windows were boarded up, as if it had been condemned. That came as a shock, though I'm not sure why. What had I expected—the girl to be out in her small front garden, jigging to and fro as she played Leapfrog and Zombie and other childish games? That was my enduring memory of her, the sheer fun she'd brought to life. The trouble was that we'd both been sixteen at the time, as good as adults. And, as an angst-ridden youth, I'd grown embarrassed by this habit of hers.

I got out of the car and strolled towards the property. I certainly hadn't expected to find Jessica living here—she'd be over forty now, surely coping with everyday burdens like my own—but would it have been surprising to discover that her parents still owned the house? I was unable to recall a lot about the couple, just that they'd been devoted to their only child, probably too much so—or at any rate, that was how I'd felt back then. Indeed, the first time Jessica had invited me to her home, she'd hopped onto her father's lap, wriggling girlishly there, and given him a sloppy kiss on the neck.

Perhaps my repressed upbringing was to blame—my own parents were unemotional, fearful of being shown up in public—but that was the first time I thought I might not get along with the young woman I'd originally met in the city centre library. We'd started talking about Edwardian history (an A-level project in her case; extracurricular interests in mine) and ended up dating. As we'd attended different schools, there was less peer pressure to deal with, just the two of us together and whether it might work out. Sadly, it hadn't.

I stepped close to the property, wondering why it had been shut up. Thick boards covered its openings, each weathered and graffitied. The building itself looked in decent shape, walls as firm as its thick slate roof. Why hadn't the place been re-marketed, sold on, bought by another family seeking a home? I was assuming that nobody since the Buntons had lived here. But that mightn't be true. Any number of other people could have occupied the place after Jessica and her parents had flitted. It was thirty years since I'd last visited, after all.

Looking up and down the street, I noticed nobody out on the pavements or even at the windows of semis similar to this one. As I lacked the opportunity to make enquiries with a neighbor, I drew in a mouthful of cool October air and then paced up a short garden path. The early evening had rendered the area gloomy, but I nonetheless observed weeds encroaching on a lawn that was more dirt than grass. Someone had kept this thicket at bay, though the surgery wasn't precise, rather hacked off at knee-height. I quickly switched my attention to the house itself.

Now I saw more clearly what I'd spotted at a distance, perhaps even the reason I'd decided to take a closer look: marker-penned words were scrawled on the board standing in for a front door.

ESSIC TH GH T TIL LIV S H RE

… read the longest of these erratic messages, and although I stared at it for several minutes, I failed to figure out what their inscriber had intended. Wear and tear had eroded it, but from the spacing I could determine that the first word was missing a first and a last letter, and the rest at least one from the various sections.

A chill wind blew, interrupting my attempt to understand what some local youth had wished to communicate. I wasted no time in trying to decode any of the other inept scrawls—most were either too faded or abusive to be bothered with—and then moved on, down the side of the building to its rear.

Had I expected the backyard to yield further clues about the absent Bunton clan? If so, I was disappointed, observing just a walled-in square of paving stones. It was darker now, and when I turned to view the property's hidden side, I had to squint through my bifocal spectacles. More boards had been attached here, covering each window featured in the building's two levels, as well as a single doorway to the right. I observed fewer examples of graffito on these, though when I stepped close to one on the left—which concealed the opening to a lounge I recalled from the past—I spotted something rather troubling. The board hung loose from its frame, rattling back and forth in a strengthening wind which suddenly caused me to shudder all over.

I used the inclement weather as an excuse for my discomfort when I paced forwards, prised back a corner of the board, and created enough space for a fully grown adult to fit through, let alone the young ruffian who must have first gained entry this way, loosening nails which held the inside in and the outside out.

What could be achieved by entering the Buntons' former home? More to the point, why was I, a respectable middle-aged man, thinking about doing so? Whatever my motivations were, I soon found myself sucking in my gut, crouching and sliding behind the dislodged board, before finally clambering over the glassless window-frame to stand again, drawing in the dry air of the house's interior.

The truth was that lately I'd been feeling wistful about the past, lamenting missed opportunities, reinterpreting events through time-jaded eyes. With my kids near school-leaving age, I'd occasionally found myself crying at night, my unsuspecting wife sleeping beside me. Being a father had proved a serious business, even during the early stages when my role was merely to entertain, playing the clown while deflecting life's many pains, at least until my son and daughter could cope without parental supervision. Later, once hormones had kickstarted their teen-hoods, my sense of loss was palpable, as if all that remained of life was a joyless crawl towards death. I felt as if I'd spent so much time being a protector that I hadn't found much fun in the task.

I stabilized my mind, trying to focus on the situation at hand. After plucking out my smartphone, I noticed that Gail had texted, asking what time I'd be back from my business trip. Her words lent me courage as I considered my next move. I sent a quick message back—"You'd better give me a few hours," I wrote, knowing that the longer I waited, the more likely the roads around our Sheffield home would thin out after the rush hours—and then switched on my phone's flashlight, animating my pitch-dark surroundings with stark illumination.

This was the very room in which Jessica had once sat coquettishly upon her daddy's lap. That wasn't the only thing I remembered about my former girlfriend. As I advanced across floorboards unhampered by furniture, I recalled the way she'd often run towards me from behind, leaping to be caught in piggy-back style. I wasn't sure she'd been aware of the sexual connotations of having her legs wrapped around a male's waist, even from the rear. In this and other matters, Jessica had struck me as naïve, quite unlike the girls who attended my own school, who'd seemed to understand even more than the boys.

I passed along the hallway from which the kitchen branched off. Pointing my phone through the doorway, I examined this room, the flashlight bringing all its crooked fixtures into dramatic relief and causing shadows to dance beyond them like restless puppets. But these bobbing shapes, frightening at first sight, were all each unit yielded. I couldn't imagine how long all the fittings had stood in such disrepair. Bedraggled spiderwebs draped across every angle while dust on work surfaces had assumed the density of soil. I backed away and returned to the stairwell, where suddenly I heard a sound from elsewhere.

I turned, lashing my phone back and forth. On the uncarpeted hallway floor, the flashlight picked out a series of markings, none of which I'd observed before crossing them. They looked like chalked squares, arranged in an alternating pattern of one and two, one and two. I saw a number scribbled in each lopsided box, but just then, before I could interpret the whole, I was distracted by a revival of that noise. It was surely coming from the upper storey of the house.

Only now did I recall that Jessica had once performed other activities unsuited to her age. Indeed, how many still indulged in such childish pursuits at sixteen years old? My question was prompted by my impression that the noise I still heard from the second level as I slowly climbed the stairs—a whiplash sound punctuated by insubstantial thuds, as if the culprit capered on the floor's bare boards—resembled that of *someone skipping with a rope.*

I continued to ascend, a reckless attempt to disprove this alarming interpretation. At the top, the layout of the building invited me to turn right, but that was when I noticed a passage to the left, one occupied by a figure which immediately raised its arms in advance of assaulting me...

Ah, but *no.* As nothing more than a jolt of horror struck home, I realized what my assailant was.

Just a mirror, by God—a grime-besmeared mirror hanging on the landing wall. The interloper appearing in the unclean glass was in fact *myself.* And now that was decided, I could refocus on why I'd advanced up here.

Standing stock-still on the landing, I listened again, trying to determine what could possibly produce a noise like someone skipping in one of the rooms up ahead. Rats scurrying across floorboards, perhaps? Or restless birds trapped among roof beams? Just as I'd begun to convince myself of these explanations, the sound ceased, whatever febrile agent had performed the activities surely becoming stationary.

The silence didn't last long, however. Indeed, was someone—and frankly, not much of someone—now edging across the floor shielded by any of three doors up here, the entrances to (I knew from memory) a bathroom and two bedrooms?

My pulse thumping in each ear, I recalled more from the past, how Jessica had liked to play Hide and Seek. She'd been good at it, always able to locate me with uncanny *nous.* We'd even once played the game in this very building. I'd always perceived a sexual undercurrent to our proceedings, a coquettish strand in my girlfriend. But I'd never been quite sure if that was the case.

I advanced for the first of the waiting rooms, the bathroom directly ahead. I'd once entered that without realizing it was already occupied by Jessica's father—Tom, he'd been called, a portly, bearded man. Fortunately, he'd been doing nothing other than trimming the bushy growth around his neck, though the moment had been embarrassing for both of us anyway. I'd had the impression that for each member of the Bunton family, many such episodes were.

On this occasion, there was no awkwardness to deal with: the room was empty, offering only a toilet, a bath, and a sink unit scattered with dislodged fragments of ceiling. My flashlight explored what little of their ceramic surfaces remained unblemished by decay. The foul smell must be of undigested sewage; none of the property's plumbing would have been attended to in years.

I moved next door, into the master bedroom where my girlfriend's parents had once slept. I'd been in here only once before—during a game of Hide and Seek, in fact, when I'd found Jessica crouching inside a wardrobe. Thirty years on, after edging open the door, I spotted no such item of furniture, nor a bed, nor any other object. The room was as empty as the others here I'd inspected.

In one dark corner, briefly illuminated when I pointed my phone that way, I noticed a dark patch splayed across the paperless plasterboards, stretching from the floor level to about waist-height. A leaking roof would surely lead to rot from the top down, but I was no expert. Pacing away, I refused to close the door behind me; that would serve as a reminder that I had nothing to fear.

Now there was only a single room left to

explore, the one I'd deliberately put off until last: Jessica's bedroom. Before ending our month-long relationship, I'd got no further than kissing the girl, and even then, only polite pecks on one cheek. There'd been no chance of anything more audacious in either of our bedrooms. My parents were uptight about such matters, and the older Buntons had always patrolled their property like chaperones. Perhaps neither of them had understood that at the time—the bawdy '80s, when sexual *mores* had slackened to the point of promiscuity—people no longer "waited until they were married."

Whatever the truth had been, a lack of progress with Jessica on an intimate plane had hastened my decision to separate from her. And if this was now an attitude for which I should crave forgiveness, I'd gladly do so.

"What did I know back then?" I said, my voice addressing the sounds of someone— or at least some*thing*—lurking behind this final doorway. "I was just a kid. I had no idea what was truly valuable in life."

As I took hold of the grease-smeared door handle and hoisted my phone to animate whatever it was I was about to see, I let myself inside my former girlfriend's bedroom.

If I was buying into the creepiest suggestions of my imagination, this wilful act served as a psychological exorcism, an effort to rid my conscience of transgressions of the past. How else to account for the way I'd just attempted to communicate with a tenant of the rundown property? Jessica couldn't be *here*. She'd be in another home, playing more of her beloved games with kids of her own. I'd been wrong to consider her penchant for fun a fault of her younger self; it had taken me three decades to understand what she'd perhaps known intuitively. At any rate, that was what I planned to tell any denizen of the dark up ahead.

But there was nothing beyond the door. My inner emotional self had again undermined any rational control, the kind I drew upon in my dull work in finance. As I cast my phone to the left and right, I no longer felt guilty but acutely foolish, as if I'd descended into the very juvenile mindset on which I'd been reflecting. Even when I spotted the wardrobe occupying one corner—the only piece of furniture this house seemed to possess—I told myself that nobody could be inside it, perhaps still enjoying, after so many years, a fun game of Hide and Seek.

All the same, as I fully entered the room, I decided to check. If I turned and left, a small irrational part of me might remain unsatisfied, constantly wondering *what if.* I could eliminate such nonsense by simply tugging open the doors, glancing inside the wardrobe, perceiving nothing of significance there, and then moving away, heading home for my wife and children, the better to get on with the rest of my humdrum life.

After pacing quickly that way, I grabbed the twin handles and gave them a firm yank. The doors parted from the carcass of the wardrobe with a sticky sound of grease separating. When I raised my flashlight, I saw only shadows retreat inside, a rapid scurrying movement which gathered in one corner like wary vermin.

But how could I account for a patch of blackness that refused to capitulate to my phone's light? The dark shape stretched up across the rear wooden panels, like a garment hanging upside down, defying gravity. At that very moment, I recalled a similar sight back in the master bedroom, the patch climbing one wall I'd taken for a stain. And had it not been that at all? Was the darkness I saw before me rather the other side of a *secret passageway* connecting the two rooms?

When I reached out a hand, my fingers, expecting the grainy resistance of timber, fell upon only emptiness. It was true. Someone had roughly fashioned a gap through both the bedrooms' dividing wall and this rotting wardrobe, a space narrower than any adult but wide enough surely to accommodate a lean teen. And what other purpose could it serve than perhaps for a game he or she liked to play?

Just then, I heard another sound from behind, out in the hallway beyond the bedroom door. If that had been a gassy giggle, it surely couldn't have emerged from anything that resembled a mouth. It was accompanied a moment later by a sharp thudding noise, as if something small and circular had just been dropped. The object proceeded to move with a rough rumble, perhaps rolling across the uncarpeted floor.

I hurried out of the room, looking downwards into the light cast by my phone. A solitary marble was just coming to a halt amid the unstirred debris of many years. I desperately wanted to believe that it had been here earlier and had only now been stirred by my intrusion. But I was unable to suspend that belief for long. Indeed, my mind quickly turned elsewhere. If someone had tossed the small opaque ball through the master bedroom's doorway, I was determined to see who it was.

I hurried across to the threshold, thinking all the while that I detected other footfalls —much less tangible than mine—scampering in the unseen room. If the sounds had been just echoes of my own paces, I'd have nothing to observe as I raised my flashlight to look inside … unless the occupant had now re-entered the slender gap in the wall from which he or she had emerged only moments ago.

What game was my tormenter playing with me? Hide and Seek seemed the most obvious choice, but as I angled my phone into that far corner, I noticed nothing other than a brief blur, vanishing inside the vaginal parting. That might have been just my vision at fault, as tears of fear gathered in my eyes. I blinked, clearing my sight of that passageway forged between each bedroom. There was nothing there, only a vague sound trailing, the same hissing expulsion I'd taken earlier for laughter.

Birds in the property's eaves, I told myself. More rats, frantically gnawing at foodstuff. At any rate, having inspected every part of this house, I was suddenly eager to flee. That marble *had* to have been on the landing the whole time, pitched into motion by the draft I felt as I hurried towards the staircase. Whatever the truth was, I was careful not to tread on the small ball as I advanced. Succumbing to such a banana skin mishap would surely amuse any playful onlooker.

"*Such nonsense … so stupid,*" I told myself, but then, the very moment I glanced into that dusty mirror at the end of the landing,

I spotted *a figure* behind me, standing in the jaws of Jessica's former bedroom.

I halted and yet refused to turn—was in fact unable to do so. The angle at which I viewed my pursuer was an acute diagonal, and so I could see only part of its body as it slowly moved ahead, the whole shielded by myself in the glass. The newcomer didn't possess much I'd describe as legs, and I'd assign similar status to the rest of a frame as tatty as any clothing I couldn't be certain it wore. It raised threadbare arms, skin covering bone less effectively than fabric concealed flesh, and then it seemed to accelerate.

As it came at me, faster and faster, it dropped an item, a lengthy wriggling thing which I took at first for a snake but then realized was a filthy skipping rope. When my assailant rushed on, the rope joined the errant marble on the hallway's bare boards.

Rapid blinking made my eyes refocus. The screech the incoming thing made was girlishly high, produced by a tattered throat that pulsed in the light I kept pointed into the mirror. That was when I saw its face. The eyes, eaten away in most places, were unsupported by intact lids, just emaciated folds that left the orbs exposed. Whatever hair it had once possessed was little more than a crazy thatch, clinging to a scalp as white as bone, if not actually composed of that substance. And its mouth—oh Christ, its *mouth*…

That was all I saw before the figure leapt upon me, flinging around my neck overly narrow limbs, each as brittle as uncoupled tree branches. It settled into its piggyback ride, pressing against my back a chest so corrugated it was a wonder the thing retained its upper structure. As I tried not gagging on a stench of decay, my rider pushed its head over one of my shoulders, showing me again what hung beneath its mess of a nose.

My terror aided perception of a chin concealed by a long spillage of black beard. A half-moist slit above opened to expose fragments of teeth barely supported by blistered gums. For a second, I thought it was about to speak but suddenly it revealed its true purpose: to deliver a single kiss on one side of my neck.

"*No!*" I cried, finally capable of a response other than disabling fright. I shrugged the thing off, hearing parts of its body crack on the ground behind me.

Then, my flashlight lashing wildly, I was away, back down that staircase and into the hallway below. As the floor of the hall passage was dramatically relit, I realized what those chalked boxes formed: a Hopscotch grid. Suddenly I realized that Skipping, Hide and Seek, and Marbles weren't the only games played by the property's gleeful occupant. Indeed, as I heard the travesty above getting back up to give dogged pursuit, I understood that it must be rather fond of Tag, too.

It wasn't an *it*, I told myself; it was a *she*. All the same, as footsteps so unstable they could only belong to some mindless puppet continued to approach, I wasted no further time. I headed for the window covered by that loose board, climbed through, dropped to the ground outside, sucked in lungs full of mercifully cool air, and finally advanced along the side of the building for my car parked at the front.

My flashlight helped me to avoid tripping on the unkempt garden path. Then I was back in the street, which remained deserted, and moments later, inside my car. I started the engine with a hand that shook so badly it took three attempts to poke the key home. Clutch, gearstick, and accelerator were handled with little more competence, but eventually I had control of the vehicle, thrusting it away from the kerbside and surging past that terrible house.

The last I saw of the place was my headlamps splashing across its vandalized frontage. That was when I read again:

ESSIC TH GH T TIL LIV S H RE

Even when I looked away, I pictured the words in my mind, was unable to dismiss them. And by the time I'd reached the end of the street, I'd solved the puzzle, as if nothing could have been more obvious.

The message disturbed me all the way home to my family, thirty miles to the south.

LATER THAT NIGHT, once my kids were in bed and my wife had turned in too, I learned what I could from the internet. An article stored in the online archives of Bradford's only newspaper revealed that in the late 1980s, a woman called Jessica Bunton, just eighteen years old, had killed herself by consuming poison. The reporter quoted her parents as saying that "yet another boy had disappointed her" and that she'd drank a toxic substance after he'd "ended their relationship." Although she'd regurgitated some of the liquid, she'd died later in hospital from "significant organ damage." The young man in question had refused to comment, though the journalist had named him as Jason Cromby.

As heartless as it might seem, I couldn't help thinking that, as these events had occurred years after I'd dated the girl, I couldn't be held responsible for the desperate thing she'd been driven to. Poor Jessica, I thought, speculating that her childlike attitude to life might have scared off a second (or even third or fourth or who knew how many) would-be suitor.

As I listened to furtive noises outside in my leafy neighborhood—maybe a cat or fox seeking quarry nearby—something about the newspaper article troubled me. I had to read it several more times before I figured out what this was. The girl's mother or father had claimed that *yet another* boy had disappointed Jessica, as if one alone wouldn't have prompted her suicide. Did that suggest that however many of us she'd dated, we'd *all* conspired to push her towards such a terrible act?

Should I feel guilty, after all?

Shutting a window to eliminate that same prowling sound—whatever lurked out there must now have entered my garden—I typed into a search engine the name of one of my romantic successors, the young man who'd been seeing Jessica just before her suicide: Jason Cromby from Bradford.

The surname was uncommon, and only a single story arose from a review of a different online resource. In the early 2000s, a guy in his mid-thirties from West Yorkshire had been driving near his new home in Manchester when his car had gone off the road, killing its driver. The cause of the accident was uncertain—no alcohol had been found in the man's blood, and no evidence of any altercation with another motorist could be identified. Friends had speculated about his tendency to pick up hitchhikers, but inspection of his vehicle had revealed DNA belonging only to himself and to people he'd known personally. Jason Cromby had left behind a wife and two children.

Was something pacing directly outside my property? The noises it (*she*) made sounded too loud to belong to any animal... But I was supposed to be focusing on my investigation. At that moment, all I was able to picture in my mind's eye was a female's gruesome face leering over the front seats of a car to offer its driver a goodnight kiss. Her chin bore bearded traces of the poison she'd expelled before the rest had scorched out her innards. Then the only thing I could

think about was my experience earlier that evening, inside that derelict property.

Perhaps the bedraggled spirit of Jessica Bunton hadn't been playing Hide and Seek at the time, after all. Perhaps she only did so *now*, drawing on the uncanny nous she'd always used to locate me on every occasion. As something—some*one*—tampered with my front door downstairs, I recalled the rules of the game: the Hider was given some time in which to find a suitable place to conceal himself. Then the Seeker began to hunt.

JESSICA THE GHOST STILL LIVES HERE, I thought as my front door handle rattled again. Yes, she continued to dwell beyond the graffitied boards of that house. But could she get out as easily as I'd got in? Could she travel the modest distance between there and here—maybe hitchhiking in body-concealing

clothes, as she must have done in the past —inside of a few hours? And might she now violate my home, stalking upstairs before I could protect my family?

I rose from my seat, stepped out of the spare room, and descended the staircase for the door. A shape was pressed up against its frosted glass panel, a moonlit outline, unspeakably crooked. The door handle jigged up and down once more.

After drawing in a panicky breath, I paced ahead.

Whatever happened next, I knew I'd struggle to find much fun in it.

Gary Fry is a semi-retired academic who lives in coastal countryside in the northeast of England. He has had published around 100 short stories, a bunch of novellas, and several novels. He was the first author in PS Publishing's Showcase range, and none other than Ramsey Campbell has described him as a "master of philosophical horror." He plays piano, loves dogs, and reads a frightening number of books each year. His web presence can be found at:

https://garyfrytalks.blogspot.com

KOLCHAK: THE NIGHT STALKER   I WALKED WITH A ZOMBIE

NIGHTMARE ABBEY

BIG PREMIER ISSUE
RAMSEY CAMPBELL
13 QUESTIONS and THREE TERROR TALES

①

STEVE DUFFY ☠ GREGORY L. NORRIS   JASON J. McCUISTON
HELEN GRANT ☠ DAVID SURFACE   ALLEN KOSZOWSKI
JOSEPH PAYNE BRENNAN   LYNDA E. RUCKER
JUSTIN HUMPHREYS   DOUGLAS SMITH
HENRY KUTTNER   ROBERT BLOCH
KURT NEWTON   A. M. BURRAGE
JAMES DORR

NOT A MUSCLE QUIVERED AS THE MAN STOOD WITH HIS GAZE FIXED ON THE DEAD WOMAN.

Through half-closed eyes he looked at the white form on the marble slab, with a red gash between the breasts where the cruel knife had entered. In spite of its rigidity, the body had kept its rounded beauty and seemed alive. Only the hands, with their too-transparent skin and violet fingernails, and the face with its glazed wide-open eyes and blackened mouth, a mouth that was set in a horrible grin, told of the eternal sleep.

The Test:
Confrontation
By Maurice Level

An oppressive silence weighed on the dreary stone-paved hall. Lying on the floor beside the dead woman was the sheet that had covered her: there were bloodstains on it. The magistrates were closely watching the accused man as he stood unmoved between the two warders, his head well up, a supercilious expression on his face, his hands crossed behind his back.

The examining magistrate opened the proceedings:

"Well, Bourdin, do you recognize your victim?"

The man moved his head, looking first at the magistrate, then with reflective attention at the dead woman, as if he were searching in the depths of his memory.

"I do not know this woman," he said at length in a slow voice. "I have never seen her before."

"Yet there are witnesses who will state on oath that you were her lover..."

"The witnesses are mistaken. I never knew this woman."

"Think well before you answer," said the magistrate, after a moment's silence. "What is the use of trying to mislead us? This confrontation is the merest formality, not at all necessary in your case. You are intelligent, and if you wish for any clemency from the jury, I advise you in your own interests to confess."

"Being innocent, I have nothing to confess."

"Once again, remember that these denials have no weight at all. I myself am prepared to believe that you gave way to a fit of passion, one of these sudden madnesses when a man sees red... Look again at your victim... Can you see her lying there like that and feel no emotion, no repentance?"

"Repentance, you say? How can I repent of what I have not done? As for emotion, if mine was not entirely deadened, it was at least considerably lessened by the simple fact that I knew what I was going to see when I came here. I feel no more emotion than you do yourself. Why should I? I might just as well accuse you of the crime because you stand there unmoved.

He spoke in an even voice without gestures, as a man would who had complete control of himself. The overwhelming charge left him apparently undisturbed, and he confined his defense to calm, obstinate denials.

One of the minor officials said in an undertone: "They will get nothing out of him. He will deny it even on the scaffold."

Without a trace of anger, Bourdin replied: "That is so, even on the scaffold."

The sultry atmosphere of an impending thunderstorm added to the feeling of exasperation caused by the struggle between accusers and accused, by this obstinate "no" to every question in the face of all evidence.

Through the dirty windowpane the setting sun threw a vivid golden glare on the corpse.

"So be it," said the magistrate: "You do not know the victim. But what about this?"

He held out an ivory-handled knife, a large knife with clotted blood on its strong blade.

The man took the weapon in his hands, looked at it for a few seconds, then handed it to one of the warders and wiped his fingers.

"That?... I have never seen it before."

"Systematic denial ... that is your plan, is it?" Sneered the magistrate. "This knife is yours. It used to hang in your study. Twenty people have seen it there."

The prisoner bowed.

"That proves nothing but that twenty people have made a mistake."

"Enough of this," said the magistrate. "Though there is not a shadow of doubt about your guilt, we will make one last decisive test. There are marks of strangulation on the neck of the victim. You can clearly see the traces of five fingers, particularly long fingers, the medical expert tells us. Show these gentlemen your hands. You see?"

The magistrate raised the chin of the dead woman.

There were violet marks on the white skin of the neck: at the end of every bruise the flesh was deeply pitted, as if the nails had been dug in. It looked like the skeleton of a giant leaf.

"There is your handiwork. Whilst with your left hand you were trying to strangle this poor woman, with your free right hand you drove this knife into her heart. Come here and repeat the action of the night of the murder. Place your fingers on the bruises of the neck... Come along..."

Bourdin hesitated for a second, then shrugged his shoulders and said in a sullen voice: "You wish to see if my fingers correspond?... And suppose they do?... What will that prove?"

He moved towards the slab: he was noticeably paler, his teeth were clenched, his eyes dilated. For a moment he stood very still, his gaze fixed on the rigid body, then with an automaton-like gesture, he stretched out his hand and laid it on the flesh.

The involuntary shudder that ran through him at the cold, clammy contact caused a sudden, sharp movement of his fingers, which contracted as if to strangle.

Under this pressure, the set muscles of the dead woman seemed to come to life. You could see them stretch obliquely from the collarbone to the angle of the jaw: the mouth lost its horrible grin and opened as if in an atrocious yawn, the dry lips drew back to disclose teeth encrusted with thick brown slime.

Everyone started with horror.

There was something enigmatic and terrifying about this gaping mouth in this impassive face, this mouth opened as if for a death-rattle from beyond the portals of the grave, the sound only held back by the swollen tongue that was doubled back in the throat.

Then, all at once, there came from that black hole a low, undefined noise, a sort of humming that suggested a hive, and an enormous bluebottle with shining wings, one of these charnel-house flies that live on death, and unspeakably filthy beast, flew out, hissing as it circled round the cavern as if to guard the approach. Suddenly it paused... then made a straight course for the blue lips of Bourdin.

With a motion of horror, he tried to drive it away: but the monstrous thing came back, clinging to his lip with all the strength of its poisonous claws.

With one bound the man leapt backwards, his eyes wild, his hair on end, his hands stretched out, his whole body quivering as he shrieked like a madman:

"I confess!... I did it!... Take me away! Take me away!"

French novelist Maurice Level's spare, 1200-word story "The Test," a retitled, English translation of his tale "Confrontation" (1910), first appeared in the author's 1920 collection Tales of Mystery and Horror.

A master of the macabre, Maurice Level (1875–1926) wrote numerous tales for French newspapers, several of which were adapted for the theatre and performed by the Grand Guignol, a Paris repertory company famous for its naturalistic horror shows emphasizing violence, blood, and gore.

"We can only admire, now almost one hundred years later," critic Philippe Gontier wrote, "the great artistry with which Maurice Level fabricated his plots, with what care he fashioned all the details of their unfolding and how with a master's hand he managed the building of suspense."

"Confrontation" was translated by the English journalist, editor, and publisher Alys Eyre Macklin (1875–1929).

Nightlight

By Ian Rogers

WHEN THE LIGHTS WENT OUT, I FELT LIKE CRYING, BUT I MADE MYSELF LAUGH INSTEAD. It seemed like the right move, sitting in a bar next to a pretty girl. If I had been at home alone, it might have been a different story.

The bar was called Smitty's or Smithy's or Smitey's. Something like that. It wasn't the sort of place I wanted to be stuck in the dark. But then I didn't much want to be there when the lights were on, either.

I had been dragged out by a friend, to use the term loosely, a guy named Jerry Baldwin who sold haunted real estate. Jerry was also a lawyer, and I occasionally retained him as my attorney. In return, Jerry occasionally retained me as his wingman. I'm not a very social person, but I thought it was beneficial to my mental health to get out every once in a while and mingle with the common folk. As a private investigator, the people I tend to meet either want something from me or want to keep something from me.

Jerry had left half an hour earlier with a tall redhead he kept calling Ginger even though she told him, repeatedly, that her name was Joanne. After apologizing in his smoothly charming way (people often got angry at Jerry, but never for very long), he told her she reminded him of the redhead from *Gilligan's Island*, then asked if she wanted to go back to his place for a three-hour tour. Normally a line like that would have resulted in Jerry getting slapped if he was lucky, or kneed in the nuts if he wasn't. But Joanne had seemed, if not receptive to Jerry's banter, then at least amused by it. And damned if she didn't end up leaving with him, much to the surprise of her friend,

a short-haired blonde who I learned, in my one and only conversational gambit, was named Christina.

With Jerry and Joanne gone, an awkward silence descended. Christina had expressed, by way of polite smiles and short, one-word replies, that she wasn't interested in anyone hitting on her this evening. Which was fine by me. I wasn't really in fighting-flirting form anyway.

When the lights went out, the silence held for another second or two, then the dam broke and the darkness was perforated by the surprised voices of the dozen or so people in the bar. I heard the bartender mutter, "Must be a blown fuse," then the sound of him fumbling around under the counter. A flashlight clicked on, shining a beam of light onto the ceiling, then down onto the top of the mahogany bar.

Somewhere off to my right I heard someone moving quickly across the room, followed by the clap of a chair falling over, and then a loud "Dammit!"

The bartender put his flashlight on the man, who was now hopping on one foot and holding his knee. "You break it, you bought it, Barry."

"I'll sue *you*," the man said in a growling-giggling voice. "Personal injury."

"Good luck. This place is insured against clumsy dumbasses."

I let out a gasping laugh. I'd been holding my breath without realizing it. Embarrassed

I turned to Christina on the stool next to me, but she wasn't there.

I was about to call out her name when the street door opened. The bartender brought his flashlight around and pinned Christina in the doorway, staring outside. In a low voice that managed to carry across the bar, she said: "I don't think it's a blown fuse."

I went over and stood next to her. The entire street was dark. No lights showed in any building and all of the streetlights were dead.

Christina and I looked at each other and spoke at the same time:

"Blackout."

EVEN THOUGH LAST CALL was only an hour away, the bartender decided to close early. Moving around the dark room like a theatre usher with his flashlight, he herded everyone out and locked the door behind us.

After the others dispersed, Christina and I were left standing together on the dark street. There were a few other bars on this stretch, and other ousted patrons were getting ready to make their respective journeys home. A couple of camera flashes pierced the darkness, followed by loud, drunken laughter.

"It's the digital age," Christina said. "Everyone has a camera on their phone, so now they take pictures of everything."

"Even blackouts."

"Do you have a cell phone?"

"I do," I said without much enthusiasm. I took it out and looked at the screen. "Dead."

"Dead?" Christina said in a tone of surprise bordering on shock. "You forgot to charge it?" She acted like it was one of the seven sins, and in the digital age of which she spoke, it probably was.

"This is an improvement for me," I said, trying to make light of it. "Usually I forget the damn thing at home."

"That's where mine is," Christina said. "I wanted to call a taxi."

"You should've asked the bartender before he kicked us out."

She looked back at the closed door, seemed to contemplate getting him to let her back in, then decided not to bother.

"I only live a few blocks north of here. It's not a bad neighborhood, and I don't mind walking it..."

"When the lights are on," I finished.

"Yeah." She looked at the door again, then back down the street, and let out a heavy sigh. "Listen, would you mind walking me home? I wouldn't ask, but I'm not really comfortable going by myself."

It was too dark to make out the expression on her face, but her tone of voice told me loud and clear she was less than thrilled to be stuck in this position.

"Sure," I said. "No problem."

I started to walk and Christina raised her hand in a halting motion. "Just so we're clear. I'm not asking you in when we get there."

"Understood."

"I'm not trying to be cute or coy. This is purely a safety-in-numbers thing, okay? It doesn't mean I'm interested in you."

"After a pitch like that, how could I refuse?"

"I'm sorry," she said, softening a bit. "That came off harsher than I intended. I just don't want you to get any ideas."

"It's all good. I'm happy to do it."

"Is it out of your way?" she asked. "Where do you live?"

"The Annex," I said. "I was planning to take a cab home, but I think cabs are going to be at a premium tonight. I'll probably end up walking, too."

"Are you sure?"

"It's no problem."

I didn't tell her, but I was glad to have the company, too.

I WISH I COULD SAY chivalry was the reason I agreed to walk Christina home. But there was another reason, and wild werewolves couldn't have dragged it out of me.

To put it plainly: I have a bit of a problem with the dark. It's not a full-on fear, more of a low-level anxiety, but still not something I mention on a first date. It was a relatively new thing for me. As a kid, the dark didn't bother me at all. One thing I've learned about irony: it's only funny when it isn't happening to you.

So when I told Christina I was happy to walk her home, I was telling the truth, but not all of it. She didn't want to be alone, and neither did I. The difference was she could admit it and I couldn't. Speaking the words out loud would force me to confront the real truth. That I'm not really afraid of the dark.

I'm afraid of the things that *live* in the dark.

CHRISTINA SAID she lived off Queen Street, about four or five blocks north of the bar. It wasn't that far during the daylight hours, or even at night with the streetlights on, but in the complete and total darkness of a city-wide blackout, it seemed miles away.

By the time we left the Distillery District, we were the only ones on the street. I suppose there were other people around, walking home like us, but it was too dark to see them. At one point a car creeped slowly by with its high beams on, but that was it for road traffic.

"Kind of spooky," Christina said.

"Yeah."

"Were you here for the 2006 blackout?"

"Yep."

"Was it like this?"

I shrugged. "I don't know. It was a blackout. They all kind of look the same." I looked to see if she smiled, but it was too dark to tell. "I was at home when it happened, so it wasn't so bad. The worst thing that happened was I had to eat everything in my fridge and freezer, and I ended up putting on about ten pounds. Were you here?"

"No," Christina said. "I was living in Guelph at the time. We lost power, but it wasn't like this."

"Like what?"

"I don't know. The dark here seems different somehow. More... total. I thought I'd be able to recognize things, but..." She trailed off, shaking her head.

I understood what she meant. A city at night was still familiar, if only because the streetlights and the lighted signs provided a reminder of what it looked like during the day. But a city at night in a blackout was as alien as the surface of Mars.

"A city never gets completely dark at night," I said. "Not even during a blackout. It's only bad luck the sky is overcast tonight. If we had a moon or some stars it wouldn't seem so bad."

Christina tilted her head back and stared at the sky. "They say you can't see the stars at night in the city. Because of the light pollution."

"That's not true," I said. "You just can't see as many of them."

"Wish we had some stars now," Christina said.

We walked on in silence. Buildings materialized out of the darkness like barges drifting through thick fog. There were no signs of life. No flashlights, no candles, not even the erratic glow from a cell phone. All the windows were dark.

I told myself there was nothing strange about this. The blackout had hit after midnight on a weeknight, and most people were probably in bed asleep.

But it wasn't the lack of human activity that bothered me. It was the silence. Despite the blackout we should have been surrounded by city noise—people talking, cars honking, dogs barking—but the only sound was our feet slapping the pavement. The darkness seemed to have muffled sound as effectively as it did light.

On the plus side, my nyctophobia wasn't bothering me as much as I thought it would. I thought that meant I was getting over it, but it was more likely I was distracted by the surreal nature of the blackout. Similar to the way a nurse will pinch your arm at the same time she slips the needle into your vein. Magicians call it misdirection. I didn't care what it was called as long as it kept me from wimping out in front of the person I was supposed to be escorting home.

I glanced over at Christina. She was hugging herself even though it wasn't cold. We were in the smoggy sauna days of August, which would probably turn out to be the cause of the blackout. It was the answer to the riddle: *How many air-conditioners does it take to shut down an entire city?*

"You okay?" I asked her.

She shrugged. "It's the dark. And the quiet. It's kind of creeping me out."

I was a little creeped out myself, hearing my own thoughts spoken back to me.

"Do you think…"

"What?" I said, and then immediately regretted it.

Christina hesitated, then said "Nothing" in a dismissive tone. I knew what she was going to say, and I didn't want to hear it.

"It's just…" she started again. "This reminds me of something." She looked over at me and I could sense the uneasy smile on her face more than I could see it. "I feel kind of silly saying it."

Then don't! I wanted to grab her by the shoulders and scream it into her face. *THEN DON'T!*

But she did.

"It feels like we're in the Black Lands."

She tried to laugh it off, not because it was funny—it wasn't—but because it was absurd. Despite that, the image it conjured wouldn't go away. Most days I tried not to think about the Black Lands. I needed someone reminding me about it like I needed a sulphuric acid enema.

"Have you ever…" she began.

"Been there?" I finished. "Of course not," I lied.

"I was going to say, have you ever had a paranormal experience?"

I was taken aback by the boldness of the question. It was a sensitive subject for some people (present company included), not the sort of thing one inquired about in casual conversation.

Christina seemed to realize this and apologized. "I'm sorry," she said. "I'm… I don't know what I am. I'm not myself tonight."

"It's all right," I said. "It's the blackout." I didn't know what I meant by that, but it was something to say.

"But doesn't it feel like that to you?" Christina said. "Like we're in the Black Lands?"

"No," I said.

"I mean, not that we'd know, right? But from what you hear on the news, what we learned in school?" She looked up at the sky again. "On a night like this… no one around… not even a little bit of light to see by… this is what it would be like, right? If all the portals ripped wide open and the Black Lands came pouring through."

"That's a pleasant thought," I said. "I'm really glad you decided to share it with me right now."

Christina said, "I'm sorry," but I could hear the smile in her voice. "They say if you talk about the things you're afraid of, then they lose the power to scare you."

"Oh yeah? Well I think 'they' are full of shit."

A hand touched my left shoulder and I almost jumped out of my skin. Christina sucked in a breath. "I'm sorry!" she said. "I didn't mean to…" She stopped talking and looked at me closely. "You're really afraid, aren't you?"

She wasn't making fun of me; she sounded thoughtful and concerned.

"I'm fine," I said. "I'm just not a fan of the dark. Or the Black Lands." I took a deep breath and let it out. "I don't think you need to worry, though. You know what the government says. *You're more likely to be struck by lightning than to encounter a supernatural.*"

"You really believe that?" Christina asked.

I shrugged. "Beats the alternative."

"The news makes it sound like it happens more often than that."

"The news doesn't always report the truth."

"And the government does?"

"No," I admitted. "But it doesn't automatically make them the bad guys."

"Do you think the government really believes that attacks by supernaturals are rare?"

I tried to pick my words carefully. "I think they know saying otherwise could cause panic at best and mass-hysteria at worst."

"I don't think that would happen," Christina said defiantly. "They don't give people enough credit."

"Maybe they're not willing to take that chance."

Christina looked at me. "Do you work for the government?"

"No." I chuckled with genuine amusement. "Not at all. I'm only saying it's a complex issue. One that goes beyond what the government may or may not be keeping from us."

"I think they should tell us everything they know," Christina said. "And if there's stuff we can't deal with, we'll jam it back in the box and forget about it.'"

"That's a nice idea," I said, "but it didn't work out too well for Pandora."

"So what DO you do?"

"What?"

"You said you didn't work for the government," Christina said. "So where do you work?"

We were standing at an intersection. The street we were walking on had come to an end and I was trying to figure out where we were. I squinted my eyes at a street sign I thought said King.

"I'm a private investigator," I said.

"Seriously?"

"Yes."

"You mean like trench coats and fedoras and femme fatales?"

"I don't have a fedora, I only wear a trench coat when it rains, and the only femme fatale I know is my ex-wife." The line came out smooth and practiced. I'd had plenty of opportunities to fine-tune it. Lots of people I met thought I was Sam Spade. It was always a little disappointing to shatter that illusion. Especially for me.

"Still, it must be exciting."

"It's a job," I said. "The movies make it out to be more than it really is. Your job is probably more exciting than mine."

"I'm a baker," Christina said.

"Never mind. I win."

"Well, I bake and I own a café."

"Okay, you beat me." I pointed at the sign. "I think we've reached King Street. Which way do we go? Left or right?"

Christina looked in both directions, even though she couldn't have seen anything beyond five feet. "Left." She hesitated. "I think."

"That sounds promising."

We started walking again.

"You want to hear something funny?" Christina said.

"Funny would be nice."

"I have a flashlight app on my iPhone, but I didn't bring it with me tonight. I left it at home."

"It's all right," I said. "It's not so bad out here."

"I wasn't even planning to go out tonight," Christina went on. "I was already dressed for bed when Joanne called and asked me to come out. She's a nurse at Sick Kids and works odd hours. She wasn't supposed to be off tonight, but someone asked to switch with her so they could have Friday off. She had a free night and nothing to do, so she decided to go out and asked me to come with her, even though I had to work in the morning. She offered to buy my drinks, and she sounded so desperate, I just couldn't say no. Then she left with your friend..."

"I wouldn't hold it against her," I said. "She might hold it against him in the morning, but that's none of our business."

"I don't mind. Jo doesn't get the chance to cut loose very often."

"I pegged you for a wingman," I said. "Or wingwoman."

"How could you tell?" she asked. "Because you're a detective?"

"No," I said. "We recognize our own."

"Your friend dragged you out, too?"

"Yep."

"No offence, but he seemed like a creep."

"Your friend went home with him," I pointed out.

"Yeah, but she's hard up."

"I'm not sure if that's an insult, and if it is, I don't know who it's against, him or her. So I'll ignore it."

"You're a good wingman."

"The best. The wingman always goes home alone."

"Sorry about that." She was silent for a moment. "Maybe I could be your partner. The PI and the baker." She giggled. "It sounds like a bad TV show."

"No," I said. "If it was a bad TV show it would be called Hot Cross Buns and I'd be a detective named Cross and you'd be my sidekick-slash-baker."

"Named Buns!" Christina said, and laughed again. It sounded very loud on the quiet street.

She stopped so abruptly I turned my head to make sure she was still there.

"What's wrong?"

"Nothing," she said. "I was just thinking. It's so dark right now, I bet you could walk right through a portal and be in the Black Lands without ever realizing it."

"You'd realize it when something ripped out your guts and started eating them while you watched."

"That's a pleasant thought."

"You brought it up," I said. "You *keep* bringing it up."

"I'm sorry," Christina said. "Really I am. But I can't stop thinking about it. You hear reports of people wandering into portals and they're never seen again."

"Accidental Tourists."

"I hate that term."

"So do I," I said. "But it doesn't happen very often. At least not as often as the media says. They hype it up, because that's what they do."

"Yeah, but it *does* happen," Christina said.

"You sound like you want it to happen," I snapped at her. "What is it, owning a bakery isn't exciting enough for you? I bet you weren't pissed at all that your friend dragged you out of bed on a weeknight. You were glad to go. It gave you an excuse because you wouldn't do it yourself. And if you didn't have a good time, then you could blame her. And if you and I did somehow end up in the Black Lands tonight, you could blame that on me. Is that it?"

Christina stared at me for a long time without saying anything. I wondered if she'd skip the snappy reply and simply slug me. I deserved it. I wasn't really angry at her, or at least not so angry to warrant such an outburst.

I stood there and waited for the punch. I welcomed it. But it never came.

I took a step closer and saw she wasn't even looking at me. She was staring at something further down the street. I followed the direction of her gaze.

And saw the light.

Then I heard the scream.

IT CAME TEARING OUT of the night like a thing alive, a high-pitched cry so loud it seemed to have been ripped out of someone's throat. It went on and on, an ululating note of terror that carved a cold, jagged line down my back.

It was Christina.

But not Christina.

Her voice, but it didn't come from her.

I could tell because she was standing right next to me; if the scream had come from her, I would've been rendered deaf. Also, her hands were clamped over her mouth.

The scream tapered off, like an air siren winding down, and the silence settled back in like an old friend.

Christina turned and looked at me with wide, panic-filled eyes. Her hands came down off her mouth, pulling it open. "That was me," she said. Her voice was small and timid, as if in direct contradiction to the scream.

I'd hoped she wouldn't have noticed, but of course she did. Who wouldn't recognize their own voice?

"That was me," she said again. Her voice warbled and trembled and finally dissolved into tears. "That was *me*." She held onto the last word, stretching it out: *meeeeeeee*.

I reached out for her and she came into my arms so forcefully she almost knocked me off my feet. I wrapped my arms around her and held her. Her body jerked and hitched like she was being electrocuted. I held her tighter.

"It's true," she sobbed into my shoulder. "We crossed over. We're there!"

"We're not in the Black Lands," I assured her. "It's the blackout. You're freaking out a bit. It's okay."

She shook her head, burrowing deeper into the nook between my neck and shoulder. "No, it's true. We went through a portal. You can't see them. It happens! It happened to us!"

"Look," I said, and tried to tilt her head up. She wouldn't let me and I had to take her by the shoulders and push her away from me. Finally she relented and I touched her chin and turned her head to look across the street.

"You see that carpet cleaning shop? Now, the last I heard they don't have carpets in the Black Lands, which means they sure as hell don't have any carpet cleaners. I don't need to be a PI to tell you we're still in the same smoggy, polluted, overcrowded city we both know and love."

I turned her head to the light I'd completely forgotten about. "See that?" I said. "No lights in the Black Lands, either. Not a one."

"What is it?" she asked in a thick voice. "A streetlight?"

That's what it looked like, but it was too high.

It was a bright dot of light, sort of orange in color like an arc-sodium streetlight, but pulsing slightly, as though it was burning. It was some indeterminate distance away. Maybe a hundred yards. Maybe half a mile. It was impossible to tell without some point of reference. But it was in our path, so we headed toward it.

One thing I knew for certain.

The scream had come from the same direction as the light.

I decided not to mention it to Christina.

"I KNOW THAT PLACE," Christina said.

We were on Power Street—the irony wasn't lost on me—headed north toward Queen, following the light like a couple of moths. It was ahead of us and off to the right, hovering in the air above a greenspace that, in the dead of night and a city-wide blackout, had become a darkspace.

"What is it?" I asked.

"I think it's called Orphan's Green. It's a dog park."

As we got closer, I could see the low wire fence running around the perimeter. There were a few trees on the inside of the park and several more on the outside, providing the place with a natural camouflage that probably appealed to the dogs and their owners.

As we approached, the light flickered once, as if it was winking at us, or telling us to hurry up. The gate was open. Christina stepped through first. I followed. Then the gate swung shut and latched. I stared at it, mildly concerned. It wasn't enough to keep us from getting out—the fence was so low I could probably jump it—but it concerned me.

I turned back and saw Christina was headed toward a picnic table in the middle of the park. The light was hovering about a hundred feet in the sky directly above it. A man was sitting on the table with his feet propped on the bench seat. He was wearing what appeared to be a hooded robe.

The light flickered again, a long stuttering flash, and I held up my hand to block it out. When it stabilized, I lowered my hand and blinked until the white blobs floating in front of my eyes were gone.

I looked back at the man and saw he wasn't wearing a robe. It only looked like he was, from the way he was sitting and the way the shadows fell across his body. *When is a hood not a hood? When it's a hoodie.* I didn't know what that meant. The words had popped into my head. But it was true. The man sitting on the picnic table was wearing a hooded sweatshirt. With his hands hidden in the pouch pocket, and his head tilted down, he looked like a monk in a deep trance.

"You're dead," he said in a clear, carrying voice.

"Who are you talking to?" I asked.

The man raised his head, which should have afforded a better view of his face, but all I could see was shadow. "You," he said. "Or her." He turned his head slightly to indicate Christina. "I don't know yet."

"That sounds vaguely like a threat," I said, slipping my hands into my own pockets, feeling for a gun that wasn't there.

"Vague is right," the man said, and laughed. It was a good-natured laugh, friendly and disarming, the kind that makes you want to join in. "But I don't make threats. I... forecast."

"Did you forecast the blackout?" I asked.

"Nope! But I'll use it."

"For what?"

"For taking one of you with me."

"We don't want any trouble," I said. "We're on our way home."

"Think of this as a detour," the man said.

"Thanks," I said, "but I think we'll pass."

I reached out and took Christina's hand.

"There's no pass," the man said, and again he turned his head, first one way and then the other, to both ends of the park. I wouldn't have been able to see what he was looking at if the light above us hadn't flared bright at that very moment. I wished it hadn't.

There were *things* in the park.

Tall. Spindly. Dark.

That was the only way I could describe them.

It was like the shadows of the trees had come alive and surrounded us. One was positioned in front of the gate. Two stood at the far end of the park, towering above the dead streetlights. They didn't make a sound.

"No," Christina said. She started shaking her head emphatically back and forth. "No no no no no."

I reached out for her, but she was too fast. She buttonhooked around me and went tearing across the park toward the gate. The light fluttered and dimmed. Darkness fell like a curtain.

Christina screamed.

It was the same scream we'd heard earlier. The exact same. High and carrying. Full of blood-chilling terror. A scream that felt like a rusty knife dragged across my soul.

Christina came stumbling back out of the darkness and collapsed into my arms. I held her and whispered in her ear that it was going to be okay. I can lie very well when I need to.

"You can't play yet, girl," the shadow man said. "I haven't even told you the rules." He laughed. "Why don't you come over here and kneel down in front of me."

I approached the shadow man with Christina burrowing into me. "Why should we?" I asked.

"You'll be here a long time if you don't," the shadow man said. "This night can go on forever or it can end right now. Time makes no difference to me. I think the young lady figured that out for herself."

Christina's body quaked and quivered against me. I wanted to ask her what she saw, but a part of me didn't want to know, thought it would be bad to know. Very bad.

"What do you want?" I asked.

The shadow man took his hands out of his pockets and spread his arms at the ground. "First, I'd like you to kneel," he said. "I've got a bad neck. Don't make me keep looking up at you." He laughed again.

I whispered in Christina's ear: "Let's just do as he asks." I started to let her go, then quickly wrapped my arms back around her as I felt her slumping to the ground. I lowered her gently, slipping my hand around her shoulder to keep her propped up as I dropped down to one knee, then the other.

"I'm heading back shortly," the shadow man said. "But I don't like to travel alone. So one of you is coming with me."

"Where?" Christina said.

"I think you know."

Christina lowered her head and sobbed.

I tried to peer into the shadow man's face. "You're saying you're from the Black Lands?"

"I don't need to say a thing."

"I don't believe you."

"You want me to invite my friends over?"

The shadow man started to raise his hand, and Christina cried out, "No! Please!"

"Why do you want to take one of us with you?" I asked. "Are you that hard up for company?"

The shadow man stared down at me, and although I couldn't see a single facial feature inside his hood, I had the impression he was grinning.

"I like you," he said. "I hope you're the one who comes with me. I think we'd have some fun."

I listened to his voice, trying to find something in it that would tell me something, anything, about him, but it was smooth and inflectionless, with no trace of an accent.

"This is the way it's going to be," the shadow man said. "One of you is going to abandon the other. I don't care who it is, but you'll have to choose. If you try to run, my friends will rip you both into bite-sized pieces for the doggies to snack on in the morning." He chuckled. "One goes, one stays. The one who stays comes with me. The one who goes"—he raised a finger and pointed at the ball of light hovering above us—"my other friend will lead you home. A word of advice to that person, whoever it turns out to be: follow the light, do not deviate, or you'll both be coming with me."

"Do you mind if we...?" I gestured with my head.

Is that what was happening here?

Did the shadow man trap us, or did we trap ourselves?

I had a feeling the answer was neither.

"Why is he doing this?" Christina asked in a low, trembling voice. "What *is* he?"

"I don't know what he is," I said. "I don't know if he's from the Black Lands or if he only wants us to think he is. Maybe he's an Accidental Tourist or someone infected by the Influence."

"He doesn't have a face!"

"Maybe he does but we can't see it."

Something clicked in my brain.

"Maybe he *is* the dark."

Christina frowned. "What?"

"The blackout. I think he was telling the truth when he said he didn't cause it. But maybe he's here because of it."

Christina's frown deepened. "Because he's…dark?"

"He wants to separate us. That's what the dark does best. It likes to get us alone."

Christina gripped my hand. She looked so tired, so completely worn out, like she'd been walking the dark streets for days. It felt like days.

"Felix, I don't want to be alone."

I gave her hand a return squeeze. "I don't want to be alone, either."

"You won't leave me?"

I shook my head. "But if you want to go… I mean, if you think you could…"

She shook her head and looked up at the light in the sky. "I don't think it would lead me home." Her eyes met mine. "I don't trust it."

I nodded. "Okay then. We'll stick together. Partners, right? The PI and the baker?"

She gave me a wan smile and nodded.

We turned together and walked back over to the shadow man.

"So," he said. "What have you decided?"

"Please," the shadow man said. "Take your time. But not too much. The planet spins."

I led Christina a short distance away. She was sniffling and wiping at her eyes. If she had told me right then and there she couldn't stand to go with the shadow man, that she hated to do it but she had to leave me, she simply *had* to, I would have let her.

Not because I'm a white knight (I'm not), and not because I have a death wish (I don't), but because I knew there was no way I'd ever be able to live with myself if I abandoned her.

But I didn't think it would come to that.

There was something about the shadow man's deal. Something I didn't like. Not so much in the deal itself, but rather in the way he had presented it to us. He made me think of a lawyer, the kind who gets you to incriminate yourself and then looks around all surprised and innocent as the guards haul you away.

"We're not leaving here," I said. "Not alone. We're going together."

"I wouldn't advise that." The shadow man spread his hands. "If you try to leave, I won't be responsible for what my friends do to you."

I turned to Christina. She nodded. I looked back at the shadow man. "Fair enough. I guess we'll stick around."

I don't know what it was, certainly not something I could see on the shadow man's face; maybe something in his posture, or the tilt of his head. Whatever it was, for the first time he seemed unsure.

After an interval that might have been several minutes or only a few seconds, he said: "That's your decision? My friends aren't—"

"We didn't make a decision," I interrupted him. "To be honest, we didn't care much for the choices. So we've decided to opt out."

More silence from the shadow man. Then, in a noticeably thinner voice: "Opt... out."

I couldn't tell if he was unfamiliar with the term or if he simply found it disagreeable.

"That is ... unfortunate."

A word that could mean different things to different people. Especially on a night like this. But I didn't say that to him.

I was done talking.

THE NIGHT PASSED.

Christina and I sat on the ground under the gaze of the shadow man and his pulsing nightlight. We leaned against each other. We didn't speak. Christina slept for a while; I could hear her soft snores. I think I dozed a bit, too. Hard to believe, under those circumstances, but I did.

The shadow man's friends remained at their posts around the perimeter of the park. They never came any closer.

The shadow man had told a lot of lies this night, but I think he was telling the truth about one thing. There *were* rules, and one of them was he couldn't take us with him, not unless one of us had made a clear decision to abandon the other.

I thought we could have probably walked right out of there and nothing would have happened. We'd made a decision to stick together, and there was nothing his friends could do about it as long as we presented a united front.

Unfortunately I wasn't confident enough in my theory to test it against our lives.

At some point I realized the sky was lightening. The dark no longer seemed as dark. Dawn was coming, but before it arrived, the shadow man had one last thing to say.

"You know you're only putting this off," he said. "You can't hold back the darkness forever."

I said I knew.

"This is your last chance to make a decision," he said.

"We'll see you around," I said.

"That you will," the shadow man said. "The planet spins."

With final words like those, I expected him to disappear. And he did. But not all at once. It was a slow fade, like watching a Polaroid picture develop in reverse. The rest of the darkness went with him, slowly, gradually, bleeding out of the air. The shadows retreated back to their corners and hollows. The nightlight hanging above us flickered and went out.

I took Christina's hand and we walked out of the park. At the gate a man came in past us walking a dachshund. "Power's out, eh?" he said cheerily.

"Oh yeah?" I said. "I hadn't noticed."

I WALKED CHRISTINA HOME.

She lived in a small white bungalow with chocolate brown shutters. It looked like something out of a fairy tale. Or maybe it was only because of the night we'd had. I stood on the sidewalk and watched her walk up the flagstone path to the front door. She stood there for a moment, then turned back to face me.

"Thank you," she said.

"Thank *you*," I said back.

"I feel different." She looked different, too, but I didn't mention it.

"You'll feel better after you get some sleep," I said.

"Will I?" Her gaze drifted away. "I think

I'll keep the café closed today."

"Good idea."

She started to turn away, then stopped. "That really happened, right? All of it?"

I nodded.

"It feels like a dream."

"I know."

"Was it a dream?"

"Not unless we had it together."

"Will I remember it later?"

"Do you want to?"

"No," she said, and gave a small shudder.

"You'll be okay. We're still partners, right?"

That got a smile out of her. A small one. "*Hot Cross Buns*," she said. "I'll make you some if you want."

"I don't even know what they are."

"Come by tomorrow and I'll show you."

I said I would, even though we both knew that I wouldn't.

Last night *was* a dream and now it was over.

I waved at her and started home.

Time to wake up.

Ian Rogers is the author of the award-winning collection, Every House Is Haunted. *His novelette, "The House on Ashley Avenue," was a finalist for the Shirley Jackson Award, and is the basis for an upcoming Netflix film produced by Sam Raimi. Ian lives with his wife in Peterborough, Ontario.*

For more information, visit ianrogers.ca

A SPECTER-HAUNTED PLACE DEDICATED TO THE CELEBRATION OF ALL THINGS THAT RESIDE WITHIN THE SUPERNATURAL HORROR REALM!

HOME IS WHERE YOU'RE HAUNTED
MY 13 FAVORITE HAUNTED HOUSE STORIES

AS YOU ARE PRESENTLY reading this volume of *Nightmare Abbey*, it's safe to assume you have a love for the horror genre. If asked to narrow such a wide field down to a single favorite sub-genre, which would you choose? That's an easy decision for me, because for as long as I can remember, I've had an unabashed adoration for the haunted house story.

I get absorbed in uncovering the mystery of what ties these spirits of the dead, or similar other-worldly entities, to such a singular location, forcing them to exert their bodiless influences in whatever fashion their environment allows. Even as young as seven years old these stories had their spectral hooks in me, as evidenced by the crayon-drawn picture book I made around that age about a house full of malicious ghosts. It was an incoherent mess, which also involved a giant octopus for some reason, but it displays how fascinated by these tales I already was at that point.

During my elementary school days, I sated my fledgling haunted house hunger through the likes of the Alfred Hitchcock and the Three Investigators books *The Secret of Terror Castle* and *The Mystery of the Green Ghost*. They were particular favorites of mine despite their hauntings being exposed as frauds. I also devoured lots of Choose Your Own Adventure books (*The Mystery of Chimney Rock* by Edward Packard being the most prominent among their haunted house offerings), or even better, the more horror-oriented Which Way books (*The Castle of No Return* and *Invasion of the Black Slime and Other Tales of Horror* by R.G. Austin were excellent, schlocky haunted house fun!). To this day I still have fond memories of a YA book purchased from the Scholastic Book catalogs which were passed out at school, *The Haunted Planet* (1980). It was a collection of short stories by DJ Arneson containing two memorable haunted house stories, "The House on Pearl Street" and "The Empty Hotel." They were so much fun and really got my young mind churning.

As I grew older, I moved away from the young adult books to more mainstream stuff. The first regular horror novel I read was a haunted house tale entitled *Night Things* by Michael Talbot (1988). It was about a sprawling mansion in the Adirondack Mountains haunted by a mysterious entity. I loved it and was soon on a mission for more. Many followed to fill my hands as years passed since then including standouts like *The Elementals* by Michael McDowell (1981), *Night Stone* by Rick Hautala (1986), *Haunted* by James Herbert (1988), *House Haunted* by Al Sarrantonio (1991), *Prey* by Graham Masterton (1992), *Nazareth Hill* by Ramsey Campbell (1996), *Apartment 16* by Adam Nevill (2010) and *It Will Just Be Us* by Jo Kaplan (2020).

Movies were instrumental as well with the first being *Poltergeist* (1982), making a

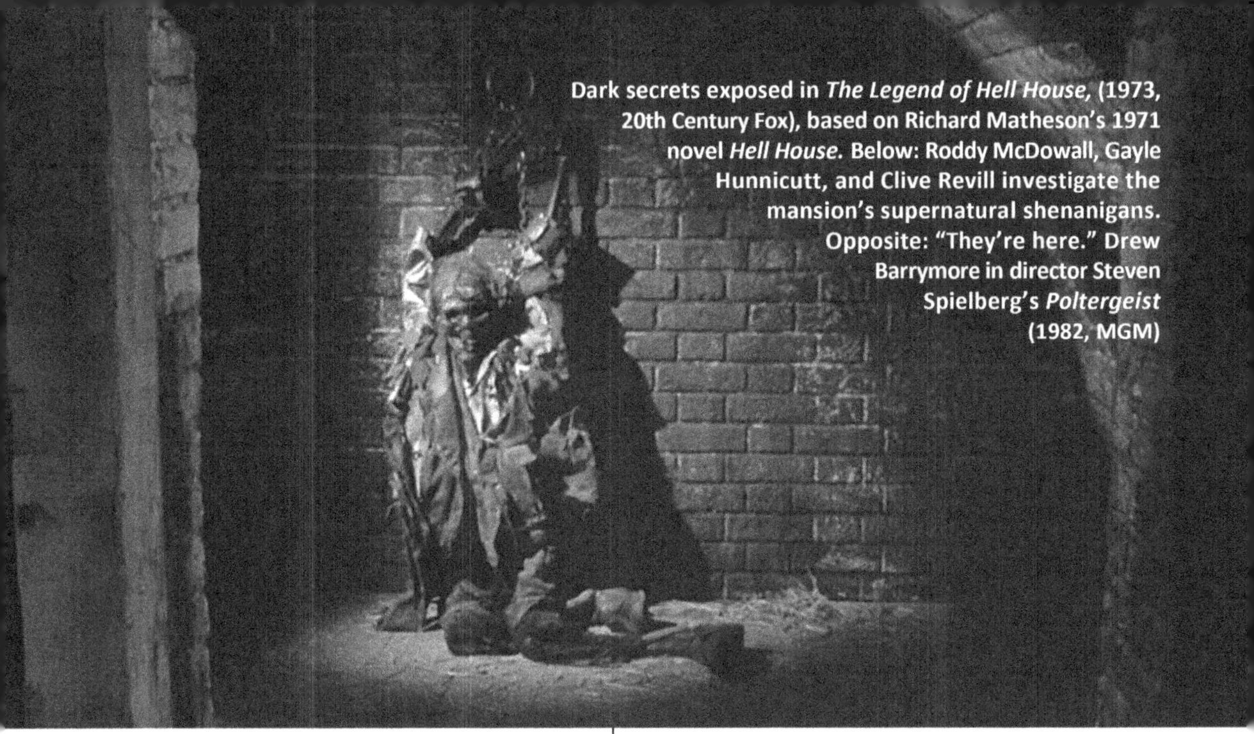

Dark secrets exposed in *The Legend of Hell House,* (1973, 20th Century Fox), based on Richard Matheson's 1971 novel *Hell House.* Below: Roddy McDowall, Gayle Hunnicutt, and Clive Revill investigate the mansion's supernatural shenanigans. Opposite: "They're here." Drew Barrymore in director Steven Spielberg's *Poltergeist* (1982, MGM)

strong impression on me when I was around ten years old. The scene where the thing haunting the house makes the paranormal investigator believe he's ripping off his own face was really strong stuff. I loved *Poltergeist 2: The Other Side* (1986) even more, with Kane as the terrifying horror assailing the family. As I grew older, I would devour as many haunted house films as I could find.

I wasn't choosy; if it involved a haunted house, I was there for it. *The Legend of Hell House* (1973), adapted from the Richard Matheson novel, about a group of paranormal investigators taking on the "Mount Everest of Haunted Houses" enthralled me. Then there was the haunting mystery of *The Changeling* (1980), which hit every note perfectly. In a similar vein, *The Innocents*

(1961) and *The Haunting* (1963) focused on unraveling the reason for the hauntings at the heart of their narratives. More recent films I feel carry on the strong tradition of those films for me include *The Haunting of Hill House* (1999), *What Lies Beneath* (2000), *The Others* (2001), as well as The Conjuring (2013–2021) and Insidious (2010–2023) series of films.

I could go on forever about more of my

Hill House, from *The Haunting* (1963, MGM), based on Shirley Jackson's 1959 novel *The Haunting of Hill House*. Above: Deborah Kerr in *The Innocents* (1961, 20th Century Fox), based on the 1898 novella *The Turn of the Screw* by Henry James.

Lili Taylor in *The Conjuring*
(2013, New Line Cinema)

favorite haunted house influences, but I need to get to the primary point of this issue's column, thirteen of my favorite haunted house short stories.

I strongly feel these tales serve as prime examples of what heights this style of story-telling is capable of attaining.

13 Haunted House Stories
(Listed in Order of Publication)

1. **"The Haunters and the Haunted"**
Edward Bulwer-Lytton (1859)

This being the only piece I've ever read by Bulwer-Lytton thus far, I really enjoyed it and can definitely see why it has remained influential so long after its original publication. While the clinical air with which it's presented hampers its ability to be scary per se, the descriptions of the bizarre manifestations in the house are excellent. It follows a fearless man, who upon hearing a notoriously haunted house is available to be let, decides to experience it for himself.

2. **"Number 13"**
M.R. James (1904)

No list such as this would be complete without the granddaddy of the ghost story himself, M.R. James. His unique brand of antiquarian terrors have inspired a host of imitators over the years, but no one has done them better. James had several worthy options of stories to garner a spot here, so it wasn't an easy decision to make. Ultimately, I'm going with "Number 13" which finds a man lodged in room number 12 of a hotel. During his stay there, he comes to realize another room manifesting in the space between his and room number 14 during certain times of night. As there is no room 13, he struggles to make sense of it. When this mysterious extra chamber is present, an eerie red glow and disturbing shadows are seen, along with the sounds of strange voices. The bizarre occurrences attached to this spectral room point to a demonic entity taking up residence within its extra-dimensional cavity.

Julie Harris in *The Haunting* (1963, MGM), based on a 1959 novel by Shirley Jackson.

"No live organism can continue for long to exist sanely under conditions of absolute reality; even larks and katydids are supposed, by some, to dream. Hill House, not sane, stood by itself against the hills, holding darkness within; it had stood so for eighty years and might stand for eighty more. Within, walls continued upright, bricks met neatly, floors were firm, and doors were sensibly shut; silence lay steadily against the wood and stone of Hill House, and whatever walked there, walked alone."
—Shirley Jackson, *The Haunting of Hill House*, 1959

5303-6

3. **"Thurnley Abbey"**
Perceval Landon (1908)

This is the story for which Landon is best remembered. Despite having been published well over a century ago, Thurnley Abbey has lost none of its power and remains one of the quintessential haunted house stories. When Alastair Colvin asks a stranger if he can share a compartment with him on the ship upon which they are about to embark, he decides he must explain why. He then relates the tale of how he went to stay at a friend's house called Thurnley Abbey. The friend says he has a task he would like him to perform, without elaborating as to what that might be. That evening the man ends up encountering a horrific specter in his room. This is a chilling haunted house story that has been anthologized often over the years. The description of the ghost and the mind-rending effect it has on Colvin and the owners of the house is palpable.

4. **"Caterpillars"**
E. F. Benson (1912)

E. F. Benson is another of my favorite authors and he wrote a ton of exceptional horror stories. I initially had his story "How Fear Departed from the Long Gallery" on the list, but then I remembered this remarkably bizarre tale. It's possibly the strangest "haunting on this list and the fact that it provides no solid explanation as to why the phenomena is manifesting actually enhanced it. It's about a man who's staying in a beautiful Italian villa overlooking the sea. He shares the place with an artist and the couple who own the house. One night, finding he can't sleep, he goes downstairs to retrieve a book and notices the only unused bedroom door standing open. What he spies piled atop the bed inside that room is freakishly bizarre. The title of the story provides a hint as to what's there but doesn't tell the whole story.

5. **"Mr. Jones"**
Edith Wharton (1928)

You can't go wrong with an Edith Wharton horror story. Just give "The Eyes," "The Triumph of Night" or "Pomegranate Seed" a read for proof. One thing I particularly love about a Wharton ghost story is how regularly her specters are capable of doing actual physical harm to their victims, which is well evidenced in her story "Afterwards," as well as with this one here. In both cases, the ghost is able to bring about the demise of a living being. Here a woman inherits a house from relatives she didn't know well. She is turned away at the door when she first goes to see it by a servant who says Mr. Jones won't allow it. When she eventually does move in, she learns Mr. Jones is an incredibly old head servant who has a stranglehold on the house and its servants. Both the house and Mr. Jones seem to be actively concealing secrets from her. The question of how old Mr. Jones must be and how he stays so well-hidden are at the core of this supernatural mystery.

6. **"The Window"**
D. K. Broster (1932)

Sadly, D. K. (Dorothy Kathleen) Broster has been largely forgotten these days, other than her much-anthologized story "Couching at the Door." That's really a shame, because she wrote a number of superb short horror stories, such as "Clairvoyance," "From the Abyss" and "The Juggernaut." Also on my list of favorites by her is "The Window," wherein an Englishman falls in love at first sight with a French woman who owns a derelict old manor he's always wanted to explore. He puts off seeing the house as he's enlisted to fight alongside her brother for the French army when war breaks out. While on leave one day, he goes to the manor alone. It has a beautiful room with a large window looking out on the sunset. He decides to sketch it but starts to feel he's not alone in the

8. "The Grey House"
Basil Copper (1967)

Copper wrote a lot of fantastic weird/horror stories ("Wish You Were Here," "The House By the Tarn" and "Camera Obscura," etc.), but I think this is his best. A successful thriller writer purchases an old, deserted estate house in Burgandy, France. Although the writer is overjoyed, his wife feels uneasy there, but stays anyway while he writes. A large wall painting is uncovered during the extensive reconstruction depicting a man wearing clothes from a long bygone era dragging a woman by her hair. The man in the painting turns out to have been a treacherous former lord of the manor. The new lady of the house begins to notice a massive, malevolent cat with yellow eyes lurking in the orchards below which glares and makes terrible noises at her. More ominous discoveries are made around the house as the tale continues.

9. "The Other Room"
Lisa Tuttle (1982)

Lisa Tuttle is a living legend of the genre who has written a number of great haunted house stories, such as "Bug House" and "Objects In Dreams May Be Closer Than They Appear." I chose "The Other Room" because it made such a strong impression which has lingered with me long after my initial reading. It's about a man who returns to a house he inherited from a long deceased grandfather he never met in hopes of finding a mysterious secret room he once discovered while he was very ill as a child. Upon doing so, he hopes to rescue his dying daughter by pulling her away from the long, pale white beings he found there so long ago. I love the unique type of specter found in this top-notch story.

10. "The Pennine Tower Restaurant"
Simon Kurt Unsworth (2010)

Simon is one of my favorite authors. He's a master of crafting terrifying stories,

empty house. The window itself is the focal point of the angry spirits haunting this house.

7. "Ghost Hunt"
H.R Wakefield (1938)

If there were a Hall of Fame for Terrifying Ghost Stories, H.R. Wakefield would be a first ballet inductee. He wrote so many magnificent haunted house stories, I had trouble deciding which to include. Ultimately, I felt "Ghost Hunt" was too iconic to be left off. In this story, a radio host broadcasts a live ghost hunt from a house in London where there has been "no less than thirty suicides." Most of the victims end up running from the house at night to cast themselves over the cliff to the river below. The investigation proves all-too successful in this chilling story which was skillfully adapted for the radio program *Suspense* in 1949.

several of the haunted house variety. His stories "The Merry House," "Scale Hall" and "The Hotel Guest" were also on my list of possibilities for this list, but ultimately "The Pennine Tower Restaurant" won out for me, and it isn't even technically a haunted house. It is, as the title suggests, a restaurant, and a marvelously haunted one at that! This oddly constructed tower has a bizarre and deadly history to it, full of deaths, disappearances, and ethereal glimpses involving the structure. It's a riveting tale presented as fact, complete with detailed, corroborating footnotes.

11. "In the Absence of Murdock"
Terry Lamsley (2011)

I haven't read much by Lamsley, but this story made a huge impression on me and I loved the strangeness of it. When successful mystery co-author Murdock suddenly vanishes from a room, Franz is tasked to go investigate. What he finds in Murdock's house is very weird, making this one of the stranger haunted house stories I've read.

12. "At Lorn Hall"
Ramsey Campbell (2012)

This was the first story which sprung to mind while compiling this list. Ramsey's ability to infuse his tales with a sense of creeping dread, subtly at first, then steadily increasing in intensity as the story progresses, is on full display here. It begins with a man seeking shelter from a rainstorm by entering a rundown manor. Inside he finds a set of headphones he puts on as he embarks on a tour of the house, "guided" by the recorded voice of its former master whose image is depicted upon various portraits hanging in every room. His eerie comments seem unsettlingly cryptic, making the trespasser think something else may be in the house with him, lurking just out of his view.

13. "In the English Rain"
Steve Duffy (2020)

I've become a big Steve Duffy fan in recent years. I discovered him through his stories in the Paul Finch edited Terror Tales series of anthologies ("Old As The Hills" and "Lie Still, Sleep Becalmed" for example) and continuing on with his stories in *Nightmare Abbey* magazine ("The Hunting Grounds" and "La Niña Atardecer"). He's consistently brilliant and this one is my favorite, especially when specifically considering his haunted house-themed ones. The narrator of this tale is introduced to a beautiful girl Sally at his school when she asks about his living near one of the Beatles, something about which he had boasted. Although the house, called Shelgrave, was purchased by John Lennon, he never actually lived there. From this initial meeting, the unnamed narrator and Sally become best friends even though he would have liked for it to be more. One day when his father is out of town, Sally insists they scale the fence and explore the now abandoned, neighboring house. This excellent haunted house tale really invests you in its characters and has a terrifying, somber finale.

That wraps up another column, horror fans. Until next time, happy hauntings.

—Matt Cowan

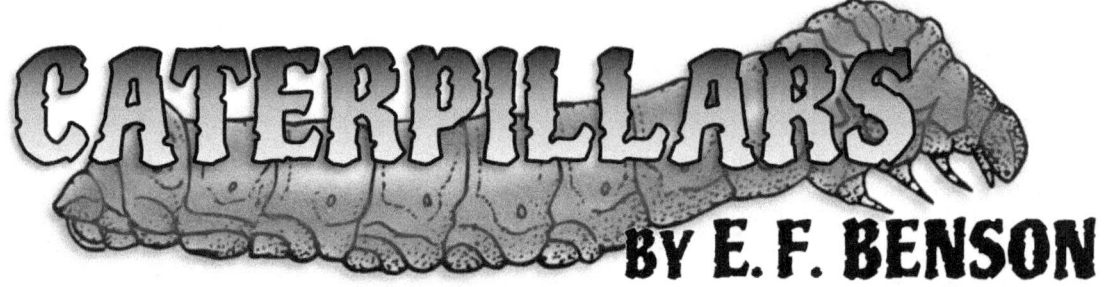

CATERPILLARS

BY E. F. BENSON

I SAW A MONTH OR TWO AGO IN AN ITALIAN PAPER THAT THE VILLA CASCANA, IN WHICH I ONCE STAYED, HAD BEEN PULLED DOWN, and that a manufactory of some sort was in process of erection on its site.

There is therefore no longer any reason for refraining from writing of those things which I myself saw (or imagined I saw) in a certain room and on a certain landing of the villa in question, nor from mentioning the circumstances which followed, which may or may not (according to the opinion of the reader) throw some light on or be somehow connected with this experience.

The Villa Cascana was in all ways but one a perfectly delightful house, yet, if it were standing now, nothing in the world—I use the phrase in its literal sense—would induce me to set foot in it again, for I believe it to have been haunted in a very terrible and practical manner.

Most ghosts, when all is said and done, do not do much harm; they may perhaps terrify, but the person whom they visit usually gets over their visitation. They may on the other hand be entirely friendly and beneficent. But the appearances in the Villa Cascana were not beneficent, and had they made their "visit" in a very slightly different manner, I do not suppose I should have got over it any more than Arthur Inglis did.

The house stood on an ilex-clad hill not far from Sestri di Levante on the Italian Riviera, looking out over the iridescent blues of that enchanted sea, while behind it rose the pale green chestnut woods that climb up the hillsides till they give place to the pines that, black in contrast with them, crown the slopes. All round it the garden in the luxuriance of mid-spring bloomed and was fragrant, and the scent of magnolia and rose, borne on the salt freshness of the winds from the sea, flowed like a stream through the cool vaulted rooms.

On the ground floor a broad pillared loggia ran round three sides of the house, the top of which formed a balcony for certain rooms of the first floor. The main staircase, broad and of grey marble steps, led up from the hall to the landing outside these rooms, which were three in number, namely, two big sitting-rooms and a bedroom arranged *en suite*. The latter was unoccupied, the sitting-rooms were in use. From these the main staircase was continued to the second floor, where were situated certain bedrooms, one of which I occupied, while from the other side of the first-floor landing some half-dozen steps led to another suite of rooms, where, at the time I am speaking of, Arthur Inglis, the artist, had his bedroom and studio. Thus the landing outside my bedroom at the top of the house commanded both the landing of the first floor and also the steps that led to Inglis' rooms. Jim Stanley and his wife, finally (whose guest I was), occupied rooms in another wing of the house, where also were the servants' quarters.

I arrived just in time for lunch on a brilliant noon of mid-May. The garden was shouting with colour and fragrance, and not less delightful after my broiling walk up from the marina, should have been the coming from the reverberating heat and blaze of the day into the marble coolness of the villa. Only (the reader has my bare word for this, and nothing more), the moment I set foot in the house I felt that something was wrong. This feeling, I may say, was quite vague, though very strong, and I remember that when I saw letters waiting for me on the table in the hall I felt certain that the explanation was here: I was convinced that there was bad news of some sort for me. Yet when I opened them I found no such explanation of my premonition; my correspondents all reeked of prosperity. Yet this clear miscarriage of a presentiment did not dissipate my uneasiness. In that cool fragrant house there was something wrong.

I am at pains to mention this because to the general view it may explain that though I am as a rule so excellent a sleeper that the extinction of my light on getting into bed is apparently contemporaneous with being called on the following morning, I slept very badly on my first night in the Villa Cascana. It may also explain the fact that when I did sleep (if it was indeed in sleep that I saw what I thought I saw) I dreamed in a very vivid and original manner, original, that is to say, in the sense that something that, as far as I knew, had never previously entered into my consciousness, usurped it then. But since, in addition to this evil premonition, certain words and events occurring during the rest of the day might have suggested something of what I thought happened that night, it will be well to relate them.

After lunch, then, I went round the house with Mrs. Stanley, and during our tour she referred, it is true, to the unoccupied bedroom on the first floor, which opened out of the room where we had lunched.

"We left that unoccupied," she said, "because Jim and I have a charming bedroom and dressing-room, as you saw, in the wing, and if we used it ourselves we should have to turn the dining-room into a dressing-room and have our meals downstairs. As it is, however, we have our little flat there, Arthur Inglis has his little flat in the other passage; and I remembered (aren't I extraordinary?) that you once said that the higher up you were in a house the better you were pleased. So I put you at the top of the house, instead of giving you that room."

It is true, that a doubt, vague as my uneasy premonition, crossed my mind at this. I did not see why Mrs. Stanley should have explained all this, if there had not

been more to explain. I allow, therefore, that the thought that there was something to explain about the unoccupied bedroom was momentarily present to my mind.

The second thing that may have borne on my dream was this.

At dinner the conversation turned for a moment on ghosts. Inglis, with the certainty of conviction, expressed his belief that anybody who could possibly believe in the existence of supernatural phenomena was unworthy of the name of an ass. The subject instantly dropped. As far as I can recollect, nothing else occurred or was said that could bear on what follows.

We all went to bed rather early, and personally I yawned my way upstairs, feeling hideously sleepy. My room was rather hot, and I threw all the windows wide, and from without poured in the white light of the moon, and the love-song of many nightingales. I undressed quickly, and got into bed, but though I had felt so sleepy before, I now felt extremely wide-awake. But I was quite content to be awake: I did not toss or turn, I felt perfectly happy listening to the song and seeing the light. Then, it is possible, I may have gone to sleep, and what follows may have been a dream. I thought, anyhow, that after a time the nightingales ceased singing and the moon sank. I thought also that if, for some unexplained reason, I was going to lie awake all night, I might as well read, and I remembered that I had left a book in which I was interested in the dining-room on the first floor. So I got out of bed, lit a candle, and went downstairs. I went into the room, saw on a side-table the book I had come to look for, and then, simultaneously, saw that the door into the unoccupied bedroom was open.

A curious grey light, not of dawn nor of moonshine, came out of it, and I looked in. The bed stood just opposite the door, a big four-poster, hung with tapestry at the head. Then I saw that the grayish light of the bedroom came from the bed, or rather from what was on the bed. For it was covered with great caterpillars, a foot or more in length, which crawled over it. They were faintly luminous, and it was the light from them that showed me the room. Instead of the sucker-feet of ordinary caterpillars they had rows of pincers like crabs, and they moved by grasping what they lay on with their pincers, and then sliding their bodies forward. In color these dreadful insects were yellowish-grey, and they were covered with irregular lumps and swellings. There must have been hundreds of them, for they formed a sort of writhing, crawling pyramid on the bed. Occasionally one fell off on to the floor, with a soft fleshy thud, and though the floor was of hard concrete, it yielded to the pincer-feet as if it had been putty, and, crawling back, the caterpillar would mount on to the bed again, to rejoin its fearful companions. They appeared to have no faces, so to speak, but at one end of them there was a mouth that opened sideways in respiration.

Then, as I looked, it seemed to me as if they all suddenly became conscious of my presence.

All the mouths, at any rate, were turned in my direction, and next moment they began dropping off the bed with those soft fleshy thuds on to the floor, and wriggling towards me. For one second a paralysis as of a dream was on me, but the next I was running upstairs again to my room, and I remember feeling the cold of the marble steps on my bare feet. I rushed into my bedroom, and slammed the door behind me, and then—I was certainly wide-awake now—I found myself standing by my bed with the sweat of terror pouring from me. The noise of the banged door still rang in my ears. But, as would have been more usual, if this had been mere nightmare, the terror that had been mine when I saw those foul beasts crawling about the bed or dropping softly on to the floor did not cease then. Awake, now, if dreaming before, I did not at all recover from the horror of dream: it did not seem to me that I had dreamed. And until dawn, I sat or stood, not daring to lie down, thinking that every rustle or movement that I heard was the approach of the caterpillars. To them and the claws that bit into the cement the wood of the door was child's play: steel would not keep them out.

But with the sweet and noble return of day the horror vanished: the whisper of wind became benignant again; the nameless fear, whatever it was, was smoothed out and terrified me no longer. Dawn broke, hue-less at first; then it grew dove-colored, then the flaming pageant of light spread over the sky.

The admirable rule of the house was that everybody had breakfast where and when he pleased, and in consequence it was not till lunchtime that I met any of the other members of our party, since I had breakfast on my balcony, and wrote letters and other things till lunch. In fact, I got down to that meal rather late, after the other three had begun. Between my knife and fork there was a small pillbox of cardboard, and as I sat down Inglis spoke.

"Do look at that," he said, "since you are interested in natural history. I found it crawling on my counterpane last night, and I don't know what it is."

I think that before I opened the pillbox, I expected something of the sort which I found in it.

Inside it, anyhow, was a small caterpillar, grayish-yellow in color, with curious bumps and excrescences on its rings. It was extremely active, and hurried round the box, this way and that.

Its feet were unlike the feet of any caterpillar I ever saw: they were like the pincers of a crab. I looked, and shut the lid down again.

"No, I don't know it," I said, "but it looks rather unwholesome. What are you going to do with it?"

"Oh, I shall keep it," said Inglis. "It has begun to spin: I want to see what sort of a moth it turns into."

I opened the box again, and saw that these hurrying movements were indeed the beginning of the spinning of the web of its cocoon. Then Inglis spoke again.

"It has funny feet, too," he said. "They are like crabs' pincers. What's the Latin for crab? Oh, yes, *Cancer.* So in case it is unique, let's christen it: *Cancer Inglisensis.*"

Then something happened in my brain, some momentary piecing together of all that I had seen or dreamed. Something in his words seemed to me to throw light on it all, and my own intense horror at the experience of the night before linked itself on to what he had just said. In effect, I took the box and threw it, caterpillar and all, out of the window. There was a gravel path just outside, and beyond it, a fountain playing into a basin. The box fell on to the middle of this.

Inglis laughed.

"So the students of the occult don't like solid facts," he said. "My poor caterpillar!"

The talk went off again at once on to other subjects, and I have only given in detail, as they happened, these trivialities in order to be sure myself that I have recorded everything that could have borne on occult subjects or on the subject of caterpillars. But at the moment when I threw the pillbox into the fountain, I lost my head: my only excuse is that, as is probably plain, the tenant of it was, in miniature, exactly what I had seen crowded on to the bed in the unoccupied room. And though this translation of those phantoms into flesh and blood—or whatever it is that caterpillars are made of—ought perhaps to have relieved the horror of the night, as a matter of fact it did nothing of the kind. It only made the crawling pyramid that covered the bed in the unoccupied room more hideously real.

After lunch we spent a lazy hour or two strolling about the garden or sitting in the loggia, and it must have been about four o'clock when Stanley and I started off to bathe, down the path that led by the fountain into which I had thrown the pillbox. The water was shallow and clear, and at the bottom of it I saw its white remains. The water had disintegrated the cardboard, and it had become no more than a few strips and shreds of sodden paper. The centre of the fountain was a marble Italian Cupid which squirted the water out of a wineskin held under its arm. And crawling up its leg was the caterpillar. Strange and scarcely credible as it seemed, it must have survived the falling-to-bits of its prison, and made its way to shore, and there it was, out of arm's reach, weaving and waving this way and that as it evolved its cocoon.

Then, as I looked at it, it seemed to me again that, like the caterpillar I had seen last night, it saw me, and breaking out of the threads that surrounded it, it crawled down the marble leg of the Cupid and began swimming like a snake across the water of the fountain towards me. It came with extraordinary speed (the fact of a caterpillar being able to swim was new to me), and in another moment was crawling up the marble lip of the basin. Just then Inglis joined us.

"Why, if it isn't old 'Cancer Inglisensis' again," he said, catching sight of the beast. "What a tearing hurry it is in!"

We were standing side by side on the path, and when the caterpillar had advanced to within about a yard of us, it stopped, and began waving again as if in doubt as to the direction in which it should go. Then it appeared to make up its mind, and crawled on to Inglis' shoe.

"It likes me best," he said, "but I don't really know that I like *it*. And as it won't drown I think perhaps—"

He shook it off his shoe onto the gravel path and trod on it.

All afternoon the air got heavier and heavier with the Sirocco that was without doubt coming up from the south, and that night again I went up to bed feeling very sleepy; but below my drowsiness, so to speak, there was the consciousness, stronger than before, that there was something wrong in the house, that something dangerous was close at hand. But I fell asleep at once, and—how long after I do not know—either woke or dreamed I awoke, feeling that I must get up at once, or I should be too late. Then (dreaming or awake) I lay and fought this fear, telling myself that I was but the prey of my own nerves disordered by Sirocco or what not, and at the same time quite clearly knowing in another part of my mind, so to speak, that every moment's delay added to the danger. At last this second feeling became irresistible, and I put on coat and trousers and went out of my room on to the landing. And then I saw that I had already delayed too long, and that I was now too late.

The whole of the landing of the first floor below was invisible under the swarm of caterpillars that crawled there. The folding doors into the sitting-room from which opened the bedroom where I had seen them last night were shut, but they were squeezing through the cracks of it and dropping one by one through the keyhole, elongating themselves into mere string as they passed, and growing fat and lumpy again on emerging.

Some, as if exploring, were nosing about the steps into the passage at the end of which were Inglis' rooms, others were crawling on the lowest steps of the staircase that led up to where I stood. The landing, however, was completely covered with them: I was cut off. And of the frozen horror that seized me when I saw that, I can give no idea in words.

Then at last a general movement began to take place, and they grew thicker on the steps that led to Inglis' room. Gradually, like some hideous tide of flesh, they advanced along the passage, and I saw the foremost, visible by the pale grey luminousness that came from them, reach his door. Again and again I tried to shout and warn him, in terror all the time that they would turn at the sound of my voice and mount my stair instead, but for all my efforts I felt that no sound came from my throat. They crawled along the hinge-crack of his door, passing through as they had done before, and still I stood there, making impotent efforts to shout to him, to bid him escape while there was time.

At last the passage was completely empty: they had all gone, and at that moment I was conscious for the first time of the cold of the marble landing on which I stood barefooted. The dawn was just beginning to break in the Eastern sky.

SIX MONTHS AFTER, I met Mrs. Stanley in a country house in England. We talked on many subjects and at last she said:

"I don't think I have seen you since I got that dreadful news about Arthur Inglis a month ago."

"I haven't heard," said I.

"No? He has got cancer. They don't even advise an operation, for there is no hope of a cure; he is riddled with it, the doctors say."

Now, during all these six months I do not think a day had passed on which I had not had in my mind the dreams (or whatever you like to call them) which I had seen in the Villa Cascana.

"It is awful, is it not?" she continued, "and I feel I can't help feeling, that he may have—"

"Caught it at the villa?" I asked.

She looked at me in blank surprise.

"Why did you say that?" she asked. "How did you know?"

Then she told me. In the unoccupied bedroom a year before, there had been a fatal case of cancer. She had, of course, taken the best advice and had been told that the utmost dictates of prudence would be obeyed so long as she did not put anybody to sleep in the room, which had also been thoroughly disinfected and newly white-washed and painted. But—

"Caterpillars" first appeared in the author's 1912 collection The Room in the Tower and Other Stories.

Edward Frederic Benson (1867–1940), a prolific English novelist, biographer, memoirist, and archaeologist, known professionally as E. F. Benson, also earned a well-deserved reputation for writing genuinely creepy ghost stories and other macabre tales of the supernatural. His short stories have been adapted for both film and television. His 1906 tale "The Bus-Conductor," for instance, served as the inspiration for two different high-profile adaptations: as part of the classic anthology film Dead of Night *(1945) and as an episode of Rod Serling's* The Twilight Zone, *"Twenty Two" (1961).*

Apparently, Benson's talent for spinning a macabre story was a family trait he shared with his brothers, Robert Hugh and Arthur Christopher Benson, who wrote some excellent ghost stories of their own. For starters, check out "Father Macclesfield's Tale" (1907) by R. H. Benson, and "Basil Netherby" (1926) by A. C. Benson.

THAT MADDENING HEAT

By Ray Cluley

THERE HAVE BEEN THREE PARTICULARLY SEVERE SUMMERS IN BOWERS DURING MY LIFETIME, THE ENTIRETY OF WHICH I HAVE LIVED IN THIS SMALL TOWN, and while I shall write to some extent of all three, it is the first that concerns these papers most. I was a child at the time, of that age where I was impatient to be considered otherwise, but Bowers has never been a town for rushing things, and my adolescence was no exception. We have always been a town where time runs a little slower than most other places. For example, it would be another five years after the summer I'm about to describe before I saw my first motorcar, though I had heard talk of them my whole young life. We've grown as a town since then, but not much, and as many people seem to move away as arrive. My mother left while I was too young to remember her, bored by the seclusion and simple living, and I was raised by a father who, though sometimes stern, raised me with love. When he passed away late last year, during the second of the three harsh summers, I inherited the store and its accounts (and its debts) along with a number of personal affects, among which were included the papers retrieved so many years previously from the home of Mrs. Winifred Dolores.

Mrs. Dolores, or Winnie as she had been less formally known to those who knew her better, had been one of our regular customers, and in that she was little different to most people, for our store was one of only two in town and of the two we had the fairest prices, if not the greatest range of goods. Mrs. Dolores lived on the outskirts of Bowers where the land begins to slope into a narrow wooded valley, a beautiful if isolated spot where she and her husband had raised goats for a number of years, but despite our willingness to deliver her groceries, she always came to the store to personally collect whatever it was she needed, as her husband had always done before her. She said it helped her feel connected to the community, and prevented her from becoming a recluse, the temptation of which grew stronger for each year that passed after her husband left. She was always very frank about his leaving, though rarely about the reasons why, seeming to accept her circumstances with admirable grace and fortitude. Of course, there was plenty of gossip to counter her reticence, and even as a child I heard some of this, for I was easily overlooked when the adults chose to talk and trade stories amongst themselves. As an adult myself now, I have very little interest in sharing the idle speculations the people of this town seem to enjoy and it is with some reluctance I tell this particular story now, except that it concerns events to which I was a witness, events that seem to have some influence on my life even now, so many years later, as I shuffle towards old age. Events that have had me dreading since boyhood a summer as hot as the one of which I write, and as hot as the one, now, in which I write of it.

My involvement in the affair begins at the end of that hot summer when Mrs. Dolores failed to come in for her usual provisions and I was sent to check on her welfare. Prior to this, my father made some rather discreet enquiries as to whether Mrs. Dolores was being supplied by our rivals in town (rivals being a term I use very loosely, and with some humor, for we had always been friendly with the McIntyres) and upon learning that she had not bought so much as a grain of salt from McIntyres Trading, and realizing that nearly two weeks had passed since her last visit to town, I was sent to her farm with instructions to both check upon her health (with polite subtlety) and to reiterate our willingness to deliver whatever goods she might need that we could provide. The most general of these I took with me, as if to prove the ease with which it could be done.

Her property was not a large one, and as such was easily maintained by husband and wife, if not quite by a wife alone. The house, I saw, did bear some minor signs of neglect, but these were easily addressed, and the opportunist in me made a mental list of the chores a young lad such as myself could

help with, such as repainting the doors and sills or realigning fences that had fallen askew. I was, that summer, trying to save enough money for a handsome saddle I had seen displayed at Pearson & Haverston's, and never mind that I didn't yet have the horse for it. Thinking of this saddle, I noted there was some weeding that could be done in the small garden of the Dolores property, and closer to the house I noticed that perhaps the windows needed some attention as well for they were all of them open. As I have mentioned, it had been a particularly hot summer and so I could have understood a desire to air the whole house through perhaps a week or so ago, but the weather had turned since the worst of it and though we were yet to know rain again, the temperature had dropped enough that a woman of Mrs. Dolores's advancing years might feel the chill of it. With her age in mind, I wondered if perhaps the wood of the window sashes had warped to such a degree that closing them had become difficult. It would be no bother at all for me to do that for her, while I was here, free of charge!

I knocked on the front door and waited.

I knocked again, and called, "Mrs. Dolores?" and waited a few moments more.

My enquiries received no answer.

I went behind the house with the intention of repeating the procedure at the back door, but upon the first knock I discovered it to be open. Not wide open, like all of the windows, but as if it had been pushed to and failed to catch upon the latch.

"Mrs. Dolores?"

I opened the door with my foot so that I could enter with my arms full of groceries, an immediate visual explanation for my intrusion should Mrs. Dolores choose that moment to appear, but still she did not answer. I set the box down on the kitchen table.

"Mrs. Dolores? It's Pip, from the store. I've brought you some things."

There was no answer to my call, nor had I expected there to be. You're probably as familiar with the feeling as I am, knowing a house to be empty even before you've checked any of the rooms. There's a silence that settles on an empty place that's different from the silence of an occupied one, and I was certain the house in which I stood was empty.

There were some papers on the kitchen table which I shall come to. I did not read them at that time, as they seemed at a glance to be of a personal nature, but I looked up from where they had been written and saw directly into the yard at the back of the building, noticing then something I had not when coming around the house to knock.

The yard at the Dolores property was a wide area trodden down to dirt that separated the main building from the fenced pen where they once kept their goats. At the center of the yard was a well. All of this I had seen already. What I noticed now, however, standing at the kitchen table and looking into the yard through the open window, was a length of rope on the ground near the well, one end of which was tied to a toppled bucket. At a glance, it would have appeared that the bucket had been discarded after water had been drawn from the well, and that whatever slack that had gathered in the rope was coiled beside it, so perhaps I had noticed it and disregarded it as unimportant, but what I was in fact looking at, still tied to the bucket handle, was a short section of *cut* rope. The rest of it I could see hanging taut to the fullness of its remaining length, disappearing into the circle of stonework, down into the well.

I knew without looking why the rope hung taut, much as you have likely guessed the cause, but I had to look to be sure of it, and on my way across the yard made another discovery. A kitchen knife had been discarded next to the bucket. I gave it little thought at the time, presuming its purpose had been to cut the bucket from the rest of the rope, though I would amend my thinking of that before too long.

Foolishly, at the edge of the well, I called as I had at the door, "Mrs. Dolores?" though I'm sure I have no idea how I might have reacted to a reply. Finally, steeling myself against the certainty of what I would find, I peered into the dark of the well and confirmed what I already knew and feared, namely that Mrs. Winifred Dolores, Winnie to her friends, had hanged herself.

It was a shock to see, and when I went to fetch my father, I did it running, though there was nothing that could be done to warrant such urgency.

MY FATHER RECEIVED the news solemnly. He asked me several times if I was all right, worried at the haste with which I tried to tell of what I'd found, and he put his hand to my forehead several times as if I might have caught a fever, though it seemed he was not satisfied by his own findings, because when he went for Dr. Crombley to tell him of poor Mrs. Dolores, he took me with him for the man to examine. Dr. Crombley was so certain of my health that when I volunteered to go back with them to the farm, he vouched that my returning might actually be mentally beneficial in processing the initial shock of my discovery, and though he would later come to regret the decision, my father was persuaded to agree.

Dr. Crombley had a cart which had served him more than once in the transportation of someone passed, and this we took with us to the farm. We no doubt inspired more than a little gossip, and several of those who saw us followed the cart a short distance so as their speculations in our absence might be better supported by our direction of travel.

"Half the town will know of her death before we even retrieve her body," Dr. Crombley said.

"And the other half by the time we return with it," my father agreed. After a moment, he added, "There'll be talk again of Gorman," meaning Mr. Gorman Dolores. "Rumors always return upon news of a death."

The doctor nodded. "Gorman, the goats, the whole mess of it."

We were a few hours yet from evening, but the afternoon sky had darkened somewhat with the promise of rain. A great deal of the heat of recent weeks had passed, but the humidity left in its wake was yet to break and we were still to know the relief of rain, so the clouds were very much welcomed.

"All her windows are open," I said as we neared the property. It was a detail I had forgotten previously, and unnecessary now when both men could see for themselves, but it was important to me upon seeing them again that we close the windows to prevent any rain from ruining the indoors, though of course, upon arrival, our priority was Mrs. Dolores.

She was in a sorry state of injury and decomposition, and I shall remember the horrors of it for the rest of my days. Or perhaps, as I should more accurately write, I shall remember it for the rest of my nights, for that is when I see her again most often. I never had the good fortune to marry, though I had been close to the occasion once, and at my age I don't dare hope it could still happen, but whenever I suffer those summertime nightmares I am glad to have no wife. Bad enough that I am tormented by remembered terrors without startling a wife awake with them, and embarrassing enough that I alone have to clean the sheets when fear regresses me to bedwetting. I record it here only inasmuch to provide as full and honest an account as I am able. There are nights when Mrs. Dolores speaks to me in dreams, and what she has to say scares me more than anything I have read in her papers, but these are the frightened fancies of an old man, and they have no place in this document.

We drew Mrs. Dolores from the dark of the well like we were drawing water, though she did not come up with the same ease. Death lends a greater heaviness to any weight and Mrs. Dolores was no exception, my father and the doctor heaving at the well handle and rope between them. My father told me to look away as the top of her head came towards us, but I have not always been an obedient child and he was too busy at his task to notice my morbid curiosity. Not until I gasped at the sight of her swollen face did he tell me again, sharp with reprimand this time, but by then I had seen her bulging eyes, wide as if with the horror of her demise. I had seen how her tongue protruded from a mouth made slack from gravity. I saw, as well, how her throat had bloated over the rope that wrapped it, as if to deny it was tied there. My attention was drawn to worse, though, when Dr. Crombley exclaimed a profanity so loaded with blasphemy I thought he'd have to confess it at church every following Sunday.

"What has she done?" he asked afterwards, though it seemed to me a rhetorical question, for the evidence plain before us. A better question would have been to ask why she had done it, and to this day I have no satisfactory answer.

Closer to the lip of the well, where the light could reach more of her body, Mrs. Dolores was revealed to be without so much as a nightgown and wore only the grotesqueries of her death, namely a horrid wound that split her across the middle, just below the stomach. It sagged open like a spewing mouth, and she hung suspended in a state of partial disembowelment.

"Look away, son."

This time I did as I was told.

"Her neck's not broken," Dr. Crombley said, and I tried not to imagine his fingers feeling at the fullness of that bulging throat, "but with a wound like that, the drop would have sent her guts slopping out—"

"Doctor, *please*."

I was sprawled on the ground a short distance from the well, leaning aside in the expectation of being sick, but I knew the look that would have come with my father's words, and I could see enough of Dr. Crombley to know that when he said, "My apologies," he was giving the words to me. My father received the same by way of a nod.

"She either suffocated her way to death, or bled to it," the doctor said, and as he was a learned man of medicine it was no difficult task for us to take his reasoning as our own when he declared, "Self-murder, albeit of a most grisly kind."

Both my father and I have since decided otherwise, or at least considered the possibility of an alternative conclusion.

Between the two of them, my father and the doctor managed to bring the poor woman out of the well shaft and lay her to the ground. I no longer wanted to see anything of her, but a sharp intake of breath from my father and another profanity from the doctor drew my attention to how the wound beneath her stomach gaped so widely, either from the force of her fall or the state of her decomposition, that she was very nearly split in two and I wondered that they were able to retrieve more than just her upper body. What looked to be tangles of bloody rope around her waist were in fact loops of what she'd once held inside, and at the sight of them I was finally (and violently) sick, my lunch heaving from me with all the burning unpleasantness you have no doubt been unfortunate enough to experience for yourself, although I hope it was with less gruesome a cause. The noise of it had me imagining the splattering sound Mrs. Dolores would have made as the rope yanked her opened body to a stop and I heaved again until all of me was empty.

I felt my father's hand, cool on the back of my neck. When I was done, he helped me to my feet.

I was grateful to Dr. Crombley, too, who had stripped to his shirt sleeves to drape his fine coat over Mrs. Dolores, concealing the worst. We had sheets in the cart with which to wrap her, but she was such a ghastly sight that he'd felt it necessary to cover her even for the short time it would take to fetch them.

"You'll never see a sight like it again, lad," he told me, "perhaps you can take some solace in that, at least." He offered me a sympathetic look to which I replied with a nod.

"Shut those windows," my father told me. "The doctor and I will prepare Mrs. Dolores for her trip back to town."

I was glad of the distraction and left the men to their grim task.

To my surprise, the windows were shut very easily, so Mrs. Dolores must have kept them open for reasons of her own or had passed during the worst of the heat. Her house was situated where the land begins to rise into the valley, and it may be that such a location trapped a great deal of heat, in which case our recent summer spell must have been insufferable. Insufferable enough that one might end their own life to be free of it, though? I did not know, and I tried to put the thought of it from my mind.

To that purpose, there was plenty in the house to remind me more of her life than her death, and as I went from room to room I took some grief-tinged relief in seeing framed pictures of Mrs. Dolores and her husband, and other personal effects such as a hair-brush and comb set on a dressing table before a mirror, a nightdress cast across the bed, a glass half full of water in the kitchen. Things that spoke of living. What I mean to say is that it was easy to believe that Mrs. Dolores might return to her house momentarily, and that in closing her windows I was merely carrying out a favor for the woman in her absence.

I was in the kitchen, closing the last of the windows, when my father and Dr. Crombley entered the house. Dr. Crombley spent some time leaning against a countertop and staring out of the window at the well. My father returned the knife from the yard to its appropriate drawer. Presuming, now, that it had been used not only to cut rope but to make that awful mortal wound, I thought the return of the knife a somewhat macabre decision and wondered who might use it again on some future day without knowing the part it played in a woman's end.

At the kitchen table, my father took up a handful of the papers I'd left alone as something private. He read the first page, and then the second, but the third and fourth he read so quickly I thought he could have only skimmed the content, at which point he gathered up the rest and folded them into a pocket. He meant to do this discreetly, and I turned away before he could see me looking, but not before I saw how pale he had become. His face could have been carved from wax, such was its pallor, and the hand with which he tucked the papers away trembled so that he couldn't pocket them with his first attempt.

He took the papers for the sake of Mrs. Dolores' reputation, to protect her from any further scandal. He told me this twice, once directly while drunk on whiskey, and again a second time (which he probably thought the first) in an indirect fashion via the reading of his will. As I have mentioned, I inherited the papers along with the store, though why he did not destroy them shall remain a minor mystery to me. Perhaps they didn't feel enough like his to do so. I will summarize them here as I move towards concluding my story, though I'm not sure how much they might explain.

THE PAPERS BEGIN like a letter written to her husband, Gorman Dolores, though before long she only writes to him in an abstract fashion, as if he is merely a useful means by which to discuss her personal concerns, and so the papers take the tone more suited to a diary, and it was with the same shameful sense of voyeurism one might feel reading another's private records that I first read them. I feel that way again now, reading them a final time so as to accurately record their details here in papers of my own.

As I say, Mrs. Dolores begins with *My dearest Gorman*, and what follows is a saddening account of the loneliness she has felt in the years of his absence. So deep is her sense of loss without him, that were I to have abandoned my reading after the first page, I would have presumed the letter a final farewell of the type often left behind by those who choose to end their own life. Come the end of the second page, however, and from the third onwards to the last, Mrs. Dolores addresses her absent husband only as one might a confidant when confessing a distressing tale. It seems in these pages that her mind takes a terrible turn towards madness, though I am no longer as certain of that as I once was. My father, too, had a change of mind in that regard.

After detailing the extent of her loneliness and expressing her wish that her husband were with her still, she writes of a mysterious figure who she claims visits the farm at night. She has seen it *creeping* about the yard, she says, sometimes bent at the back like someone keen to remain unseen, other times crawling on all fours as if tracking a scent across the muddy ground.

I must confess that my earliest reading of this was affected by the sadness I felt for how her mind had so badly turned, though even in presuming thus, I must also confess to the shiver of fear I felt in imagining such a visitor, and I did so while safely embedded in the heart of town. It must have been a thousandfold worse for a woman alone at that isolated farm.

It seems Mrs. Dolores coped initially, and rather desperately, by longing for this figure to be her husband, come back to her after all these years. Be him alive or something altogether more ghostly, she shares her hopes that the figure she sees by the light of the moon is her lost love, and declares how she can love him, still, however unsubstantial a form he might be forced to take, so long as he chooses to remain with her. Even when her strange visitor behaves like something animal, sly and snuffling, this good woman is still willing to believe it may be her husband and reminds him in her writing that were he now of unsound mind, she accepted him *in sickness and in health*. Alas, the figure is *not* her husband, as she realizes very quickly, is in fact something altogether very *different* to Mr. Dolores or indeed any other man, for she notes how it *proved beyond a doubt that it was not of heaven or of this earth, but elsewhere*, though how it proved this to her she does not reveal. Instead, and with a shaking hand, she writes *I fear not so much for my life as for my soul, for why else should such a thing appear if not to strike me damned?*

Content, at first, to limit its visit to exploring only the yard, there is yet an instance in which it looks at the house *with some awful intention* that troubles Mrs. Dolores, even as it seems to excite her. She writes that she has seen the figure several times but offers very little by way of specific detail, combining all but one of her sightings in a single line of writing, and it is in this line she notes of its new interest in the house. *I have seen it skulking in shadows, hunched in hiding,* she writes, *seen it creeping in circles, snorting at the ground like a beast with a scent, and once, to my awful wonder, it stood boldly by moonlight, staring at the house with some awful intention, the anticipation of which seems to please it.* She adds, *I wait for its return to see what such intentions, and my role in them, might be.*

I understand now, at least to some extent, the strange thrill she must have felt then, though she waited for its return in a braver state than I could ever manage. I, who writes this with my doors locked and a bar across my shuttered windows, though in this heat I'd like to throw them wide for any coolness of air they might offer, despite the consequences.

THERE IS A MOMENT in Mrs. Dolores's papers when she blames this skulking, creeping figure that visits for luring her husband away. In a brief interlude she remembers with some regret her accusations that he had been continuing some torrid affair with someone from town, though she never puts a name to this woman, and while it may seem an error on my part to presume it truth and not simply the creation of a jealous, abandoned wife, let me note here that I have learnt in subsequent years that Gorman Dolores was indeed rumored to be a man of questionable moral rectitude regarding his marriage vows. With that recorded, I should also note that it appears the affairs he allowed himself were few, and brief, and for the most part without consequence beyond the slow and silent breaking of poor Mrs. Dolores's heart over a period of years. I say for the most part because there was one incident that may be of some relevance regarding the events I write of now, and Mrs. Dolores herself alludes to it briefly.

As I have mentioned, Mr. and Mrs. Dolores used to keep a number of goats, selling the milk and cheese and sometimes the meat, until one year, over a short period of time—I believe it was no longer than a week—they were all slaughtered, down to the last. This was not an intended butchering for market, as they might carry out themselves, but a violent attack, or rather a sequence of attacks, that saw every animal gutted and crudely displayed. Do I need to write that the week had been a particularly hot one? That the animals had been slaughtered at the height of a terrible heatwave?

Upon the first awful occurrence, Mrs. Dolores and her husband suspected it to be the work of some savage predator, perhaps driven into ferocious frenzy by the severe heat, but with subsequent attacks Mrs. Dolores's thoughts went to her husband's suspected adulterous affairs, and she considered the possibility of someone who might bear them grievance, such as a scorned woman or a jealous partner, though it seems in her writing of it that she never put a voice to such suspicions. In each instance, they saved what they could of the meat, though none of it made the market price they could have normally expected and they were never able to replace any of the animals.

There were those in town (and are, still) who supposed it was this loss of livestock and livelihood that drove Mr. Gorman Dolores to abandon his wife, perhaps to seek work, perhaps because he saw the slaughtering of the goats as a threat to his own person, whereas others were (and are) of the opinion that he merely saw it as an opportunity to leave a woman he no longer loved, despite having sworn quite the opposite in till death do us part. Whatever his reasons, Mr. Dolores was soon gone, and Mrs. Dolores remained alone, resigned to never knowing why.

That said, and as I have mentioned already, there is a moment where she blames the figure in her yard for luring her husband away, admitting that even a married man might find himself lonely and seeming to forgive her husband for any previous indiscretions before turning her attention to one who might encourage them. It makes for distressing reading, the sudden shift in tone to a voice so angry and resentful that her handwriting becomes jaggedly erratic on the page, and it is at this point that she imagines a different reader for a short while, no longer addressing her husband or recording events in a diary-like fashion but rather speaking directly to the figure she claims to see in her yard. *You took him from me*, she writes. *You drew him to you with the coolness of one who has no want for what might come so easily, though you crept in the night with the manner of one intent on stealing.* While there is evidence of control in her word choices and syntax, nevertheless there is a vehemence to her script that nearly presses her pen through the paper.

She is far less aggressive when accusing the nocturnal visitor of driving Gorman Dolores away in fear. Indeed, she writes of this possibility with such calmness and clarity that it seems she harbors no regret at all that this was so and may even be relieved by such a prospect. I would go so far to suggest there is even some joy in how she writes of her realization that her strange visitor was in fact *mostly male*, an observation that allows her *to sleep at last, despite the maddening heat that keeps me fidgeting*. What she means by *mostly* is never disclosed, nor do I have the imagination for it.

The final pages of her account are filled with such woeful accounts of loneliness and rejection (and, as I understand it now, frustration) that reading them without pity is an impossible undertaking, all the more so because of how much her mind seems to have deteriorated by this time. How long must the poor woman have suffered so privately? There were more than a few people in town who could have offered companionship, had they only known.

It was a thought that troubled my father a great deal in the last years of his life, which was when he turned more frequently to the comfort of drink. Could it be that Mrs. Dolores came personally to the store not only to collect her groceries but to see my father, similarly abandoned by one he once loved? McIntyres Trading were, after all, better stocked. And had he, also, looked forward to her visits? I know, with certainty, that I did. She had no children herself but she had a motherly nature I appreciated, and I had always been fond of her; perhaps my father had been, as well. I remember finding him more than once, in his chair by the fire, quite melancholy with the thought that for each day that Winnie (as he still fondly called her) came into town to fetch her food and other supplies, she spent six more in isolation at her farm without so much as even a single goat for company, at which point, depending on his temperament, he might launch into a violent deconstruction of her husband's character. Come the morning he would always apologize for his recollections of Mrs. Dolores (or for his diatribe regarding her husband) as he knew the memory of her upset me, but the truth of the matter is I welcomed such drunken monologues, for they reminded me more of the woman herself than the state in which we found her, and I took some comfort in witnessing a more emotional side of my otherwise stoic father, for it helped me understand that my own occasional lapses into an unhappy mood were not unusual.

He was troubled, too, by another detail. "How was the knife so clean?"

Though he talked of this less frequently when troubled, the knife he meant was the one found in the yard. The knife Mrs. Dolores likely used to cut the bucket from the rope for which she had a darker purpose. The knife which I'd presumed she'd used to commit awful violence upon herself so as to be certain of her death at the end of that rope. It was the knife my father had returned to the kitchen, because as he said, and as I remembered again at his prompting, it had been clean.

"Long knife like that, and such a wound, and no blood upon the blade? Not a single drop?" my father would ask. "There had been no rain for days. Not for *days*."

I have mentioned the lack of rain already, though it came the very night we brought Mrs. Dolores back to town. Prior to that, the week had been uncomfortably warm, the summer heat settling upon us like a hot, stifling blanket. Just as it does again now, as the curling of these sweat-damp pages upon which I write this evening testify. And so it is I am almost brought to the end of this tale.

For Mrs. Dolores, the tale ends at the end of a rope, the horrid details of which I have already provided, but her papers end with a few paragraphs more detailed and distressing than the others, which I reproduce here in full. It concerns the final sighting not included in the compression of one line like the previous visits, and Mrs. Dolores gives it an entire page of her writing.

Yesterday, I witnessed for the first time its arrival and later its departure. I had always supposed that it appeared as if by magic, prowling out from the dark like it was made of the same shadows or riding down on a moonbeam or some other such fanciful method, and no doubt you would blame the fiction I enjoy, Gorman, for having put such ideas in my mind, but having seen the truth of the matter I wish that there had been more substance to such imaginings. Instead, what I saw as I watched my visitor's arrival was how it climbed out from the very well from which I daily fetched my water. A graceless thing, it grasped at first with long-taloned hands the edge of the well wall and then hooked more with the thin crook of its elbow to pull itself out of the dark. There followed, then, a scant thigh and bony knee, and then a shin like a goat's rear cannon, before it fell into the yard. From there it crawled, low to the ground, not on its forearms and knees but upon its palms and feet. A bent-backed thing as thin as a reed, it shuffled as much sideways as forwards, its rump on proud display until the moon appeared and bathed its sickly skin with silver, at which point it stood without shame or modesty despite its obvious nudity, and I fully saw how wicked it was. Though in its eventual departure it returned to the well, yet was I glad to see it go, for the sight of it that moonlit night was almost too much for my mind to bear. Better that it should fold itself over that wall and descend, headfirst into the well, crawling spider-like down out of view, than remain a moment longer in the yard with every detail of its form exposed. And in that form, I had some idea of its intentions, and, oh, how foul a feeling that aroused in me.

Before it went—and this is the worst of it, dear Gorman—before it went, it said something I'd been keen to hear for many years. Its voice was like water, slow and trickling, and though in writing this I can no longer remember a single word it spoke to me, I understood its want and find I must give it what I can, and all I can, just as I understand, now, that I want too.

There is a declaration of love, a plea for forgiveness, and a signature, but those details aside, such is how the story of Mrs. Winifred Dolores comes to its end. With a hitherto unseen grammatical error that provides some ambiguity as to the meaning of her final sentiment.

My own end will come soon enough, and I fear that applies to more than my writing, for I, too, have seen this thing from the well these last few nights. Perhaps it comes to me from the old Dolores farm, but if it does then I wonder that there might be more than one, for the individual that visits me is far from *mostly male*. Indeed, were I inclined to provide a detailed description (which I am not) I would note there are prominent if ill-proportioned *female* attributes. It is yet to speak, and I am glad of that for now, though the silence in my house is beginning to feel like an empty one despite my occupation of it and I am concerned that I will soon long to hear whatever this visitor might choose to say. That I shall succumb to it as I have that maddening heat that had me, at last, opening all the windows.

I shall watch for it and write what more I can in the time that remains to me. There are some details yet to tell.

First, to conclude the mystery as to the whereabouts of Mr. Dolores, they found his body in the very same well, which is to say, they found bones enough to suggest a human skeleton, albeit with some minor deformities. The well was filled shortly after, though considering my own nocturnal visitor I find myself wondering how thoroughly.

I should, as well, offer some more detail regarding my father's passing. He suffered a fatal heart attack one night, collapsing in the store yard where he was discovered the next morning by one of our traders. The most likely explanation is that he had been investigating the possibility of an intruder (and perhaps had found one and been more startled than they upon the discovery) as he had confided with several customers, as well as myself, that he suspected someone was loitering in the yard in recent nights. Do I need to add that this was during the second of those bad Bowers summers? Perhaps the heat was why he had stripped himself down to only the most minimal of clothing when his heart so abruptly stopped.

Upon inheriting the store, I moved back into the rooms above the business and it is from the open window of one of these that I have the view of that same yard where my father died. I don't pretend that it is he who comes again now, while the nights are hottest, to crawl in the moonlight down there or to beckon me to follow, and I do not think I imagine the rank, stagnant smell of brackish water, though I do suppose that should I be visited again, and should the visitor speak, that smell will become at once cool, and welcoming, and impossible to resist on a night as stifling hot as this.

I have no one, and leave these papers to you, whoever shall find them. Please do not judge me too unkindly and know that though I am (and have been for some time) very lonely, I go to my new friend sound of mind.

I can see her now, shimmering in that maddening heat, and her voice, when she speaks, will be as welcome as the rain.

Ray Cluley's work has appeared in various magazines and anthologies. It has been reprinted several times, including in Ellen Datlow's Best Horror of the Year *series, Steve Berman's* Wilde Stories 2013: The Year's Best Gay Speculative Fiction, *and in Benoît Domis's* Ténèbres *series. He has been translated into French, Polish, Hungarian, and Chinese. He won the British Fantasy Award for Best Short Story ("Shark! Shark!") and has since been nominated for Best Novella (*Water For Drowning*) and Best Collection (*Probably Monsters*). His second collection,* All That's Lost, *is available now from Black Shuck Books.*

STORE IN A COOL, DARK PLACE

BY GREGORY L. NORRIS

THERE ARE THINGS THE LATE LAWRENCE WILSON'S IMDB PAGE WILL TELL YOU—BARE-BONES DETAILS AND CELLULOID NUGGETS MEMORIALIZED AND LEFTOVER FROM HIS THIRTY-PLUS YEARS IN THE FILM BUSINESS. You'll see he's credited with directing such celluloid cult gems as *Flying Saucer Invasion, Fiend at the Window,* and *Margaret's Monster,* among others. The write-up includes the summation: *Wilson was never as bad as Ed Wood or as great as Roger Corman could be, and is today mostly forgotten for that very reason.* There's even a photograph of my father in black and white and mostly gray, a lit cigarette clutched between two fingers, staring offstage, his expression intense. More than once, I've wondered what he was thinking in that moment. What dark dreams plagued him?

What his IMDB page doesn't tell you is that the director was distant, more ghost than father. It doesn't reference how, after walking away from his last project before a frame of film was shot, he loaded up a moving van and drove east to settle as a recluse in an old New Englander in a town no one's heard of. Oh, it lists his death—that got updated eleven days ago after the news broke. But it doesn't say how he left me burdened with property I didn't want and a house full of relics to sift through and dispose of.

I DON'T KNOW WHY he chose Redfern, New Hampshire as the place for his escape from

California and everything that was. Maybe, in the throes of a breakdown, he opened an atlas, randomly pointed, and that was that.

A light snow fell on the day I landed. I rented a car, keyed the address in the GPS to a house I'd never visited or been invited to, and drove through the bone-chilling grayness. Emotions sat heavy in my gut. Part of it was hunger, sure, but the fast food burger I wolfed down en route only added to the malaise. My father had died at a respectable age of ninety-one. I was fifty-five and still resented his role as a stranger. Why couldn't he have fathered other children out of wedlock and blessed them with the corpse of his estate? There was money, some, and the house. But I didn't want any of it.

"*Turn right*," the GPS's robotic female voice urged, shocking me out of my thoughts.

I turned right. Six hundred feet later, I'd reached my destination.

The place might have once been white, but its exterior looked gray in the early afternoon's overcast. The shutters were supposed to be red. Now, they were the shade of charcoal. A small memorial in plastic had been laid at the chain link fence's gate. A puddle of hard wax was frozen around the remains of a candle set on the concrete walkway. As I opened the gate and it complained with a creak, I found myself wishing the bearer had lit that candle closer to the house. Close enough that only ashes would remain, and I wouldn't have to be here.

The key was where I was told it would be, left under an empty flowerpot. I entered through the kitchen door, expecting the worst. It was only half as bad as I'd prepared myself for.

There were dishes in the sink, only a few, and the faucet dripped a slow leak. Bread in a bag had sat on the counter long enough to show a fine crust of neon green. The appliances were classic white, the table and chairs survivors from another era— metal frames, hard surfaces in blue. Along with the faint mustiness that owed to the leaking faucet was the yellow smell of mice. At least one had taken up residence according to the droppings I noticed on a strip of otherwise clean counter.

The sad, sinking feeling deepened as I wandered past the kitchen and into the rest of the downstairs. There, to my left, was a dining room with table and six chairs looking quite sterile and unused, a living room with tired furniture and a dinosaur of a TV hooked to a VCR. A bookcase crammed full of old VHS tapes stood beside it. I imagined my late father, no cell phone, no cable, no streaming services, bleakly staring at old reruns of TV shows and movies, maybe even some of his own video offspring.

There was a downstairs bedroom with a bed and unfolded piles of clothes, a bathroom in need of the local haz-mat unit, and laundry tucked behind a door with plantation slats.

My father was dead and, standing there, he truly felt gone. I glanced around at the walls, which bore no family photos or movie posters from his career, and the first tears I'd managed since getting the news of his passing spilled down my cheeks.

As I ALREADY SAID, that day was gray, cold. I'd paid for home heating oil so the pipes wouldn't freeze and asked the estate lawyer to set the thermostat on 58-degrees; at that moment, the chill in the air worked past my clothes, my skin, my bones. The oppressive stillness inside the house struck me, a pall broken only by the low moan of the wind as it whisked around the angles of the roof.

Upstairs was a front bedroom, sparsely furnished—a lone easy chair turned toward a blank wall. A moderately clean bathroom filled the center. And at the back of the house...

It was a room with a single bed. Shelves lined the walls. Upon those shelves was all the memorabilia he'd accumulated over the years of his career. The rubber head of *Margaret's Monster* sat propped and staring blankly outward. As I neared, I detected the foul smell of the rubber along with an acrid note of sweat left over from the uncredited actor who'd worn it. The music box from one of my father's more psychological horror pictures, *Siren's Song*, was on another. I lifted the lid, but no music played. One entire shelf contained movie scripts, three-hole punched and bound at the top and bottom but not the middle by brass brads. Most of the scripts had white cardstock covers—which identified them as shooting copies. Some of the covers were black, one pale green.

There were trophies and plaques, all of them minor, fan-produced stuff, nothing from the academy. The cheap, plastic flying saucer that had so terrified the good citizens of his most famous effort had crashed and now collected dust among them.

It was a kind of museum. A sad reliquarium with no visitors apart from me.

The room contained a closet that conformed to the slope of the ceiling. Standing confused, the light cast from a single bulb illuminating some things that didn't make sense like a jumpsuit made of silver fabric, it struck me that I had discovered a kind of wardrobe department, more relics from past film projects.

There were boxes inside filled with studio ephemera—call sheets, clippings from newspapers with more advertisements and reviews of films, contracts, and, in one dark, forgotten corner, an ancient movie reel canister. Hexagonal in shape, its surface had oxidized. I picked it up and gave it a shake. What sounded like dried leaves shifted inside. I figured the contents had decayed and were now detritus.

A faded paper sticker on the outside of the canister read:

Ghost of the Gorilla.
Dir: Lawrence Wilson.

I'd never heard of that particular project. A quick search online revealed nothing. None of the fringe podcasts referenced it. Neither did the handful of websites dedicated to my father's body of work. It wasn't listed on his IMDB page or any other.

I returned the canister to the cool, dark corner of the closet where I'd discovered it, shut off the light, and closed the door. Outside, an empty twilight fell, helped along early by the dregs of the snowstorm.

I FOUND A DINER not far from the house and ordered soup to drive out the chill and meatloaf and mashed potatoes for the comfort. The soup was salty and greasy but worked; the meal removed some of the dark emotion though not all. I enjoyed a slice of chocolate cream pie and a hot cup of decaf, no closer to deciding what to do about my father's possessions. An image crossed my mind— *The Lawrence Wilson House, a historical landmark—see the horrors of Margaret's Monster! Listen to the terrifying song of the Siren! Feel the chills of the Gorilla's Ghost! Honor system—please leave donation in the box.*

Exhaustion overwhelmed me. I drove back through the dusting of new snow to my late father's house.

THERE WAS NO WAY I'd sleep in his bedroom downstairs on the same mattress and bedclothes he'd sweated and died upon. Same for the lumpy downstairs sofa, which had taken on the bas-relief of his body from all those hours of sitting. I remembered the single bed upstairs in the museum and made my way there, my suitcases in tow.

The comforter smelled dusty but clean. I brushed my teeth in the bathroom, stripped down, and watched part of an episode of a new TV show on my phone. All of the miles and, more so, the years caught up with me. I passed out in the dark unfamiliar upstairs room in a dead stranger's house.

At some untimed point in the night, I heard the muffled scraping sound from somewhere close by. *Mice,* I assumed until, playing in counterpoint with it, came a deep and guttural growl. I jolted up, forgetting how to breathe. In the void, I didn't know where I was—the house where I grew up in California, the one that haunted my dreams? No. My awareness did a reset. A house that haunted my waking self in the present. Time blurred as I waited for the sound to repeat.

Creak...

I remembered my phone and, hands shaking, activated the flashlight app. I trained the beam toward the source of the sound—the closet door, which now stood the slightest bit ajar despite my having closed it earlier that afternoon.

I SCRUBBED THE coffee pot, filled it with water, and brewed morning Joe with the filters and can of cheap grounds I found in the cabinet.

There was no way I'd risk eating anything in the fridge. By the time the pot finished percolating, I'd stuffed an entire garbage bag full with old lettuce, condiments, and freezer-burned meat. I carried the trash out back to the pair of barrels I'd spied near the flowerpot. An inch of fresh snow coated everything on another gray morning at the farthest end of the known world.

The list of must-do's I'd assembled in my mind scattered on my return to the kitchen. A dumpster? I forgot whether I'd agreed to dispose of it all and list the house for sale as-is. An exterminator to deal with the mouse problem or inexpensive wooden traps from the local hardware store?

Then I recalled what I'd heard. Mice didn't growl like jungle predators. The cold from outside had followed me past the threshold and wrapped me in its unwanted, chilly embrace.

"Maybe what I heard was the ghost of the gorilla," I whispered aloud and punctuated the statement with a humorless chuckle.

Blinking, I came out of the sudden fugue enough to down a bit of coffee, black, and exit my late father's house for necessary provisions.

I TRIED TO EXPLAIN it away on exhaustion. Or it could have been the stress of being *there*. And, I reminded myself, that for all of its cheesiness, *Margaret's Monster* had terrified me as a boy and, yes, into adulthood—and I'd slept in the same room as the monster's head.

But as I unpacked plastic bags and sent fresh cold cuts into the meat drawer and bread to the top of the fridge, an invisible finger stroked my backbone. That movie about the gorilla—I'd never heard of it. According to the Internet, it didn't exist. And yet there it was, a relic all but forgotten by history. My father was dead. I figured, too, so was anyone else associated with the project. The studio my father worked for, Federal Films, had gone out of business decades earlier. There was no way to confirm anything.

I fixed a sandwich, downed another cup of coffee—this time with a splash of milk thanks to my haul, and tabled my plans of phone calls and trash runs for that day. I wandered upstairs to the room at the back of the house.

Again, the sense of isolation struck me, coaxed along by the soundtrack of the wind whistling around the angles of the roof and a car's horn in the distance. The room was as I'd left it—bed unmade, the closet door shut, the head of Margaret's Monster staring blankly from a bookshelf. Now the finger tickling my spine had pierced my flesh and traveled far deeper. I felt it wiggling around inside my stomach.

I opened the closet door and pulled the light chain. The film canister was where I'd left it in its cool, dark corner. I picked it up and shook it. The same dusty, dead leaves sound filtered out. I attempted to open the case. The edges had rusted shut. I yanked harder only to wince and lose my grip. I *heard* the splinter of fingernail on my right pointer snap. When I glanced down, I was bleeding.

I ran it under the upstairs bathroom faucet, dried it off on a towel, and located a box of old bandage strips beneath the sink. The tiny wound itched more than stung. Undaunted, I returned to the back bedroom.

My focus drifted over to the shelf filled with screenplays. I grabbed a stack and flipped through them—the shooting script for *Fiend at the Window*, *Siren's Song*, my father's attempt at a noir murder mystery, *Belfast Road*, and others were there, all containing notes jotted on the sides, my father's version of the Dead Sea Scrolls. I tossed the handful of scripts onto the floor and suffered the thunderclap produced. Another stack. The shooting scripts for *Margaret's Monster*, *Swamp Dwellers*, *Canary Yellow*—the irony in that it was shot in black and white, and others. But no *Ghost of the Gorilla*.

Not until I pulled out that lone script with the pale green cardstock cover.

And there it was, 102 pages thick. How long I stared at the cover, seeing not only my father's name credited as Director but also Writer, I can't say. The world outside the windows grew noticeably darker.

I thawed enough to crack open the script. Until that moment, I'd dismissed the concept as your typical low-budget, lowbrow monster movie about a man in a gorilla suit. That first page of script altered my perception.

FADE IN:
EXT. House – DAY

A typical two-story New Englander behind a mote of chain link fence and gate.

A car pulls up to the curb. A MAN (WARREN, 50s) gets out. He studies the house, his expression grim.

                    WARREN
                    Dad...

Warren enters through the gate. He walks up to the front door and tests the knob. It's locked. Warren wanders around to the back-door, lifts an empty flowerpot on the back steps located near two garbage barrels.

A key is hidden beneath the flowerpot. Warren inserts it into the backdoor lock and enters the house.

INT. KITCHEN – DAY
Warren stands in the kitchen. He—

I dropped the script. It landed on the floor beside the others, splayed open atop bent pages.

FRAMES OF FILM crackled through one of those old projectors. The sound caught up—muted, in the background, and traveling a second behind the actors, who played out in black and white across the screen.

There was Warren, walking around the inside of his late father's house.

"Dad?" he called. "Dad, where are you?"

The camera tracked him through the downstairs, up to the second story, and into the back bedroom.

"Dad? You're scaring me!"

Warren turned his back to the room's closet. In the strangulating silence that fol-lowed—and unseen to the film's star, the closet door opened. Wider. Wider yet.

The gorilla charged out, and oh, how terrifying to behold that stir of living shadows was! No man in a cheap gorilla suit that zipped up the back, it seized hold of unsuspecting Warren and sank its long teeth into the back of his skull. The screams caught up to the spray of black blood and Warren's death struggle, echoing and un-forgettable.

I jumped awake and found myself in that other upstairs room, having fallen asleep in the chair turned to the wall, facing the blank screen upon which the movie had been projected in my nightmare. Soaked in sweat that had grown clammy, I screamed.

And screamed.

I ENTERED THE back bedroom. The head of Margaret's Monster still eyed me blankly. Old scripts littered the floor. The closet door remained shut.

Only a dream, my inner voice attempted to reassure me. It also tried to sell me on the lie that I'd willingly chosen to sleep in that other room, in that chair, when I knew I'd gone to bed in the museum.

I opened the closet door. The hexagonal film canister was where it should have been. I stared at it until my eyes burned from not blinking.

When I roused enough to enter and lift the film canister, gone was the dry-leaves shuffle of its contents. What shifted around inside was solid, weighty, and I imagined its sound as that of an intact film reel.

The reel for *Ghost of the Gorilla*, my father's opus, finished at last.

A low moan built in my belly and clawed its way up my throat. I returned the canister to its spot and switched off the light, shut the door.

Go, that same inner cheerleader now urged.

I walked out of the room, not bothering to pack up my things. Down the stairs. To the living room. I'd sell the house. Hell, I'd let the town take it for back taxes. Anything so long as I was free of it and my father's legacy.

Two steps toward the front door, I heard the footfalls pounding overhead—heavy, hastening after me. And in counterpoint came the gorilla's growl.

I hurried out of the house and to my rental, not bothering to close the door behind me.

I'VE KEPT HAVING THE DREAMS.

The ones about a house, a son and dead father, and something sinister that sneaks out of the closet in the upstairs back bedroom. Where one dream leaves off, the next picks up. I'm over 1400 miles from that place, but I've also heard *it*—the footsteps, the growls.

I released it from that film canister. *The Ghost of the Gorilla*, my late father's movie. The copy restored, the film almost complete, I'm just about at the end of the third act when the monster emerges from the closet. Then? Fade out. God help me.

Raised on a healthy diet of creature double features and classic SF TV, Gregory L. Norris writes regularly for numerous short story anthologies, national magazines, novels, and the occasional episode for TV or film. Gregory novelized the NBC Made-for-TV classic by Gerry Anderson, The Day After Tomorrow: Into Infinity *(as well as a sequel and a forthcoming third entry into the franchise for Anderson Entertainment in the U.K.), a movie he watched as an eleven-year-old sitting cross-legged on the living room floor of the enchanted cottage where he grew up. Gregory won HM in the 2016 Roswell Awards in Short SF Writing. He once worked as a screenwriter on two episodes of Paramount's Star Trek: Voyager. Kate Mulgrew, Voyager's "Captain Janeway," blurbed his book of short stories and novellas,* The Fierce and Unforgiving Muse, *stating, "In my seven years on* Voyager, *I don't think I've met a writer more capable of writing such a book—and writing it so beautifully."*

In late 2019, Gregory sold an option on his modern Noir feature film screenplay, Amandine, *to the new Hollywood production company Snarkhunter LLC, owned by actor Dan Lench, a devotee of Gregory's writing. In late 2020, Snarkhunter optioned Gregory's tetralogy Horror film based upon four of his short stories,* Ride Along. *That same month, his short story "Water Whispers" was nominated for the Pushcart Prize.*

Gregory lives and writes at Xanadu, a century-old house perched on a hill in New Hampshire's North Country with spectacular mountain views, with his rescue cat and emerald-eyed muse. Follow his further literary adventures at: www.gregorylnorris.blogspot.com

AN ABSENCE OF MALICE

BY JOHN LLEWELLYN PROBERT

"IS THAT HIM?"

The Reverend Mr. James Kendall peered through the window of the hospital side room at the emaciated figure lying on the bed. The man's eyes were closed, but his jaw was active, lips constantly rolling over and against one another as if he was desperate to cry out but the depth of his sedation prevented it. As the man's head jerked from side to side, straggles of his moist black hair left grey stains on the crisp clean pillow. The white hospital gown was muddy and very crumpled. The man's right wrist had been chained to the upraised guard rail of the bed, the other to a young bullet-headed policeman who nodded in acknowledgment as the young doctor who had met Kendall at the hospital entrance waved from the other side of the glass.

"No," said the medic. His name was Carstairs and at twenty-nine he considered his current post in this tiny district general hospital in the middle of nowhere strictly a stepping stone to greater things. "That's Corrigan—the serial killer."

Kendall frowned. In his thirty-three years as vicar of the county parish of Beesford the only crime in his community had been the occasional episode of shoplifting. Serial killers were something to be read about in paperback novels or watched on television drama programs, both of which he assiduously avoided.

"What's he doing here?"

"They recaptured him a couple of hours ago." The two men made their way further down the brightly-lit corridor. "He'd lacerated his leg quite badly falling into a nearby river and this was the closest hospital. They brought him here to be tidied up and get a tetanus booster, and I took the precaution of giving him a big dose of his regular anti-psychotic medication as well. That's why he keeps slapping his lips like that, in case you were wondering."

Kendall had been trying to forget it. "So is it safe to have him here?"

Carstairs shrugged. "He should sleep for hours, and if he does wake up Sergeant Wilton has assured me that he has a large truncheon on hand. They'll be taking him back to Rampton in the morning by helicopter. Did you think you were here to see him?"

"For a moment I did, yes." Kendall was already visibly relaxing.

"Oh no. The chap who was asking to see a vicar is down here. I'm sorry to have had to call you out on such a filthy night by the way, but under the circumstances I thought you were the best person for him to talk to."

"That's all right," said Kendall, still a bit unhappy at his having been prised away from a planned evening of model ship-building. "Is Mr. Teasdale of a similar disposition to your Mr. Corrigan?"

Carstairs pondered for a moment before replying. "No, I'm certain he's harmless. He talks a lot, though, and what he says doesn't make an awful lot of sense. Not to me, anyway, and seeing as I'm the closest thing this place has got to an on-call psychiatrist I think all he really needs is a sympathetic ear. I would spend more time with him but I'm the only one here tonight and there are already another three emergencies waiting."

Carstairs eased open the door of the third sideroom to reveal a man in his late twenties lying on the bed. He was wearing a very creased dark blue suit and his blonde hair was in disarray. A large absorbent dressing had been taped just above his right eye.

"Mr. John Teasdale, this is Reverend Kendall." The politeness of Carstairs' introduction quickly turning admonitory. "And may I ask who gave you permission to get dressed again?"

"I thought it would be best under the circumstances," said Teasdale, fingering the bandage. "Once I've talked to the vicar I really need to get out of here."

"We'll see about that," Carstairs shook his head at Kendall before closing the door. The vicar pulled up a chair and sat as Teasdale eyed him nervously. Kendall spoke in the calm, soothing tones of someone who has had many years of practice talking to the distressed. "How can I help you, Mr. Teasdale?"

"I don't really know if you can." Teasdale got off the bed and walked over to the rain-streaked window. As the man gazed at the heavy drops of water trickling down the glass Kendall caught the word *inevitable*.

"I beg your pardon?"

Teasdale turned. "The raindrops on the window. It's inevitable that they will run downwards. They may stand still for a while, or be buffeted to the side a little by the wind, but eventually, given time, they fall. Inevitable, you see?"

Kendall nodded, hoped his expression looked sufficiently understanding, and tried again. "Is it a spiritual matter you need help with?"

Teasdale ran both hands through his hair before looking up at the cracked ceiling. "I don't know, Reverend. But I'm not mad. I'm just trying to provide you with an analogy that will help you understand what I'm going to tell you. Then perhaps you might be able to offer me some advice." Teasdale sat back down. "It all started with the accident."

"The one that brought you in here, you mean?"

"No, no, no." Teasdale shook his head furiously and then paused for a moment, waiting for the nausea the action had brought on to subside. "I had an accident with the car a couple of days before the one that brought me in here. It was after that first accident that I started to see...the things."

Kendall leaned forward in his chair. "What things?"

JOHN TEASDALE BEGAN his trip to Farrowdale Conference Centre on a rainy Wednesday morning with the intention of reaching the northern English town sometime during the afternoon. By lunchtime he was in Derby Royal Infirmary being assessed by a cheerful casualty officer as Teasdale recounted how the lorry driver behind him on the M1 motorway had failed to notice the lines of traffic were slowing rapidly to a crawl just south of Nottingham. Teasdale's car had been involved in a "minor collision," according to the traffic policeman who had arrived at the site of the accident within minutes of it occurring. The bump had been just enough to crumple the rear of Teasdale's car and give him a nasty jolt, and the officer had insisted that Teasdale be medically assessed "for insurance purposes if nothing else." Fortunately Teasdale had not been knocked out and his skull X-Ray showed no evidence of fracture, so he was discharged with a card listing the symptoms of acute brain injury, and instructions to come back at once if he began to experience any of them.

He made it to Farrowdale driving a slightly more crumpled vehicle than the one he had set out in, and was viewed with amusement by hotel patrons as he parked and removed his luggage from the boot, doing his best to hold the sides of his bruised suitcase together. He checked in, explained that he was part of the "Health Economics in the UK—A Plan for the Future" group, and was shown to one of the single rooms on the third floor.

The first thing he did was clear the clutter of individually wrapped teabags and packets of coffee and sugar that had been crammed into one of those horrible stainless steel teapots Teasdale had always felt should be given some sort of "poorest design of all-time" award for their ability to get more tea on the table than into the cup. There was also a couple of colorful brochures telling you about sites of local interest. Teasdale didn't think he would have either the time or the inclination to visit "World of Apples" or the "Edwardian Frog Museum," whatever that was, and so the leaflets all went into the bin. Once he had some space clear he took the framed photograph of Lisa from his suitcase and propped it by the bedside. He hardly needed it to remind him of his wife, especially now that she was pregnant, but he had got so used to taking her picture with him on trips that it would have been difficult to leave it behind.

His mobile rang. It was one of his colleagues letting him know that he had been spotted entering the hotel twenty minutes ago. Why was he not getting a round of drinks in at the bar? Oh, and everyone was dying to know what he had done to his car.

Despite what the doctor had said, Teasdale reckoned a couple of drinks would help to get him over the shock of his accident. He rang Lisa and told her what had happened, reassuring her that he was unhurt. After admitting that he was off to the bar he ignored her comments about whether that was wise, and promised to ring her the following evening.

THE NEXT MORNING Teasdale was profoundly grateful for the hotel's all-you-can-eat breakfast which, along with the copious amounts of coffee he consumed, helped to temper the colossal hangover he had from the exploits of the previous evening. He drank very little normally, but he had done an admirable, if inadvisable, job of keeping up with his more booze-hardened colleagues. As he stumbled into the lecture theatre for the first talk he wondered when the painkillers he had swallowed before coming down to breakfast were going to kick in. Two slide presentations passed with him just about managing to sit upright and keep his breakfast down. After the coffee break his head felt clearer, and on going back in he found he could concentrate better on what was being said.

The presentation finished. As the speaker fielded questions, Teasdale found his attention being drawn to the projection screen. Here in the dimness of the auditorium, he almost fancied that the shadow of the speaker cast by the podium light was the profile of some otherworldly entity, the jutting lapel of the speaker's suit and the arrangement of the papers before him adding to its malignant, crooked appearance. With one final question about quality-adjusted life years answered, the young man, whose name Teasdale had missed, stepped down from the podium to allow a tired-looking individual in a grey suit named Geoffrey Harris to take his place. As Harris introduced himself prior to putting up his first slide, Teasdale noted with interest how this speaker, too, had somehow managed to orientate himself such that he was producing exactly the same shape of shadow on the expanse of whiteness behind him. Harris was obviously a little nervous and when he dropped the first page of his notes, Teasdale felt sorry for him.

When the man bent down but the shadow did not, Teasdale felt the first pang of uneasiness.

He chided himself as Harris began his speech. The pattern on the screen must have been caused by something else. Teasdale looked behind him but couldn't make out anything that could be responsible. Turning back to view the presentation he was relieved to see the first slide was now on display. In the split second between the first and second slides, Teasdale was sure he saw the shape again, and by the time the seventh slide left the screen there was no doubt in his mind that something was there.

It was nonsense, of course. Teasdale was well aware that images could remain on the retina for a short time and persist, particularly if the eye was exposed to a very white or black background shortly after being shown a picture. But the slides had been of text only, not of a human figure.

A figure with the thinnest of arms and legs.

A figure with a bald, bulbous head far out of proportion to its body, one that, as it turned its head to the side, seemed to possess a monstrous blunted semblance of a beak.

The talk ended. Teasdale made his way out of the auditorium and into a nearby washroom. He splashed cold water on his face, rubbed his eyes and stared at himself in the mirror. His slightly disheveled but essentially healthy-looking twenty-seven-year-old self stared back. He wiped his face with a paper towel, wished he hadn't had so much to drink last night, and returned to his seat.

A plump, power-dressed girl named Fiona Worthington was just starting to speak about health economics for the twenty-first century, illustrating her talk with pie charts, bar graphs and some tricolor box diagrams that Teasdale could make neither head nor tail of. She got as far as the fifth slide before Teasdale saw the shape again. As the talk continued he gave up following what Ms Worthington had to say and instead gave in to the urge to study it. Rather than mere shadow, he could see now that the figure was an outline of absolute blackness.

No, not just blackness. More like nothingness. An absence, rather than a presence. It almost felt as if the space occupied by the stooped figure, its horrible swollen head swaying slightly from side to side between pictograms, was somehow gone, as if the substance of the screen, the brick wall behind it, and perhaps even the world beyond no longer existed. Teasdale's hallucination began to raise its right arm. He looked at the crude vestige of a hand, two spiny protuberances serving as fingers, and felt a chill at the thing's undoubted malefic intent.

Slide twenty-two of Ms Worthington's talk clicked colorfully by and suddenly the shape was gone. Teasdale twitched, disturbing the person next to him. He coughed to cover his surprise, then relaxed, hoping that the bizarre ill-effects of his hangover were finally clearing. Then he realized that the shape was standing next to Fiona, the tip of one claw resting delicately on her lectern as it swung its head from side to side, the obscene beak-like protuberance searching for something.

Teasdale was still convinced he was seeing things, particularly as no one else seemed to have noticed anything, and so he kept quiet as the thing lifted itself into the air and glided down to the floor of the auditorium, up the left-hand aisle, and to the third row from the back. Teasdale craned his neck to try and see where it was going, much to the consternation of his neighbor who, like everyone else, remained oblivious to the spectral intruder within their midst.

The thing was hovering in front of a dark-haired, jowly, middle-aged man in a charcoal grey suit who was busy scribbling notes. What if it was Death, Teasdale suddenly found himself wondering. Perhaps the individual it had picked out was about to die from a welter of cholesterol clogging one of his coronary arteries. As Teasdale watched, the shadow-thing extended its right arm and laid its twin finger-prongs upon the man's forehead, just above the bridge of his nose. Then, with one swift movement, it drove them into the man's skull before pulling them back, briefly inspected what it had removed, and then vanished.

THE MAN'S NAME was Henry Stebbington. He was fifty-one, and apart from being overweight as a result of no longer playing as much rugby as he did in his youth he was otherwise quite fit.

"It's very kind of you to ask if I'm all right, old boy," Stebbington said, biting into one of the cucumber and mayonnaise sandwiches that was the catering department's idea of a healthy lunch, "but I can assure you I feel perfectly fine. Apart from the after-effects of last night's introductory party, of course. Excuse me, won't you?"

Stebbington's mobile phone had started to emit a tinny melody. Holding his sandwich in one hand and the phone in the other, the man made his way out of the function room to the quieter surroundings of the hotel foyer.

Teasdale watched him leave, all the while feeling hugely embarrassed. That bang on the head combined with the alcohol he had stupidly drunk last night was causing his mind to play tricks. He sipped at a glass of orange juice and tried to involve himself in two different but similarly stultifying conversations about the talks that had just been presented. It wasn't long before he decided he needed to lie down for half an hour.

Henry Stebbington was sitting on a white marble bench in the foyer, just to the left of two huge rotating doors that led into the hotel. Teasdale had intended to go straight to his room, but the man's expression caused him to halt. Stebbington was staring at the black and white checkerboard pattern of the floor tiles, or rather beyond them at nothing in particular, like a little boy whose mother had forgotten to pick him up from school.

"I hope it wasn't bad news," said Teasdale as he reached Stebbington's side. He had to repeat the words before the seated man registered his presence, and when he did he regarded Teasdale with the eyes of someone who has experienced a personal tragedy.

"My mother," he said. Then, to qualify what he meant. "She died this afternoon."

With a bit of a squeeze there was just room on the bench for two. Teasdale tried to ignore the chill from the icy surface as he sat.

"I'm sorry to hear that. Please accept my condolences." Stebbington acknowledged his words with a nod and resumed staring at the floor. "Was it expected?"

"Not exactly," was the reply. "I mean, she was seventy-two, but as far as I know she'd never had a day's illness in her life. That's why they were more than happy to give her the hip replacement. Apparently she had a heart attack under the anesthetic and never came round. It's taken them an hour to get through to me because you can't get a phone signal in that auditorium."

"Will you be okay?"

Stebbington assured Teasdale that he would, and thanked him for his concern. "It's silly, you know," he said, "but even though we hadn't got on for a while, it still feels as if a part of me is missing. Does that sound ridiculous to you?"

Rather than ridiculous, his words caused a clawing sensation deep in Teasdale's gut. Particularly when he realized that it was just over an hour since he had seen the shadowy image tear something from Stebbington's unsuspecting, unfeeling body.

HENRY STEBBINGTON left early that afternoon after assuring Teasdale he was fine to drive home to Manchester. Teasdale retired to his room and succumbed to the urge to sleep. He was woken several hours later by the ringing of his bedside telephone. It was Bill Richards, the conference organizer, who told him everyone was planning to watch the football down in the bar if he was interested.

"I'm not sure, Bill," said Teasdale, "I've been feeling a bit under the weather today."

"Nonsense," came the reply. "You just need another couple of beers to clear those post hangover blues. Come on—we've got a big-screen TV set up."

An hour and a half later Teasdale was feeling the benefit of a shower, a soft drink, and the company of over a hundred English men and women waiting for the European championship quarter finals to begin. As he sipped at another lemonade, he congratulated himself on his decision to come down from his room. This was just the sort of thing he needed to take his mind off the events of the past two days, which is why it was a shame that, five minutes before the match was due to begin, there was a fizzle and a *phut* and the screen went blank.

There was a roar of disappointment from the assembled crowd. Everyone turned to the barman, who gave an exaggerated shrug before making for the exit, saying he would be back in a minute with the manager. The nineteen-year-old girl he left to look after things did her best to fulfill the sudden surfeit of orders. Meanwhile, some of the more technically astute members of the clientele (in their own minds if no-one else's) had huddled around the projection unit to see if they could fix the problem.

The television screen briefly flashed a brilliant white.

"I think you've got something there!" Teasdale cried, to which the attractive young woman standing next to him asked what he was talking about. Teasdale gestured to the ghost of a shape moving onscreen. Then he realized that nobody else could see it.

The thing was bigger this time, but maybe that was because he was closer. Once again its head swayed a little before it detached itself from the blank surface. Teasdale gripped his glass tightly as the thing moved towards him, then realized it was closing in on the girl. His desperate attempt to push her out of the thing's path sent her careering into a wooden table cluttered with empty glasses.

"What the bloody hell do you think you're doing!" An arrogant young executive who had been doing his best to chat the girl up all evening now saw John's clumsy behavior as his chance to act as her knight in shining armor.

"I'm sorry," said John, his eyes on the shape as it swung from side to side, trying to locate the girl again, "I slipped."

"Yeah, right," said the executive. The shadow thing homed in on her once more. As the girl was picking herself up from the sodden carpet and brushing fragments of glass from her navy-blue suit Teasdale tried to approach her again, but this time he was held back.

"You don't understand!" he cried as he watched the thing gently lay two ebony razor-sharp prongs against her temple.

"Yes I do, mate," said his captor, man-handling Teasdale out of the bar. The last thing Teasdale saw before he was shoved through the doorway was the thing gloating over what it had taken from the unwary young woman.

"AND THE NEXT DAY it turned out that her sister had been killed in a traffic accident."

"Is this before or after they let you out of the cell?"

Teasdale took a deep breath. "Lisa, I told you. They didn't arrest me, I got a caution, just like the other bloke. As long as we agree not to have any dealings with each other for the rest of the time we're here the police have said they aren't going to do anything about it."

"Well anyway," said the voice on the other end of the phone, "let's go back to this thing you think you keep seeing."

Teasdale tensed. He hadn't realized it would be so difficult to talk to his wife about what had been happening. It was only because she was a psychologist that he had even brought it up, otherwise he would have happily kept the bizarre occurrences from her. Usually he could talk to her about anything, but now, in his cramped hotel room, the Anglepoise lamp beside the bed casting a dim pool of yellow light on the bed and leaving the rest of the room in darkness, he found himself unexpectedly lost for words.

"It's probably due to that bump I had," he said eventually.

"Have you been back to the hospital?"

He had. Straight after the police had left last night he had got a taxi to the local infirmary where they had checked him over thoroughly and taken another X-Ray of his skull. Once again he had been given the all clear.

"Well that's something at least," she said, the relief in her voice obvious. "Let's talk about what you actually think you saw."

Teasdale sipped at the instant coffee he had made for himself and thought hard as the bitter liquid burned his mouth.

"I think it's some kind of harbinger. It seems to know when someone close to you is going to die. Then it comes and takes something from you."

"What do you think it's taking?"

John ran a hand through his hair. "I don't know. But haven't you ever talked to a person who's lost a loved one? Don't people often say that learning of their death was like losing a part of themselves? Isn't it just possible that this combination of events has allowed me to see things that normal people can't see? After all, things like radiowaves and mobile phone signals are all around us, we just lack the ability to see them. I think this thing sucks a part of you into itself, the part that 'belongs' to the person who's died, only for some reason it's not until you consciously receive the news that you realize what a terrible aching hole has been left behind."

"If what you say is true," said Lisa, "why is it that you've only seen this thing when you've been staring at a blank screen?"

He admitted he didn't know. "Maybe there are too many visual distractions under normal circumstances. I can only see it if I'm focusing my attention on a blank surface. Once I do I can keep my attention on it and that's why I can see it touch people."

"John," Lisa was doing her best to remain authoritative, but traces of concern were creeping into her voice. "I still think this is an hallucination. I believe you think you're seeing this creature, but it's far more likely a combination of the bump, the journey, the really bad idea of getting drunk when you got there, and the unconscious anxiety you're feeling over the fact that I'm pregnant. Try and get some rest now, but if it doesn't go away will you promise me that you won't drive? I'd hate for something to happen while you were on the motorway. Get the train home or something."

At least he could promise her that. "I will," he said. "And if it doesn't go away I'll go back to the hospital. Fingers crossed I should be home in a couple of days anyway, right as rain."

Teasdale put the phone down and switched off his bedside lamp. Before he did, he was tempted to glance at the blank screen of the portable television set perched in the far corner of his room.

Then he realized he was too afraid to.

THE NEXT MORNING Teasdale seriously considered leaving the conference and heading back home, but his boss had made a point that all employees were to attend all the presentations, and there was the threat of dismissal if he didn't sign the register at the beginning of each day's program. He nibbled on a few slices of toast before joining the queue outside the lecture theatre. As soon as he had signed the form he turned round and headed for the hotel exit. Teasdale

was not the sort of man who usually did such things and he still had no intention of leaving the conference before it was over, but just then he knew he could not face sitting in that darkened auditorium with the chance of that obscene figure appearing again to him.

The sun was shining and a warm breeze blew gently across his face as he stepped out of the hotel. Almost before he realized it, he was walking out of the car park and taking the footpath that ran along the main road into Farrowdale.

After ten minutes of pleasant walking beside green fields dotted with cows, during which only one car passed him, John found himself in the village. Farrowdale was nothing special, and after he visited a local shop and looked at the war memorial that sat proudly in the village square, there was little else to explore but the village church. It was locked, and so he sat on a bench displaying a brass plaque that stated in proud letters, "In Memory of Edna Liddle, Church Warden 1991–2004." He gazed out across the fields. The breeze had grown stronger and the sky had darkened since he had reached the village, but he wasn't worried. If there was to be an imminent repeat of the storm he had witnessed before breakfast he could shelter in the church porch.

Before leaving, and to waste a little more time, Teasdale decided to look at some of the gravestones. The oldest he could find dated back to the early eighteen-hundreds, although he presumed that the one he found by the lychgate was much older. Because of the softness of the rock from which it had been hewn and the constant buffeting of the wind and the rain in the spot where it stood, it had been worn smooth. It was probably so old that there was no one left to remember who it was intended to mark the passing of. He was about to move on when it started to rain. At the same time a shaft of sunlight broke through a gap in the inky black clouds to the south. The combined effect almost made him think for a moment that the surface of the gravestone was moving.

Then he realized with horror that it was.

In the drizzling rain, the darkened area he had taken as simply being a damp patch of stone began to expand and move. As it became larger and more defined he might have assumed it was the shadow of someone coming up behind him, except that he knew he was alone in the graveyard. With mounting terror he realized it was the thing he had seen before.

As it swung its bulbous head in his direction and slid sideways off the stone, John Teasdale ran, away from the church, back through the village, along the main road and back to the hotel. He didn't stop until his bedroom door was bolted behind him, although what little defense that might offer he didn't like to guess. He checked around the room, looked out of the window, and then breathed a sigh of relief when he realized that the thing seemed to have lost him for the moment.

When he glanced at the blank screen of the television set he realized it had found him again.

While it was still just a trace of darkness in the glass, Teasdale picked up his coffee mug and threw it at the screen. He was surprised when the television didn't explode, but the noise of glass shattering was likely enough to cause someone to come running. He left his belongings where they were and headed to the hotel car park, all the while his mind racing. His parents were long dead, his only surviving relative being his younger brother Tom who lived in Leeds. Could that be who was in danger?

Or was it Lisa?

He got into his car, knowing he had promised his wife he would not drive, but all he could think of was to get to her. Perhaps together they could ward off whatever this thing was, escape its clutches. Surely it was not impossible? The thing hadn't touched him yet, so presumably Lisa was still safe.

He drove out of the hotel and was soon on the main road that led to the motorway. He regarded with horror the sign that explained that due to a combination of road works and a recent breakdown, the lanes going south were closed. He took the diversion suggested by the traffic news on the radio and soon found himself driving on a single lane carriageway through the heart of the English countryside. He was passing through the village of Beesford when he saw the shadow before him on the windscreen, an incipient darkness reflected a thousand times in the rain drops that were constantly being cleared from the glass.

He had little memory of what happened after that. The next thing he knew he was waking up in a hospital side ward with a large bandage on his head, having had, according to Dr Carstairs, seven stitches administered to the laceration in his scalp where it had collided with the windscreen after his car had done the same thing with a nearby tree.

"And that more or less brings you up to date," said Teasdale. "I was just wondering whether there is any record of this sort of thing happening before, if perhaps what I'm seeing is some manifestation of the afterlife. Perhaps this thing is an instrument of God," Teasdale paused. "Or the devil."

Kendall raised his eyebrows and coughed.

"Mr. Teasdale," he said, "I may be the vicar of a small country parish, but during my youth I worked with inner city communities. I have been to Uganda, Tanzania, and Bosnia. I have seen some of the most appalling suffering and done my best to alleviate the spiritual element of it in any way that I can. I have talked to thousands of people in many parts of the world, but none has ever related the kind of story you have just told me. If I may be so bold, do you think you have managed to evade this creature you believe is pursuing you?"

Teasdale twitched, jerking his head to look all around the room.

"For the moment, yes I think so."

"Why?"

Teasdale gestured to the walls, the scratched paintwork and pockmarked plaster desperately in need of redoing. "No blank surfaces. Plus I think it knows that I can see it. For some reason it's not going to take what it wants without making sure I'm aware. As long as there is enough distraction here I'm safe, and that means my wife is safe as well."

"And do you believe you can escape this thing?"

"I don't know, but I've been thinking about that. Haven't you ever known someone who had a near-miss? A lucky escape from something? At the moment, I'm relying on the slim hope that it may tire, or even go after someone else. If I can perhaps evade it for long enough then it might run out of energy, or find an easier victim."

They were interrupted by Dr. Carstairs poking his head around the door.

"How are you getting on?" he asked.

Teasdale shrugged.

"He's had a lot to tell me," said the vicar.

"Well when you've finished," Carstairs looked at Teasdale, "your wife's outside waiting to see you."

"She's here?" A mixture of relief and horror crossed the man's face.

"Of course. Her telephone number was in your wallet so we rang her a couple of hours ago. She's just arrived. Now if you could just fill in these forms so we can send a summary letter of everything that's happened to your local doctor you can be on your way."

"If, that is," said Kendall leaning forward, "I can be of no further help?"

Teasdale reached for the blue clipboard. "No, Reverend," he mumbled, "I don't think you can."

Carstairs was showing Kendall into the cramped staff coffee room when a young staff nurse came in clutching a sheaf of papers.

"The forms for Mr. Teasdale, doctor—you left them lying next to Mrs. Johnson—the lady who's had the fall."

"Thank you, nurse," he said, taking them from her. "They must have slipped from the clipboard."

A thought struck Kendall. "What's Teasdale looking at, then?" he asked.

"Oh, don't worry," said the doctor. "There's nothing confidential on there, just some blank paper I was using to aid in performing some higher mental function tests on our rather demented Mrs. Johnson."

There was a terrible scream from down the corridor.

Carstairs rushed to Teasdale's room, Kendall close behind, only to collide with Teasdale coming the other way.

"Where is Lisa?" he cried. "Where is my wife?"

There was another scream, higher in pitch this time, from near the hospital entrance. Teasdale didn't wait for their reply. Carstairs and Kendall followed, only to be stopped by Sergeant Wilton, a large bruise beginning to bloom on the left side of his head.

"God knows how it happened," he said.

"How what happened, man?" shouted Carstairs.

The police officer looked confused.

"I thought that's why you were coming here in such a hurry, doctor. It's Corrigan. Somehow he got loose and belted me over the back of the head. It can't have happened more than five minutes ago, but I've only just managed to stop my head from spinning enough to raise the alarm. He can't have got far."

No, thought Kendall, but maybe far enough to make young Mr. Teasdale's fears warranted after all.

"Where is the waiting room?" the vicar asked.

"What?" said Carstairs.

"The waiting room—where you asked Mrs. Teasdale to sit."

"On the left by the front entrance. You don't think—"

The three of them ran down the corridor. As they rounded the curve they saw the front door of the hospital swinging open, banging in the wind of the storm that had considerably worsened since Kendall's arrival.

The waiting room door was open too.

Both Carstairs and Kendall breathed a sigh of relief as Wilton took the lead, gently pushing the door open as far as possible and edging slowly into the room.

It was empty.

Empty that is, save for the streak of blood on the ripped green vinyl cover of the nearest chair, and a pool of water beneath the open window over on the far side of the room.

"Right," said Wilton, "This is now a designated crime scene. If I could ask you gentlemen to leave the area, I need to get hold of backup." The policeman took out his radio, speaking rapidly while Carstairs and Kendall shuffled back into the corridor. The front door was being thrown back and forth now by the unforgiving elements, banging loudly against its neighbor every time it was blown shut. Both of them moved to close it at the same time.

The two of them stood in the doorway for a moment, the man of science and the man of God, as the wind whipped round them and the hammering rain washed away whatever footprints may have been left by the poor tormented souls who had run from the building that night.

"They can't have got far," said Carstairs.

"No," said Kendall.

"I hope that poor woman's all right," said the doctor.

"I'm sure she is," said Kendall. But he sounded unsure.

They stared into the impenetrable, hazy darkness for a while, saying nothing, before turning and closing the door properly behind them.

John Llewellyn Probert is the published author of nine novellas, six story collections, two novels and two non-fiction film books, all horror-related. He is the winner of the British Fantasy Award and the Children of the Night Award. He has two new short story collections due out in late 2022 (from NewCon Press and Black Shuck Books respectively). He writes about new film releases at his site, House of Mortal Cinema, and has a major new film book planned to launch in August 2023.

"An Absence of Malice" was the concluding tale in the author's 2008 Ash-Tree Press collection Coffin Nails *and he has welcomed the opportunity to present a slightly revised version in* Nightmare Abbey.

HEH HEH. SO YOU ENJOY THE GREAT OUTDOORS, DO YA? FANCY YOURSELF A REGULAR FRONTIER SCOUT. YEAH, YOU'RE A LATTER-DAY DANIEL BOONE IN THE DUST, AREN'T YOU? WELL, HEH HEH, BEFORE YOU TAKE THAT NEXT CAMPING TRIP, YOU MAY WANT TO READ THIS LITTLE TERROR TALE! IT'S CALLED . . .

The Pioneers of Pike's Peak

By Basil Tozer

IT WAS A PERFECT NIGHT ABOUT THE END OF JUNE, THE SORT OF NIGHT COMMON ENOUGH IN **COLORADO AT THAT TIME OF THE YEAR.** At the end of the game, I rose from the card table and strolled out into the cool, refreshing air. The stars were shining with extraordinary brilliance in a sky so clear that one seemed almost to hear them winking. The moon had not yet risen above the range of mighty peaks which tower into the heavens until their crests gradually vanish into great belts of clouds, and at night seem to touch the lowermost of the celestial bodies; but a sort of halo, gradually broadening, served to show that presently the moon herself would shed a flood of light from the very summit of the highest peaks down into the little village nestling at the feet of the mighty range. No sound broke the perfect stillness without. The very houses seemed to sleep.

It was only when I re-entered the heated atmosphere of the smoky bar saloon, where our companions, grown tired of card-playing, were now quietly talking, that we noticed an odd-looking and apparently elderly stranger seated alone beside a little window at the further end of the room. The window was open, and he was staring through it vacantly, only interrupting his reverie now and again in order to blow a long cloud of smoke into the air. My friend cast a glance of inquiry in his direction.

"He came in five minutes ago," one of the card-players said.

"Who is he?"

"Some crank, I suppose. He has hardly stirred since he sat down there."

"What is he staring at?" someone asked, presently.

"Pike's Peak, apparently," replied Watson, the man who had called the stranger a crank.

Though the words were spoken in an undertone, the "crank " evidently overheard them, for he turned his head and frowned. Then he resumed his former position—his vigil. Watson tapped his forehead significantly, and presently conversation drifted from one topic to another, until the subject of the Rocky Mountains in particular engrossed our attention.

"And who really was the first to reach the top of Pike's Peak?" Watson asked, looking round at us.

"Not Pike himself," answered a man named Norton. "They say that some man— Look out, you fellows!"

The stranger had left his seat and was approaching us with a slow, stealthy tread, his eyes oddly dilated. We all turned to face him. He was a man of immense proportions, well over six feet in height, an could not have been over fifty years of age, though he looked quite sixty. His hair was white and rather long. He had evidently been handsome in his day, but now the face, neck, and hands were disfigured with numberless little sunken blotches not unlike the pits left by smallpox. He wore an old drab suit, a coon cap, thick boots, and leather leggings.

"Who did you say first reached the top of Pike's Peak?" he asked, in a threatening, hollow voice. He had dropped into a chair on the opposite side of the table beside me. Norton, whom he had interrupted, came to the rescue.

"I believe that—"

"*I* was the first to reach it! You know the story of our ascent?"

"I know only what I have read and been told," Norton said.

"You yourself have been up Pike's Peak?"

"I have."

"You have seen the summit, then."

"Yes."

"And what did you notice there that struck you most—there, fifteen thousand feet above the sea's level?"

"Scenery that was perfectly grand."

"Yes, yes, I know—grand, magnificent, marvelous scenery. I know all that. But what else did you see?"

He paused. "Surely it is there," he muttered, "surely it is still there—it must be there—it must be there. Who could have removed it, eh?" he continued, aloud; "who could have taken it away? Tell me that"

Norton had an inspiration. "Do you mean the stone?"

Instantly the stranger's expression changed. He looked round at us all quite intelligently.

"It *is* there, then?" he inquired eagerly, bending forward across the table.

"Of course it is there," Norton replied. "I can give you the inscription word for word."

"Do! What is it? Tell me, what is it?"

"The inscription says: '*This stone is erected in memory of William Dawkins, James Weston, and Walter Hellier, Pioneers of Pikes Peak, who were devoured by mountain rats while endeavoring to reach this summit.*'"

"Ah!" he cried, greatly relieved. "I am glad it is there—I am glad it is still there. Do you know the story of my friends, the story of those pioneers?"

He had grown suddenly calm. He seemed suddenly to have regained his reason. Our interest and curiosity were now thoroughly aroused. We could see that the stranger was quite sober though his mind seemed unhinged, he had now a lucid interval.

He poured brandy into his tumbler until it was three parts full. Just then the moon shone over the summit of the famous peak, and from where we sat the outline of the glorious mountain could be clearly discerned. Watson drew the stranger's attention to it, and an odd, bitter smile flitted across his face. It was the first time we had seen him smile. He sighed once, but did not utter a word. Then his gaze became again riveted on the gigantic peak.

"Pike never would—never could have reached it. He tried to several times. Finally he stood upon a hill near the stalactite caves at the base of my mountain, and, pointing with his finger at the summit, said: 'No mortal man will ever tread that Peak!'

"But we—*we* were determined to. Our friends shook us by the hands and bade us farewell.

"'But you are fools,' they said. You will never come back. You don't know what you may meet in those mountains. You know what Pike said when he came back. You know the tale he told. And some things he would not tell.'

"'Don't go, oh! don't go,' my wife cried in agony.

"I loved her, yet I forced her from me. She was but a unit. In the success of our enterprise lay the welfare of thousands. I told her that to comfort her. It was the last time I saw her alive.

"Early in the morning we started. We took with us arms, food and drink for many days, and the bare necessities of life. We carried everything ourselves. We knew where and how Pike had failed. We should succeed.

"A week later we were fairly in the midst of difficulties. The work was terribly severe, but we had determination, strength, and courage. We had expected to find obstacles, and in this we certainly were not disappointed. Here, enormous boulders which had to be circumvented; there, unlooked-for waterfalls and ravines that delayed us, besides vegetation so thick that in places we had to hack our way through it. All this impeded our progress enormously. And then the unknown dangers that Pike had hinted at. There might be snakes concealed among those immense boulders; there might be death-dealing plants all around us—such plants flourish in South America—indeed, we did not know what there might not be. But of course we did not pause to consider those things."

"Over a fortnight went by. As we gradually mounted higher and higher, our spirits steadily rose as if in sympathy. Far down in the valley we had once or twice during our progress caught glimpses of this very townlet, now called Colorado Springs, also of the village of Manitou. Tiny villages, indeed, they were in those days; and as we saw them from those great heights they looked like chessboards stretched out upon the vast expanse of prairie. And still we fought our way upward.

"How long our expedition had been started I cannot quite remember, when the nature of the surroundings gradually changed greatly. In place of rock and black soil we now found vast tracts of a sandy formation. The undergrowth was still dense, however, though here and there thousands upon thousands of slim fir trees lay rotting upon the ground, evidently swept down by some terrific storm, for storms in these mountains sweep down trees as a reaping machine sweeps down standing corn. Sometimes we came upon broad, open spaces—spaces swept clear apparently in early days by giant waterfalls long since dried up. Then, as we penetrated still higher, and the vegetation decreased in density, even the boulders grew smaller. Indeed, they now looked as though in prehistoric times they had all been flung together by a tremendous seismic disturbance.

"'Have you noticed,' one of my comrades remarked one day, 'what a quantity of insects there are up here? And the rats are getting more plentiful. We seldom see any of those grey squirrels now.'

"As he spoke he stamped his foot upon an immense brown spider that was running away. Its body burst with a crack, and glutinous liquid spurted out all round his boot. Almost instantly several more spiders ran out from beneath a large stone as if to ascertain what had happened. They stopped. For a moment they seemed for all the world as if they looked at us—looked at us with a malignant, vindictive expression. Then they scuttled away.

"'I believe I felt several of those spiders scampering over my face last night,' he continued. You had better be careful; they bite like mischief. These mountains are famous for them, and—just look at that!'

"A couple of large rats were chasing an enormous spider across a long, flat boulder. A moment later, spider and rats disappeared over the edge.

"'They say that mountain rats will devour any living thing,' Weston said presently. 'They will eat *us* if we don't watch them!' he added in jest.

"During the early part of the afternoon we had made good progress, when suddenly we came upon a large sloping tract of bare white sand. The sun, still high in the heavens, shone down upon it, and at first sight the sand seemed to be alive with small, moving bodies.

"'Talk of spiders!' Dawkins said, laughing. 'Did you ever see anything like that?'

"We had long ago, in previous expeditions, grown accustomed to surprises. Few things astonished us now. Never in our lives, however, had we seen such an assemblage. There must have been thousands upon thousands of them running about in every direction, colliding with one another and tumbling over one another apparently for no reason. The sight made me think of a gigantic ants' nest overrun with mammoth ants, and an odd sort of smell that for several days had pervaded the air struck our nostrils with renewed strength.

"Now, as we stepped forward into this open tract, a strange thing happened, for the entire space which a moment before had been alive, became in an instant motionless. The spiders were all there, right before us, but of one accord they had stopped running. Oddly enough, too, every spider was now facing us. Instinctively we felt that we had become objects of intense curiosity. And as we stood there, interested and amused, we could distinctly see the spiders' great eyes sticking out and evidently watching us. The sight would have given some people the 'creeps,' but we rather enjoyed it.

"'*Pish!* you hideous things,' Dawkins said, pitching a pebble into their midst. In less than a minute hardly a spider was to be seen.

"'If we describe that sight when we get back we shall be called liars,' Weston said, glancing at his watch. 'I've seen insects in my time, but never anything like that.'

"The offensive smell was still strong in the air, and as we progressed it increased. Once or twice it became almost unbearable. We had now a long stretch of clear going before us, so we hastened to avail ourselves of it by advancing briskly. And still we saw spiders at every turn, spiders by the thousand sunning themselves on every rock and boulder—great brown spiders, with fat, oval bodies, and with thick, hairy legs bent in grotesque curves. I kicked over a stunted little tree that lay rotting—ugh! Quite two or three hundred spiders must have scuttled away from under it.

"'This is getting beyond a joke,' Hellier, who seldom spoke and was generally considered surly, suddenly said. 'I tell you what it is: these spiders will go for us.'

"'Like Weston's rats!' Dawkins said, laughing at him; and we were still chaffing Hellier and Weston when Dawkins happened to look round.

"'Harry!' he exclaimed.

"There was anxiety in his tone, and I felt his hand grip my shoulder. And no wonder. Though anything but a coward, Dawkins could not help at once realizing what we all realized a moment later—that Hellier's evil omen was more than likely to come true, and a sickening sense of fear had come over him.

"For there, barely fifty yards away, a reddish-brown mass gradually assuming the form of a crescent was steadily, swiftly gliding over the sand, steadily and swiftly overtaking us. And as it approached, we could see thousands upon thousands of spiders hastening towards it from every side and quickly increasing its size. The swarm when first we saw it must have covered between twelve and fifteen square feet. Before it had glided over another twenty yards of sand the entire mass was nearly one-third as large again. Yet a sort of horrible fascination kept us rooted to the spot where we now stood watching the swarm approach. In order to brace up our courage we told one another that the spiders could not be pursuing us at all; that if we moved aside they would pass us by. But in our hearts we knew that we tried to think a lie. And when we moved aside in order to convince ourselves, the creeping crescent immediately swayed round towards us and seemed if anything to advance more quickly.

"Suddenly the intense horror of the situation flashed across my mind and struck terror into our hearts. For what could we do to avert the terrible fate that threatened us? Savage animals we might have coped with; treacherous human beings, even, we might have bested; but now we were face to face with a peril totally unexpected, utterly loathsome and unassailable.

"'Our only chance lies in flight,' Hellier said bitterly.

"'Flight! and where shall we fly to? The top of the mountain, I suppose! Look there, Hellier.'

"It was Dawkins who spoke, and he spoke in tones of scorn. Looking round us, we now saw what we had not noticed before. We were surrounded. Everywhere we saw spiders—spiders approaching in brown, gliding crescents of varying sizes. And over a hundred yards away the largest and darkest mass of all could clearly be distinguished, also winding its way along the sand, also approaching, also closing us in. And as this great crescent surged undulatingly, unswervingly across the hillocks and irregularities in the surface of the soil and sand, it resembled the great wave of a sluggish, turbid stream leaving a factory sluice.

"'Fire into them!' I exclaimed, slipping a couple of shot cartridges into my gun. The two charges cut a lane into the approaching wave, but almost instantly the lane closed up, and the undulating mass advanced as if nothing had happened. Together Dawkins and Weston fired four barrels. Rather a broader lane this time; but again it closed up. I had reloaded.

"'Give them a volley,' Weston called out; 'that may turn them.'

"We did so, but by the time the smoke had cleared, the swarm had well-nigh resumed its former size and shape. Could we sweep a lane with our eight barrels and then rush through it? No, that was obviously impossible; the width of the wave was too great. And still recruits were pouring in upon every side, and as we fired volley after volley into the quickly approaching swarms, in the vain hope of turning them, the distant ravines rang again and again with echoes.

"'My God, we are done for!' came despairingly from Hellier, as for the twentieth time he closed his gun with a snap.

"Our barrels had now become almost too hot to hold, and still the hideous, crawling waves, which must have contained trillions of spiders, were fast approaching with a strange swaying motion, and rapidly narrowing our little circle. In a few minutes they would be upon us, overrunning us, dragging us down. Already many stragglers were running up our legs and over our bodies. Now the first swarm was so near that we could distinctly hear it rushing up us, and—ah! the smell, how it still hangs in my nostrils...."

For a moment the stranger stopped. His eyes were widely distended. His limbs trembled. He clutched the table frantically, in order to support himself.

"Suddenly I saw several spiders run up Weston's face and fix upon his eyes. With a scream he dashed them away, but as he did so his eyes began to swell, for the brutes had bitten him badly."

He stopped again. He was quivering all over with excitement. Suddenly he dashed

from his seat to the farthermost corner of the room.

"Keep them from me! Keep them off!" he cried, glaring wildly all round the floor. "Look at them now—look at them—ah! God help me!—help me!—help me...!"

He sprang to right and left, then towards the door. Perspiration was pouring down his face. Then suddenly he snatched wildly at imaginary spiders running up his sleeves and legs, running up his body, running over his head, over his face, over his eyes, into his mouth. It was a dreadful sight.

"Stop him!" Watson cried, jumping from his seat and rushing towards the old man, but as he approached the maniac a blindly directed blow from the stranger's fist nearly stunned him, and the innkeeper and two rough-looking men entered the room.

"Hold him, boys," the innkeeper said calmly, and as the two men pounced upon the stranger the innkeeper sauntered towards us.

"Poor fellow," he said, "I always have to be ready for him—look at him now, yet the doctors pronounce him sane. He often is sane, of course, but when I heard him starting on the spiders, and saw him drinking brandy, I knew what to expect."

"Is there any truth in his spider story?"

"Any truth? It's all truth—at least, that's my belief. Though I was quite a lad at the time the expedition started, I can remember it well. Four of them there were, all strong and hearty when they set out. Two months later *he* came back."

"Did he alone escape?"

"He alone came back—came back quite done for and disfigured all over with red blotches. Afterwards they turned into pits. Look at them now on his face and neck, but they are all over his body, too—all over every inch of him. Some years later another expedition went up and reached the summit, but they always maintained that rats, not spiders, devoured those poor fellows, so they set a stone with an inscription upon it at the top of the mountain—you have seen it, no doubt?"

"What do you yourself think they were killed by?"

"I don't think anything. As sure as you are standing there they were eaten up by swarms of great spiders, as Mad Harry has told you. I have heard him tell the story often enough, and he always tells the same story. Besides, those marks are not rats' bites. They are not a bit like rats' bites.

"It's a horrible place, that mountain," he said, looking at its rugged peak so clearly outlined in the moonlight. "Though you can go up it now by the winding funicular, which is eight miles long, you don't know what horrors may exist in other parts of it. Many a man has gone into those mountains, but few have ever returned."

☠ ☠ ☠

"The Pioneers of Pike's Peak" first appeared in the September 1897 issue of The Strand Magazine. *(Original* Strand *illustrations by Gordon Browne. Above art by Allen K.)*

British author, journalist, and publicity agent Basil (John Joseph) Tozer (1868–1949) trained steeplechase horses, and is primarily noted for his scholarly 1908 book The Horse in History. *"The Pioneers of Pike's Peak" is his only known work of fantastic fiction."*

GRAB NIGHTMARE ABBEY 2 -- BEFORE IT GRABS YOU!

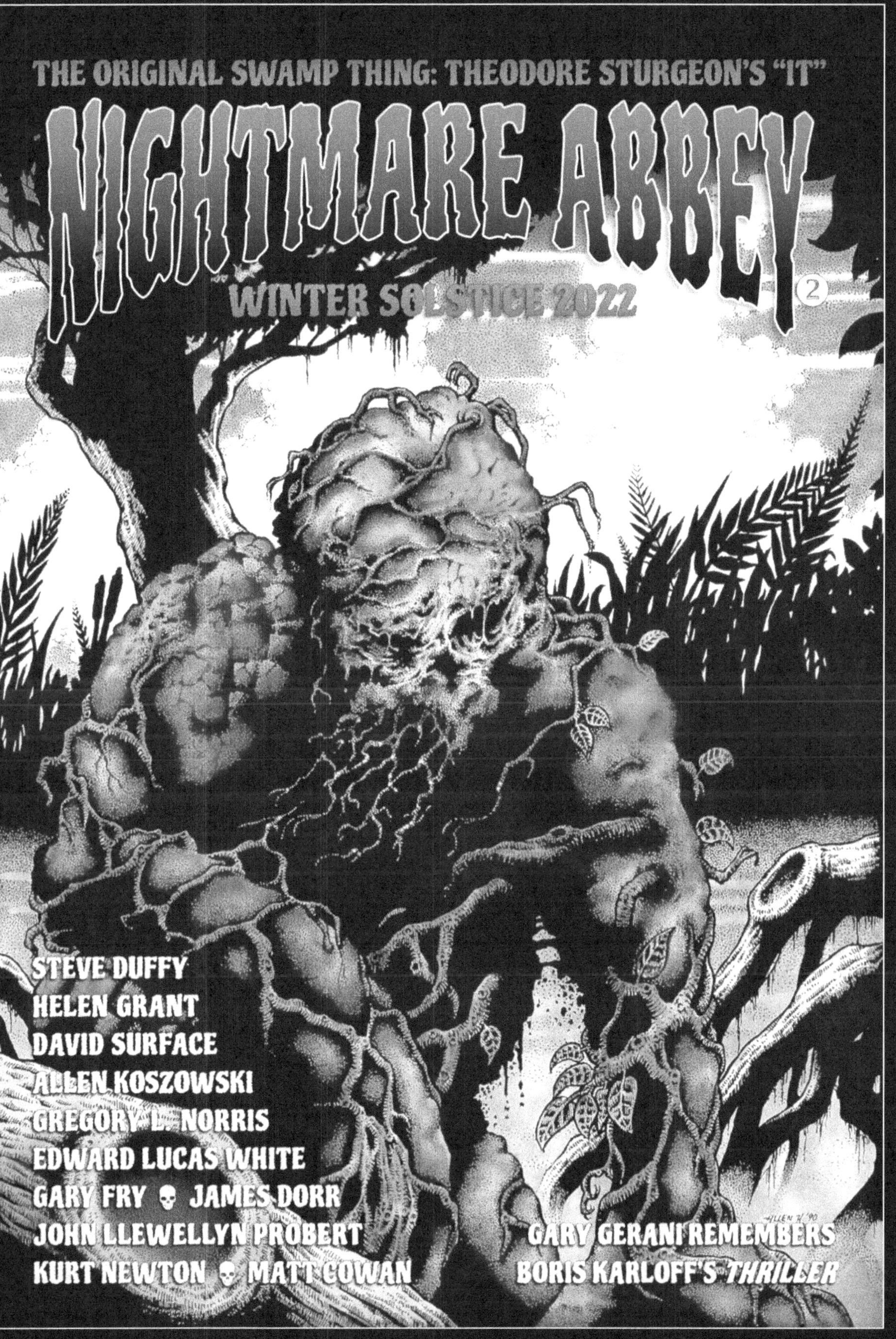
THE ORIGINAL SWAMP THING: THEODORE STURGEON'S "IT"
NIGHTMARE ABBEY
WINTER SOLSTICE 2022
2
STEVE DUFFY
HELEN GRANT
DAVID SURFACE
ALLEN KOSZOWSKI
GREGORY L. NORRIS
EDWARD LUCAS WHITE
GARY FRY ☠ JAMES DORR
JOHN LLEWELLYN PROBERT
KURT NEWTON ☠ MATT COWAN
GARY GERANI REMEMBERS
BORIS KARLOFF'S *THRILLER*

HORROR FLYING HIGH:
REVISITING *NIGHT OF THE EAGLE*

By John Llewellyn Probert

In the late 1950s through to the early 1960s, magic was at work in the British film industry, weaving its spell with almost careless abandon and resulting in a cluster of movie classics, many of which remain unparalleled in their quality and effectiveness to this day. As well as Hammer Films kickstarting the horror renaissance, the span of just a few years would see Jacques Tourneur's *Night of the Demon* (1957), the company that would become Amicus (calling itself Vulcan at that point) giving us *City of the Dead* (1959), Jack Clayton's *The Innocents* (1961) and Robert Wise's *The Haunting* (1963) all being filmed in the UK. From Nat Cohen and Stuart Levy's Anglo Amalgamated would come three films grouped loosely by academics as their "Sadean trilogy" consisting of the Herman Cohen-produced *Horrors of the Black Museum* (1959), Michael Powell's *Peeping Tom*, and Sidney Hayers' *Circus of Horrors* (both 1960). Shortly after, and with some input from American International Pictures, would come cinema's second attempt at bringing to the screen the first novel of one of literary fantasy's greatest writers. However, whereas 1944's *Weird Woman* had been a B-movie programmer (albeit one of the better entries) in Universal's Inner Sanctum series, *Night of the Eagle* (US title: *Burn, Witch, Burn*, about which more in a bit) would finally give Fritz Leiber's *Conjure Wife* an adaptation worthy of its source material while also affording the book sufficient acknowledgement that its author's name was positioned just beneath the main title card.

Let's have a quick look at those main titles before we delve into the meat of the movie. The screenplay for *Night of the Eagle* was originated by noted authors and screenwriters Charles Beaumont and Richard Matheson, who had decided they wanted to work together and adapt Leiber's novel. Beaumont took the first half, Matheson the second, and a draft was completed and taken to James H. Nicolson and Samuel Z. Arkoff at AIP, who did a deal with Universal who still owned the rights at the time. AIP had a relationship with Anglo Amalgamated in the UK. Anglo passed the actual production of the film over to Independent Artists who had also made *Circus of Horrors* for them. That's why *Night of the Eagle* is credited as "A Julian Wintle–Leslie Parkyn Production." George Baxt, who had written *Circus of Horrors*, was brought in to work

DIRECTED BY
SIDNEY HAYERS

on the screenplay and presumably "British it up" as the Beaumont–Matheson script was set in New England, although Baxt claimed he did a complete rewrite whereas Matheson argued he didn't change a thing. It's likely we shall never know the real story behind the screenplay. Finally, another *Circus of Horrors* alumnus, Sidney Hayers, was brought in to direct.

Night of the Eagle's credits play out to the left of an image of a female eye, which nowadays may remind viewers of similar opening titles to Roman Polanski's *Repulsion* (1966)—another classic horror from a British independent. Whose eye it is we won't know until the end of the film, but it's a beguiling spectacle as we read through the cast (including poor Bill Mitchell, whose surname is misspelt *Mitcthell*) and crew.

Then we are at Hempnell Medical College. In one of the classrooms Norman Taylor (Peter Wyngarde, who had just come off playing Peter Quint in Jack Clayton's *The Innocents*) is lecturing on something that doesn't seem to be connected to medicine at all, despite the anatomy illustrations on the walls. "I do not believe" are the first words of dialogue uttered, both significant in themselves and in that they are uttered over the stone statue of an eagle which will become increasingly important as the film reaches its climax. We later learn that Taylor is a lecturer in sociology and very much a realist,

as he emphasizes in his lecture by writing in capitals and circling the word *believe*. These are the four words, he says, which are necessary to destroy the forces of (and again he has listed them in capitals) the supernatural, witchcraft, superstition, and psychics, with etc., etc. added after for good measure. These, he says, are things entertained by

Above: Hempnell's stone mascot watching over the campus; Peter Wyngarde playing the skeptic. Previous pages: Janet Blair and Wyngarde. *Night of the Eagle* and all associated images © MGM and StudioCanal.

individuals who have "A morbid desire to escape from reality." Taylor claims this is a quote, but if so, it's certainly not one that can be easily researched and it's likely he may be quoting himself.

In the next shot we are introduced to more of the university staff, where we learn that the departmental chair in sociology is up for grabs. Norman arrives home to find his wife

Faculty carpooling: Kathleen Byron, Margaret Johnston and Anthony Nicholls. Below: Colin Gordon

Tansy (Janet Blair, who would appear in the "Tourist Attraction" episode of *The Outer Limits* the following year) waiting for him. She seems perturbed and Norman jokes that she's pining for "that old warlock Corabius and his phony black magic" whom they encountered on a trip to Jamaica a couple of years ago. They are preparing for a bridge evening, which may not sound the most dynamic of situations in which to further develop plot and characterization, but Beaumont, Matheson, and Hayers make it work beautifully.

Lindsay Carr (Colin Gordon, best known for playing Number 2 in two episodes of Patrick McGoohan's *The Prisoner*, including the classic "The General") is married to Flora Carr (Margaret Johnston, whose career was

mainly on the London stage, although she did take time out to appear in both this and Amicus's *The Psychopath* in 1966) who is a professor in the sociology department. Lindsay's dialogue helps give us some background on Norman, and his line about Norman seeming to have a charmed life is especially significant. "What have you done?"

Lindsay asks, "Sold your soul to the devil?" Perhaps that would be the case if this film were made in the 1970s but not here, where there's something rather different going on. Later that night after everyone has left, Tansy starts searching for something in the living room while upstairs Norman unsticks a dresser drawer and finds a dead spider in a ceramic pillbox. Apparently, it's a gift from the Jamaican warlock, and Tansy jokes that it's the reason Norman has had all the good luck he has enjoyed. Later, while Norman sleeps, Tansy turns the living room upside down and eventually finds what she has been searching for—a tiny doll secured to the tassels of a lampshade, revealed through a nicely lit, twirling, almost fairground ride-style effect. She burns it and the doll erupts in a shower of sparks.

Next morning Norman is working on his latest manuscript "Neurosis and the Modern Man" while his cat (which will play an important part later on) sits by his typewriter as, perhaps in this case, an unwitting good luck charm. The laundry man calls and Norman gives him a coat to be dry-cleaned,

discovering first (at the cost of pricking himself) that a small sachet of powder has been pinned to the inside of the collar. Norman searches the house and by the time Tansy gets home he has a tableful of fetishes, bells, cemetery dust and other bizarre trinkets to confront her with. Tansy admits she has been using "Conjure Magic" which she started using in Jamaica after Norman had a near-fatal accident. She recounts how she saw the warlock Corabius bring a child back from the dead, and how she was willing to sacrifice her own life if it meant Norman could live. Fortunately, he regained consciousness before such a need arose, but since then, and especially since their arrival at the college, Tansy has been using magic to influence and combat what she sees as the hostility she and her husband have been met with by other faculty members.

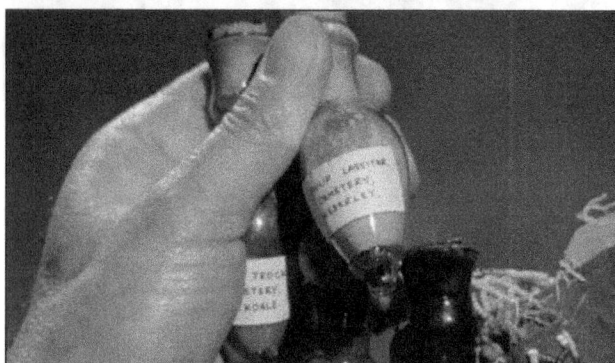

What's especially effective about this scene and much of what has gone before is the mundane surroundings in which all this talk of possible witchcraft is being discussed. Despite also being set in contemporary England, even Jacques Tourneur's *Night of the Demon* is packed with atmosphere, and we have no doubt from the very beginning that strange things are afoot. So far, Hayers has admirably downplayed any suggestion that what Tansy might be up to is anything other than the affectations of someone who has taken belief in the supernatural a bit too seriously. One of the new movements in British cinema of the time was the "kitchen sink" drama where stories would be told in realistic settings (a prime example is Karel Reisz's 1960 *Saturday Night and Sunday Morning* starring Albert Finney), and it adds considerably to the effectiveness of what is to follow that many of the conversations in the first act of *Night of the Eagle*, including Lindsay's accusation of soul-selling, take place in a brightly-lit, ordinary kitchen with not a hint of macabre devilry at work.

Norman convinces Tansy to destroy her entire collection of "magic" items, accidentally burning a tiny photograph of himself in the process. Finally, the dead spider and its ceramic container are consigned to the flames, incurring much displeasure from the cat as Norman does so. Almost immediately the telephone rings and a breathy female voice tells Norman she loves him. Norman slams down the receiver as a very familiar-looking but now living spider crawls from the ashes.

The following morning, Norman's world swiftly begins to fall apart. He is nearly run down by a van, and once he is in his office he is accosted by one of his students, Bill Jennings (Bill Mitchell) who accuses him of deliberately failing him in his exams so Norman can have Bill's girlfriend Margaret Abbot (Judith Stott) to himself. Meanwhile Margaret herself is in Professor Flora Carr's office, claiming Norman has "violated her." Eventually she concedes that she has made the story up, but this doesn't stop Bill from threatening Norman with a gun later that night. Defusing the situation Norman arrives home to find a tape waiting for him.

Norman wants to play it to Tansy as it's a lecture of his. She urges him not to put it on but he does anyway. We get the lecture, but Norman's voice is accompanied by an

Norman (Wyngarde) sternly refutes Margaret's (Judith Stott) false accusation, as Flora Carr (Johnston) and college dean Harold Gunnison (Reginald Beckwith) bear witness. Below: Outside Norman's office window, the Hempnell eagle seems to watch over his shoulder, as Bill Jennings threatens to kill his professor.

undercurrent of strange sounds which, it soon transpires, is causing *something* to be summoned to the house. The juxtaposition of Norman's rational voice explaining scientific facts, advocating against the concept of the very thing that is accompanying his talk on the recording, is a splendid device that's going to be used to tremendous effect at the climax. Tansy begs Norman to switch off the tape but when he does the telephone rings, only for the same sounds to be emitted from the receiver—modern technology again being used as a conduit for forces Norman refuses to believe in.

As the lights go out and we hear the full force of the storm raging outside, there's a terrible roaring noise from just outside the front door. Norman, still the rationalist, goes to open it despite Tansy's (and the audience's) pleas. He pulls open the door just as Tansy rips the phone cord from the wall, resulting in Norman being confronted with nothing but the wind and the rain in a shot that could easily be taken from a movie version of W. W. Jacobs' story "The Monkey's Paw."

Tansy gets Norman drunk and while he is passed out she casts a spell that confers "all that he has" to her, presumably including any spell that has been cast on him. When Norman wakes the next day, Tansy is gone but there's a taped message telling him she plans to die in his place. Norman learns she has taken a bus to their seaside holiday cottage. His attempts to attract her attention from his sports, car racing alongside the bus she is in, allows for a change of style and pace with a brisk bit of thrilling driving action in the style of Cy Enfield's *Hell Drivers* (1957) before it's back to the atmospherics as Norman gets to the cottage. It's close to midnight. He calls for Tansy but all

he hears in return is the crashing of waves on the rocks below the cliffs. Inside the cottage, Norman finds a number of books on demonology as William Alwyn's score does its very best Gustav Holst impersonation, adding in a bit of the "Dies Irae" for good measure.

Learning what he has to do in order to save his wife, Norman heads for the cliff path that leads to a crumbling cemetery. He breaks into a crypt and performs a ritual over Tansy's photograph. Meanwhile his wife has been making her way across the beach and into the sea. Norman saves her but she remains catatonic. As a local doctor (Norman Bird) examines her, Tansy regains consciousness and demands to be taken home.

At this point the viewer may wonder why much of this scene is shot from Tansy's point of view, and it's only when we get back to the Taylor house and we see, in a nice overhead shot, Tansy taking a knife from the kitchen drawer after which she tries to stab Norman, that the person looking through Tansy's eyes in the previous scene was not her.

It's Flora Carr who has been behind it all. Norman confronts her in her office and plays the "cursed" tape, threatening to summon the creature Flora had intended for him in an echo of the ending of Tourneur's *Night of the Demon*. But Flora has other tricks up her sleeve, and in her Tarot deck. This climactic confrontation between Norman and Flora is effectively staged by Hayers, cutting between the two players and having Flora's face lit from below in a suggestion of her unearthly and wholly evil potential. He keeps the angle high on both of them as Flora builds a house from Tarot cards and sets it on fire, leading to a beautiful shot of Flora through the flames. Meanwhile the Taylors' cat (I said it would be important later) has caused a fire to ignite at their home.

"Burn, witch, burn!" Flora mutters as Norman leaves her office to save Tansy from the flames. Flora turns the tape back on and channels it through the

public address system, turning the entire university campus into the battleground between Norman's rationalism and the forces of black magic. Norman is chased by something that is quickly revealed to be an enormous eagle. As with *Night of the Demon* it could be argued that not showing what is chasing Norman at all might have been more effective. On the other hand, throughout the film we have seen recurrent shots of the stone eagle that presides over the college entrance, guarding the gateway to rational scientific thought. Now it's being used against one of its proponents, and it does make for a satisfying climax.

Pursued through the college, Norman eventually takes refuge in his classroom. His words I DO NOT BELIEVE are still on the blackboard from earlier, as is the circle around the word BELIEVE, now giving an entirely different message to that conveyed at the beginning of the film. Does Norman believe by now? He surely does, and as if to hammer the point home that the most

rational of individuals cannot save themselves from the forces of the supernatural, Norman doesn't save himself at all. Instead, it's the chance (or is it?) intervention of Lindsay, Flora's husband, who switches off the public address system, and prevents Norman

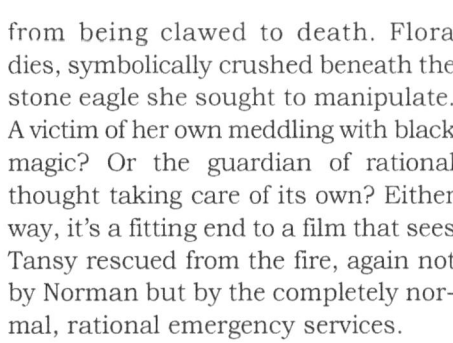

from being clawed to death. Flora dies, symbolically crushed beneath the stone eagle she sought to manipulate. A victim of her own meddling with black magic? Or the guardian of rational thought taking care of its own? Either way, it's a fitting end to a film that sees Tansy rescued from the fire, again not by Norman but by the completely normal, rational emergency services.

Night of the Eagle was released in the US as *Burn, Witch, Burn*, a title thought up by AIP boss James H. Nicholson and very much in keeping

with distributor AIP's philosophy of down-playing subtlety in favor of promising exploitative thrills. Of course, there isn't actually any witch burning in the film, and to further confuse members of stateside audiences with a literary bent, Burn, Witch, Burn also happened to be the title of an unrelated 1932 novel by Abraham Merritt that provided the inspiration for Tod Browning's 1936 movie *The Devil-Doll.* To add further exploitation value, the US version also added on an opening voice-over (by Paul Frees) that allegedly cast a protective spell over those about to watch the film, adding just over two minutes to the running time. It failed to detract from the sheer class of the movie that followed, though.

Night of the Eagle benefits from a tight, skillfully written script by Beaumont and Matheson (and Baxt), as well as resourceful direction by Sidney Hayers, who at that time had only a few directorial credits to his name. Those only familiar with the pulp horror antics of his 1960 *Circus of Horrors* must have been surprised at the restraint shown here. Composer William Alwyn's music score is similarly subtle except for the moments when it helps to ratchet up the suspense immensely. The film was Alwyn's only work in the horror genre. He was better known for scores to films like Roy Ward Baker's *A Night to Remember* (1958) and Ken Annakin's *The Swiss Family Robinson* (1960), and *Night of the Eagle* was one of his last. For anyone who might be wondering, he was not related to Kenneth Alwyn who conducted the 1996 Silva Screen CD collection of British soundtracks entitled *Horror!* Reginald Wyer was the director of photography responsible for the film's moody and atmospheric lighting, shooting in black and white at the behest of Anglo Amalgamated, who saved their color film stock for what they considered to be "bigger" pictures. Wyer would go on to shoot John Krish's remarkably atmospheric science fiction picture *Unearthly Stranger* (1963) as well as a number of films for Tom Blakely's Planet Productions, including *Island of Terror* (1966) and the following year's *Night of the Big Heat.*

All this technical expertise would, of course, be little without some riveting performances to bring the story to life, and *Night of the Eagle* is fortunate in having Peter Wyngarde as its leading man (getting the job after both Peter Cushing and Peter Finch turned the role down). A few years from gaining worldwide fame (and shortly thereafter worldwide notoriety) in his role as jet-setting author Jason King in the ITC TV show *Department S*, Wyngarde initially rejected the script but relented when he needed a new sports car and realized the salary would provide just the amount of money he needed to buy it. Even though he

brings an almost aristocratic gravitas to the role of Norman Taylor, he allegedly made filming somewhat difficult by his insistence on wearing trousers so tight Sidney Hayers was sometimes forced to shoot him only from the waist up. In the UK Wyngarde was top-billed, whereas in the US the film's American star, Janet Blair, was put first as per an agreement with AIP. The film went through a number of title changes before the ones UK and US audiences were to become familiar with. The original script kept the title of Leiber's source novel, and it will likely surprise no one that in the UK the title *Night of the Eagle* was adopted with the success of Tourneur's *Night of the Demon* in mind.

Released in Britain on a double bill with the lighthearted gentle comedy *She'll Have to Go,* it's perhaps not surprising that the film did nowhere near as well as it did in the US, where AIP paired it with Roger Corman's *Tales of Terror.* Despite the fact nothing was made of it in the publicity, it was a most fitting combination—a black-and-white adaptation of a novel by a modern American master of the macabre combined with a color version of stories by one of its all-time greatest practitioners. While the tales of Edgar Allan Poe have been adapted endlessly and exhaustively, apart from a couple of short stories ("The Dead Man" and "The Girl with the Hungry Eyes," both for Rod Serling's *Night Gallery*—first and third seasons respectively) *Conjure Wife* remains the only major work of Fritz Leiber's to have reached the big screen. Another version appeared in 1980 under the title *Witches' Brew,* starring Teri Garr and Richard Benjamin, but it, like Universal's 1944 *Weird Woman,* is really only for Leiber completists. *Night of the Eagle,* however, stands as one of the high watermarks of literary horror adaptation, a credit to its author and all those involved in its making, and remains essential viewing for the horror connoisseur, no matter what title you get to watch it under.

CLIMBING

by Darrell Schweitzer

IT WAS THE SORT OF THING THAT SHOULD HAVE HAPPENED TO A CHILD, IN THE FINEST TRADITION OF *ALICE THROUGH THE LOOKING-GLASS* or the Narnia kids with their wardrobe; but I was eighteen at the time, a newly arrived freshman at Villanova University in Pennsylvania.

The beginning was a botanical excursion. Maybe it was because I was from Arizona that I didn't believe the casual reports of gigantic *blue* trees on campus. I went to see for myself as soon as I could, and there they were, dominating the lawn that sloped down between the chapel, Tolentine Hall, and Route 30, like massive interlopers from another planet.

Blue beeches, they were called, their leaves not really blue, but an equally unnatural reddish purple, and the bark was indeed grayish blue. The long heavy branches touched the ground all around, giving the impression of mountainous skirts or petticoats, layer upon layer. I resolved to penetrate same, and, I thought, having already survived a week of Intro. Psych., I'd let the Freudians make of that what they would.

Yes, it was something of the child in me which remembered and yielded to the impulse: on all fours, I crawled under the outer branches, then stood up *inside*, among the strange leaves, my back against the enormous, curiously lumpy trunk. It was like being inside a wonderful cave, a secret little world beneath the canopy of leaves, silent but for the slight rustling of the leaves and, once, briefly, a squirrel scurrying somewhere overhead. I couldn't hear the traffic from the highway, or the shouts from the impromptu baseball diamond down the slope, or the conversations of passers-by on the nearby path. I was alone.

I wanted to be alone much of the time. *Animal House* was setting standards of student behavior that year. I couldn't stand beer. I didn't care about the frats any more than they cared for me. Even before I turned around suddenly on arrival day and collided with my new roommate, my nose buried in his chest since he was a foot taller than me and easily twice my weight, I had misgivings.

"Hiya punk!" he said. His meaty slap of a greeting nearly dislocated my shoulder. It was time to slip even lower on the evolutionary scale than such neanderthals and return to the trees.

I did much of my studying under the largest of the blue beeches. One hot, late September afternoon I sat there, back against the trunk, a book open on my lap, shoes off, toes idly digging in the dust. The air was absolutely still, the light and shadow of the leaves motionless.

I was beginning to doze but not yet asleep. If what followed was somehow a dream, I have never awakened from it.

A twig dropped onto the page of my book. Then another and another, in measured succession, one, two, three.

Laughter, *from above.*

I looked up, suddenly angry that someone had discovered my hideaway.

Up among the foliage, something deft as a monkey swung from branch to branch.

More giggling, decidedly feminine laughter.

I blushed with embarrassment and got to my feet, still holding the book.

"Hello? Is anyone there?"

A larger twig fell in my hair. I brushed it away. "Hey!"

The branches above me were completely motionless once more. I peered into their depths, but saw no sign of my unwelcome company.

Then a heavy branch came plunging right at my face like a spear. I yelped and jumped aside, sending the book fluttering.

"Stop that! Leave me alone!"

She replied, whoever she was, in a high, almost musical voice, very sweet, completely unintelligible. Branches rattled. I shielded my eyes from the steady rain of twigs, leaves, and bits of bark. She was climbing higher. Her voice receded.

"Hey! Is this some kind of joke?"

Why I just didn't pick up my things and leave, and find a quiet spot in the library or an unused lounge, I do not know. I shall never know. Perhaps I was feeling possessive about my tree.

I put my shoes on, then started climbing. Beeches are so easy to climb, with numerous thick branches close together. Above me, leaves rustled. She scrambled higher, faster. I followed patiently. After all, we would soon run out of tree and I'd meet her at the top.

I thought of Rima, the bird-girl from *Green Mansions.* But what if I got to the top and there was no one there? What if this tree was haunted? The *Twilight Zone* theme drifted through my head.

I didn't call out anything more, but continued on with grim determination. One of the few advantages of being skinny is that the muscle-to-body ratio is quite different. You're all arms and legs. Skinny people make good climbers.

On I went, with no thought of how high up I must be. Each branch led immediately to the next, and the next, and the next. Slowly I circled the great trunk, craning my neck to gaze upward. Once I caught the briefest glimpse of a pale, bare thigh.

Oddly, the trunk didn't seem to be getting any narrower. It was still a slowly curving wall, far too large for me to be able to see around the other side.

Up, until I was soaked with sweat and itchy from bits of bark and leaves clinging to my skin.

Up, until something in the back of my mind told me: ignore what you see, ignore what you feel. None of it is really happening. No tree is *this* high.

I tried to look out through the branches at the campus below, but the purple leaves closed everything out. This was, truly, a world unto itself.

Up. I counted a hundred more branches.

A hundred and fifty. My hands were rubbed raw. My knees ached. Up. Impossible.

So maybe I was going to come out in the clouds and battle giants, the way Jack did. No, I was too tired. Where two particularly large branches sprouted upward from the tree, forming a sort of cradle, I paused for breath in their embrace.

Far above, my quarry also paused.

I clung to those branches, breathing hard, eyes closed, thinking, no, no, it's all impossible.

I opened my eyes and looked down. I couldn't see the ground below. The tree was like an ocean, dark, endless, shifting with the wind.

Experimentally, I broke off a stick perhaps three feet long and an inch thick, trimming it of twigs and leaves, and let it drop, watching it turn and bounce off a branch and tumble some more, until it vanished from sight. The sound of its passage faded slowly. I never heard it hit bottom.

Now I was afraid, and my fear grew worse as the sun set, as my little world darkened. I had been climbing for *hours*, which was impossible, maybe half a mile into the air, which was ridiculous, on an impulse I couldn't explain. I wondered if I'd ever be missed. Would someone come looking for me, and find my books down below there…somewhere?

I thought, briefly, of Judge Crater, of space-warps, of people carried off in UFOs.

I considered, just as briefly, climbing back down the way I had come. No, not in the dark. It was too far.

Was there even any ground to return to?

So I spent the night lying on a branch, my arms around it tight, my feet dangling in space. I couldn't sleep. If I lost my grip, if I rolled over, such a fate was unimaginable—to be battered to death, branch by branch, falling, I was somehow insanely certain, forever.

It wasn't a joke. I wasn't amused. I desperately, desperately wanted this to end.

I listened to the utter darkness, to the night birds, a hooting owl, the eternal wind among the leaves, and to *her*, so near I could almost feel her breath as she spoke gentle words I didn't understand and sang something that might have been a lullaby.

Perhaps it was the wind, or else she actually did reach out and touch me on the cheek, wiping away a tear.

I awoke with a start. It was dawn. I *had* been asleep, and she sat beside me now, holding firmly onto my arm to make sure I didn't fall.

She might have been two or three years older than me, thin but not gaunt, muscular in a long-limbed way, her hair white, her skin pale as paper; almost naked, clad only in the remnants of what might have been rags or even animal skins.

What a contrast we made. I wore blue jeans, sneakers, and a striped polo shirt. I tried to joke about it—*One Million B.C.* meets *Brewster McCloud*—but she only shook her head and chattered on.

I tried a few words of first-year French on her. She paused, as if almost recognizing something. Then I tried Latin, an even worse smattering of Church Latin and classical.

She gasped, eyes wide, and crossed herself.

Up. She started to climb.

"Hey! Where are you going?"

She shouted something in reply. I climbed after her, heaving myself from branch to branch until I finally caught hold of her ankle.

"Stop!" I gasped. "I'm not ready for this. This is just *too* weird. We've got to go *down*." I pointed and said again, "Down."

She pulled her ankle free and crouched just above me, shaking her head fiercely. I pointed down again. She pointed up.

Impossibly, we climbed throughout the day, pausing only a few times for rest, driven on by an impulse I could feel but couldn't begin to put into words. She showed me where to find rainwater cupped in the hollows where the great branches joined the trunk, where to find birds' eggs and even edible mushrooms growing out of the bark.

She was showing me how to survive, as if we were going to be here for a long time. As if she already had been.

Still the tree never diminished; and the purple canopy admitted no outside sound, allowed not even a glimpse of the clear sky.

The top drew no nearer. The bottom receded, infinitely far. Once a flock of startling white birds invaded our little universe, fluttering around us, settling far out on the branches, gazing silently as we climbed past.

Up.

I thought I saw a cloud drifting through the branches. Odd, it came to me. We should have been practically in the stratosphere by now, where there are no clouds. It might have just been my breath fogging my glasses. I paused to clean them on my shirt, fumbled with stiff fingers, and lost them to the depths below. Indeed, the world was filled with soft fog now. My friend kept on climbing. I followed. There was nothing else I could do.

That second night we lay together in a cradle of branches, and she spoke to me once more, softly, in long, warbling sentences, and I replied in French, Latin, and English. It didn't seem to matter which. After a time, we had a few words in common. I told her my name. She told me hers, a garbled *Mmm*, as if she had not spoken it in so long she had forgotten how to shape that particular sound, which might have been Marie or Marla or even Martina.

I considered all the supernatural explanations, that she was a ghost or some kind of tree spirit who had already lured me to my doom, and all of this was a near-death hallucination as I lay broken at the base of the tree.

She clung to me. She was cold and smelled of leaves and bark and moss. She shivered. I felt her heart beating as I held her.

I thought of praying then, but couldn't. That made no more sense than anything else.

In the morning, we climbed again. I lost my grip once, and dangled screaming for help while she came down and rescued me, tearing the front of my shirt in the process, scraping my chest and belly against a sharp, broken branch. She touched the blood with her finger and held the finger up in amazement, as if she had never seen such a thing before.

Toward evening, two days later, we found a human skeleton huddled as if sleeping in a concavity where the tree's trunk was shaped like a cupped hand. She regarded it solemnly for a long time, and, once more, crossed herself. I repeated the gesture, then held up the little silver crucifix I wore around my neck. She took the crucifix gently in her fingers, then released it. I think she was close to weeping then, as if she knew or recalled some terrible truth she couldn't find the words to tell me, or was afraid to speak even to herself.

At the very last I picked up the skull, examining it, as if the answer could be found in its empty eyes. But there was nothing. Somehow the act of putting it back disturbed all the other bones, sending them clattering down through the branches, until the skull alone remained.

When we started climbing again, I led the way.

I think we had been climbing for several weeks before we came upon a second skeleton, this one with a few scraps of hair and clothing on it. The hair was very long, gray, and rough as straw. Several months later, we found a third.

I was losing all sense of time. It should have been January or February. We should have been freezing, I in my ragged summer clothing, she in almost nothing. But the leaves did not change color. Snow never fell. There was only the eternal succession of the daytime sun sparkling through the swaying branches, the purple twilight, and the impenetrable night.

As we climbed, we assembled our own private language, until she could tell me what little she remembered of where she had come from. None of the places or names meant anything to me, but I think she was talking about castles, famines, and wars. She wasn't sure if she truly remembered anything like that, anything other than climbing, and the day when she first saw me seated so absurdly, so hilariously...on the ground? Had she seen the *ground?*

We couldn't find the words between us. A turn of the screw, a useless hint, yielding nothing. She didn't understand, anymore than when I told her about America, or television, or cars.

I imagined her a refugee from some

barbarous Dark Age village, wandering into a forest, hearing voices she took for witches or ghosts, beginning to climb out of fear or wonder, no more able to explain what was happening to her than I was.

But that was my imagination. The truth remained, as ever, beyond any grasp.

Up. Thus the rhythm of our existence, the eternal climb, punctuated by rest and the scantiest of meals. I suspected that we didn't actually have to eat, but only did so out of a sense of ritual; that we had become mere airy nothings, slowly losing form, habitation, and half-forgotten names.

I wondered if I had ever been missed, if the police had come looking and found my books beneath the blue beech on the Villanova campus.

What had they told my parents?

"Dieu," my friend whispered one night in her sleep. *"Dieu."*

"Is that it?" I asked her, though she still slept. "Are we going to see God? Is this some kind of purgatory, to work off our sins?" She stirred, half awake. Her hand slid along my bare chest until she found the silver crucifix. She wept softly.

Or were we in Hell?

Up.

Years must have passed between that time she wept and fingered the crucifix and my realization that we were no longer young; but it was a subliminal thing, something you know the instant a dream ends, then almost, but not quite, forget when fully awake. It was almost impossible for me to recognize that her face was growing lined and her hair streaked with silver, to envision her any way other than she appeared *now,* at the given instant. But her face *was* increasingly lined, her hair changing color even as the eternal leaves never did. I had a bristly gray beard. I could feel the bare spot on the top of my head where my hair was thinning. In all this while, I had not seen my own face, and could only imagine what I looked like: some wholly arboreal creature, pale and gnarled, hard as the twisted branches, naked now, my clothing long since worn away.

I tried to think back to the boy who liked to study under a tree and imagine what sort of life he might have had, if he'd chosen a remote recess of the college library instead. I couldn't remember much about him.

"The blue beech," I said to my companion once, "is such a strange tree. The color just isn't right."

"I see it as an oak," she said without surprise. "The world's axle, turning."

I think there was actually a time when we were content, midway on the journey of this life, with no more uncertainty before or behind us than anyone else, our lives reduced to a pleasing rhythm, a comforting routine. But I cannot recall. The mind shuts down. It sinks into numbness. Up. Climbing. Up.

There was only one possible conclusion. All she could do was die. The sickness came upon her subtly, but relentlessly. She coughed. She paused more often to rest. She shivered in my arms each night, and one morning she could no longer climb. I placed her gently in the crook of a branch and tended her as best I could, bringing her water and birds' eggs in my cupped hand.

She left me, closing her eyes, whispering words I still could not make out. Her head rolled back, and she lay there, her white hair streaming into space. I took the silver crucifix from around my neck and pressed it in her hand. I wanted her to smile. But she was already dead.

Up. I reconsidered all my old notions, of Judge Crater and space-warps and UFOs and alternate universes; of an infinite tree, expanding in all directions, or, quite the opposite, endlessly recurring, the upper branches coming into existence only as I touched them, the lower dissolving back into nothingness one by one.

No. There was no logic here, no possibility of rational understanding.

I thought of witchcraft and enchantments and mischievous spirits; of my adventure as life's allegory, an eternal, symbolic striving toward the light.

I weighed all these and found them wanting.

No thematic coherence, no possible morality.

We blunder through random holes in the world sometimes. It doesn't mean anything.

The mind shuts down. Consciousness fades. Only the unthinking motion continues.

Upward. Ever upward. Toward the awful, merciless mystery that has no end.

"Climbing" first appeared in After Hours #25 *(1995).*

Darrell Schweitzer had a story in Space & Time *in 1970, one in* Weirdbook *in 1971, and one in* Whispers *in 1973. He has since published about 350 short stories, in publications ranging from* The Twilight Zone Magazine *to* Amazing Stories *to* Interzone, *plus numerous anthologies. His most recent story collection is The* Children of Chorazin and Other Strange Denizens, *from Hippocampus Press (2023). In 2020 PS Publishing issued a two-volume career retrospective of his work,* The Mysteries of the Faceless King *and* The Last Heretic. *His four published novels are* The White Isle, The Shattered Goddess, The Mask of the Sorcerer, *and* The Dragon House. *He has also published non-fiction books about Lord Dunsany and H. P. Lovecraft, collections of essays, poetry, interviews, etc. He was co-editor of* Weird Tales *between 1988 and 2007. He has been nominated for the World Fantasy Award four times and won it once (for* Weird Tales).

THURNLEY ABBEY

BY PERCEVAL LANDON

THREE YEARS AGO I WAS ON MY WAY OUT TO THE EAST, AND AS AN EXTRA DAY IN LONDON WAS OF SOME IMPORTANCE, I TOOK THE FRIDAY EVENING MAIL TRAIN TO BRINDISI INSTEAD OF THE USUAL THURSDAY MORNING MARSEILLES EXPRESS. Many people shrink from the long forty-eight-hour train journey through Europe, and the subsequent rush across the Mediterranean on the nineteen-knot *Isis* or the *Osiris*; but there is really very little discomfort on either the train or the mail-boat, and unless there is actually nothing for me to do, I always like to save the extra day and a half in London before I say goodbye to her for one of my longer tramps. This time—it was early, I remember, in the shipping season, probably about the beginning of September—there were few passengers, and I had a compartment in the P. and O. Indian express to myself all the way from Calais. All Sunday I watched the blue waves dimpling the Adriatic, and the pale rosemary along the cuttings; the plain white towns, with their flat roofs and their bold "duomos," and the gray-green gnarled olive orchards of Apulia. The journey was just like any other. We ate in the dining-car as often and as long as we decently could. We slept after luncheon; we dawdled the afternoon away with yellow-backed novels; sometimes we exchanged platitudes in the smoking-room, and it was there that I met Alistair Colvin.

Colvin was a man of middle height, with a resolute, well-cut jaw; his hair was turning gray; his mustache was sun-whitened, otherwise he was clean-shaven—obviously a gentleman, and obviously also a preoccupied man. He had no great wit. When spoken to, he made the usual remarks in the right way, and I dare say he refrained from banalities only because he spoke less than the rest of us; most of the time he buried himself in the Wagonlit* Company's timetable, but seemed unable to concentrate his attention on any one page of it. He found that I had been over the Siberian railway, and for a quarter of an hour he discussed it with me. Then he lost interest in it, and rose to go to his compartment. But he came back again very soon, and seemed glad to pick up the conversation again.

Of course this did not seem to me to be of any importance. Most travelers by train become a trifle infirm of purpose after thirty-six hours' rattling. But Colvin's restless way I noticed in somewhat marked contrast with the man's personal importance and dignity; especially ill-suited was it to his finely made large hand with strong, broad, regular nails and its few lines. As I looked at his hand I noticed a long, deep, and recent scar of ragged shape. However, it is absurd to pretend that I thought anything was unusual. I went off at five o'clock on Sunday afternoon to sleep away the hour or two that had still to be got through before we arrived at Brindisi.

Once there, we few passengers transshipped our hand baggage, verified our berths—there were only a score of us in all—and then, after an aimless ramble of half an hour in Brindisi, we returned to dinner at the Hôtel International, not wholly surprised that the town had been the death of Virgil. If I remember rightly, there is a gaily painted hall at the International—I do not wish to advertise anything, but there is no other place in Brindisi at which to await the

---

* A variation of the Wagons-Lits ("sleeping cars") Company founded by Belgian innovator Georges Nagelmackers in 1872. Nagelmacker created luxury sleeping cars for trains serving the European continent, and later started the Orient Express.

coming of the mails—and after dinner I was looking with awe at a trellis overgrown with blue vines, when Colvin moved across the room to my table. He picked up *Il Secolo*, but almost immediately gave up the pretense of reading it. He turned squarely to me and said:

"Would you do me a favor?"

One doesn't do favors to stray acquaintances on Continental expresses without knowing something more of them than I knew of Colvin. But I smiled in a noncommittal way and asked him what he wanted. I wasn't wrong in part of my estimate of him; he said bluntly:

"Will you let me sleep in your cabin on the *Osiris*?" And he colored a little as he said it.

Now, there is nothing more tiresome than having to put up with a stable-companion at sea, and I asked him rather pointedly:

"Surely there is room for all of us?" I thought that perhaps he had been partnered off with some mangy Levantine, and wanted to escape from him at all hazards.

Colvin, still somewhat confused, said: "Yes; I am in a cabin by myself. But you would do me the greatest favor if you would allow me to share yours."

This was all very well, but, besides the fact that I always sleep better when alone, there had been some recent thefts on board these boats, and I hesitated, frank and honest and self-conscious as Colvin was. Just then the mail-train came in with a clatter and a rush of escaping steam, and I asked him to see me again about it on the boat when we started. He answered me curtly—I suppose he saw the mistrust in my manner —"I am a member of White's." I smiled to myself as he said it, but I remembered in a moment that the man—if he were really what he claimed to be, and I make no doubt that he was—must have been sorely put to it before he urged the fact as a guarantee of his respectability to a total stranger at a Brindisi hotel.

That evening, as we cleared the red and green harbor-lights of Brindisi, Colvin explained. This is his story in his own words:

"When I was traveling in India some years ago, I made the acquaintance of a youngish man in the Woods and Forests. We camped out together for a week, and I found him a pleasant companion. John Broughton was a lighthearted soul when off duty, but a steady and capable man in any of the small emergencies that continually arise in that department. He was liked and trusted by the natives, and his future was well assured in Government service, when a fair-sized estate was unexpectedly left to him, and he joyfully shook the dust of the Indian plains from his feet and returned to England. For five years he drifted about London. I saw him now and then. We dined together about every eighteen months, and I could trace pretty exactly the gradual sickening of Broughton with a merely idle life. He then set out on a couple of long voyages, returned as restless as before, and at last told me that he had decided to marry and settle down at his place, Thurnley Abbey, which had long been empty. He spoke about looking after the property and standing for his constituency in the usual way. Vivien Wilde, his fiancée, had, I suppose, begun to take him in hand. She was a pretty girl with a deal of fair hair and rather an exclusive manner; deeply religious in a narrow school, she was still kindly and high-spirited, and I thought that Broughton was in luck. He was quite happy and full of information about his future.

"Among other things, I asked him about Thurnley Abbey. He confessed that he hardly knew the place. The last tenant, a man called Clarke, had lived in one wing for fifteen years and seen no one. He had been a miser and a hermit. It was the rarest thing for a light to be seen at the Abbey after dark. Only the barest necessities of life were ordered, and the tenant himself received them at the side-door. His one half-caste manservant, after a month's stay in the house, had abruptly left without warning, and had returned to the Southern States. One thing Broughton complained bitterly about: Clarke had wilfully spread the rumor among the villagers that the Abbey was haunted, and had even condescended to play childish tricks with spirit-lamps and salt in order to scare trespassers away at night. He had been detected in the act of this tomfoolery, but the story spread, and no one, said Broughton, would venture near the house except in broad daylight. The hauntedness of Thurnley Abbey was now, he said with a grin, part of the gospel of the countryside, but he and his young wife were going to change all that. Would I propose myself any time I liked? I, of course, said I would, and equally, of course, intended to do nothing of the sort without a definite invitation.

"The house was put in thorough repair, though not a stick of the old furniture and tapestry were removed. Floors and ceilings were relaid; the roof was made watertight again, and the dust of half a century was scoured out. He showed me some photographs of the place. It was called an Abbey, though as a matter of fact it had been only the infirmary of the long-vanished Abbey of Closter some five miles away. The larger part of this building remained as it had been in pre-Reformation days, but a wing had been added in Jacobean times, and that part of the house had been kept in something like repair by Mr. Clarke. He had in both the ground and the first floors set a heavy timber door, strongly barred with iron, in the passage between the earlier and the Jacobean parts of the house, and had entirely neglected the former. So there had been a good deal of work to be done.

"Broughton, whom I saw in London two or three times about this time, made a deal of fun over the positive refusal of the workmen to remain after sundown. Even after the electric light had been put into every room, nothing would induce them to remain, though, as Broughton observed, electric light was death on ghosts. The legend of the Abbey's ghosts had gone far and wide, and the men would take no risks. On the whole, though nothing of any sort or kind had been conjured up even by their heated imaginations during their five months' work upon the Abbey, the belief in the ghosts was rather strengthened than otherwise in Thurnley because of the men's confessed nervousness, and local tradition declared itself in favor of the ghost of an immured nun.

"'Good old nun!' said Broughton.

"I asked him whether in general he believed in the possibility of ghosts, and, rather to my surprise, he said that he couldn't say he entirely disbelieved in them. A man in India had told him one morning in camp that he believed that his mother was dead in England, as her vision had come to his tent the night before. He had not been alarmed, but had said nothing, and the figure vanished again. As a matter of fact, the next possible *dak-walla* brought on a telegram announcing the mother's death. 'There the thing was,' said Broughton.

"'My own idea,' said he, 'is that if a ghost ever does come in one's way, one ought to speak to it.'

"I agreed. Little as I knew of the ghost world and its conventions, I had already remembered that a spook was in honor bound to wait to be spoken to. It didn't seem much to do, and I felt that the sound of one's own voice would at any rate reassure oneself as to one's wakefulness. But there are few ghosts outside Europe—few, that is, that a white man can see—and I had never been troubled with any. However, as I have said, I told Broughton that I agreed.

"So the wedding took place and I went to it in a tall hat which I bought for the occasion, and the new Mrs. Broughton smiled very nicely at me afterwards. As it had to happen, I took the Orient Express that evening and was not in England again for nearly six months. Just before I came back I got a letter from Broughton. He asked if I could see him in London or come to Thurnley, as he thought I should be better able to help him than anyone else he knew. His wife sent a nice message to me at the end, so I was reassured about at least one thing. I wrote from Budapest that I would come and see him at Thurnley two days after my arrival in London, and as I sauntered out of the Pannonia into the Kerepesi Ut to post my letters, I wondered of what earthly service I could be to Broughton. I had been out with him after tiger on foot, and I could imagine few men better able at a pinch to manage their own business. However, I had nothing to do, so after dealing with some small accumulations of business during my absence, I packed a kitbag and departed to Euston.

"I was met by a trap at Thurnley Road station, and after a drive of nearly seven miles we echoed through the sleepy streets of Thurnley village, into which the main gates of the park thrust themselves, splendid with pillars and spread-eagles and tomcats rampant atop of them. From the gates a quadruple avenue of beech-trees led inwards for a quarter of a mile. Beneath them a neat strip of fine turf edged the road and ran back until the poison of the dead beech-leaves had killed it under the trees. There were many wheel-tracks on the road, and a comfortable little pony trap jogged past me laden with a country parson and his wife and daughter. Evidently there was some garden party going on at the Abbey. The road dropped away to the right at the end of the avenue, and I could see the Abbey across a wide pasturage and a broad lawn thickly dotted with guests.

"The end of the building was plain. It must have been almost mercilessly austere when it was first built, but time had crumbled the edges and toned the stone down to an orange-lichened gray wherever it showed behind its curtain of magnolia, jasmine, and ivy. Farther on was the three-storied Jacobean house, plain and handsome. There had not been the slightest attempt to adapt the one to the other, but the kindly ivy had glossed over the touching-point. There was a tall flèche in the middle of the building, surmounting a small bell tower. Behind the house there rose the mountainous verdure of Spanish chestnuts all the way up the hill.

"Broughton had seen me coming from afar, and walked across from his other guests to welcome me before turning me over to the butler's care. This man was sandy-haired and rather inclined to be talkative. He could, however, answer hardly any questions about the house: he had, he said, only been there three weeks. Mindful of what Broughton had told me, I made no inquiries about ghosts, though the room into which I was shown might have justified anything. It was a very large low room with oak beams projecting from the white ceiling. Every inch of the walls, including the doors, was covered with tapestry, and a remarkably fine Italian fourpost bedstead, heavily draped, added to the darkness and dignity of the place. All the furniture was old, well made, and dark. Underfoot there was a plain green

pile carpet, the only new thing about the room except the electric light fittings and the jugs and basins. Even the looking-glass on the dressing-table was an old pyramidal Venetian glass set in heavy repoussé frame of tarnished silver.

"After a few minutes cleaning up, I went downstairs and out upon the lawn, where I greeted my hostess. The people gathered there were of the usual country type, all anxious to be pleased and roundly curious as to the new master of the Abbey. Rather to my surprise, and quite to my pleasure, I rediscovered Glenham, whom I had known well in old days in Barotseland: he lived quite close, as, he remarked with a grin, I ought to have known. 'But,' he added, 'I don't live in a place like this.' He swept his hand to the long, low lines of the Abbey in obvious admiration, and then, to my intense interest, muttered beneath his breath, 'Thank God!' He saw that I had overheard him, and turning to me said decidedly, 'Yes, thank God I said, and I meant I wouldn't live at the Abbey for all Broughton's money.'

"'But surely,' I demurred, 'you know that old Clarke was discovered in the very act of setting light to his bug-a-boos?'

"Glenham shrugged his shoulders. 'Yes, I know about that. But there is something wrong with the place still. All I can say is that Broughton is a different man since he has lived here. I don't believe that he will remain much longer. But—you're staying here?— Well, you'll hear all about it tonight. There's a big dinner, I understand.' The conversation turned off to old reminiscences, and Glenham soon after had to go.

"Before I went to dress that evening I had twenty minutes' talk with Broughton in his library. There was no doubt that the man was altered, gravely altered. He was nervous and fidgety, and I found him looking at me only when my eye was off him. I naturally asked him what he wanted of me. I told him I would do anything I could, but that I couldn't conceive what he lacked that I could provide. He said with a lusterless smile that there was, however, something, and that he would tell me the following morning. It struck me that he was somehow ashamed of himself, and perhaps ashamed of the part he was asking me to play. However, I dismissed the subject from my mind and went up to dress in my palatial room. As I shut the door a draught blew out the Queen of Sheba from the wall, and I noticed that the tapestries were not fastened to the wall at the bottom. I have always held very practical views about spooks, and it has often seemed to me that the slow waving in firelight of loose tapestry upon a wall would account for ninety-nine percent of the stories one hears, and certainly the dignified undulation of this lady with her attendants and huntsmen—one of whom was untidily cutting the throat of a fallow deer upon the very steps on which King Solomon, a grey-faced Flemish nobleman with the order of the Golden Fleece, awaited his fair visitor—gave color to my hypothesis.

"Nothing much happened at dinner. The people were very much like those of the garden party. A young woman next to me seemed anxious to know what was being read in London. As she was far more familiar than I with the most recent magazines and literary supplements, I found salvation in being myself instructed in the tendencies of modern fiction. All true art, she said, was shot through and through with melancholy. How vulgar were the attempts at wit that marked so many modern books! From the beginning of literature it had always been tragedy that embodied the highest attainment of every age. To call such works morbid merely begged the question. No thoughtful man—she looked sternly at me through the steel rim of her glasses—could fail to agree with me. Of course, as one would, I immediately and properly said that I slept with Pett Ridge and Jacobs under my pillow at night, and that if *Jorrocks* weren't quite so large and cornery, I would add him to the company. She hadn't read any of them, so I was saved—for a time. But I remember grimly that she said that the dearest wish of her life was to be in some awful and soul-freezing situation of horror, and I remember that she dealt hardly with the hero of Nat Paynter's vampire story, between nibbles at her brown-bread ice. She was a cheerless soul, and I couldn't help thinking that if there were many such in the neighborhood,

it was not surprising that old Glenham had been stuffed with some nonsense or other about the Abbey. Yet nothing could well have been less creepy than the glitter of silver and glass, and the subdued lights and cackle of conversation all round the dinner-table.

"After the ladies had gone, I found myself talking to the rural dean. He was a thin, earnest man, who at once turned the conversation to old Clarke's buffooneries. But, he said, Mr. Broughton had introduced such a new and cheerful spirit, not only into the Abbey but, he might say, into the whole neighborhood, that he had great hopes that the ignorant superstitions of the past were from henceforth destined to oblivion. Thereupon his other neighbor, a portly gentleman of independent means and position, audibly remarked 'Amen,' which damped the rural dean, and we talked of partridges past, partridges present, and pheasants to come. At the other end of the table Broughton sat with a couple of his friends, red-faced hunting men. Once I noticed that they were discussing me, but I paid no attention to it at the time. I remembered it a few hours later.

"By eleven all the guests were gone, and Broughton, his wife, and I were alone together under the fine plaster ceiling of the Jacobean drawing-room. Mrs. Broughton talked about one or two of the neighbors, and then, with a smile, said that she knew I would excuse her, shook hands with me, and went off to bed. I am not very good at analyzing things, but I felt that she talked a little uncomfortably and with a suspicion of effort, smiled rather conventionally, and was obviously glad to go. These things seem trifling enough to repeat, but I had throughout the faint feeling that everything was not square. Under the circumstances, this was enough to set me wondering what on earth the service could be that I was to render—wondering also whether the whole business were not some ill-advised jest in order to make me come down from London for a mere shooting party.

"Broughton said little after she had gone. But he was evidently laboring to bring the conversation round to the so-called haunting of the Abbey. As soon as I saw this, of course, I asked him directly about it. He then seemed at once to lose interest in the matter. There was no doubt about it: Broughton was somehow a changed man, and to my mind he had changed in no way for the better. Mrs. Broughton seemed no sufficient cause. He was clearly very fond of her, and she of him. I reminded him that he was going to tell me what I could do for him in the morning, pleaded my journey, lighted a candle, and went upstairs with him. At the end of the passage leading into the old house he grinned weakly and said, 'Mind, if you see a ghost, do talk to it; you said you would,' He stood irresolutely a moment and then turned away. At the door of his dressing-room he paused a moment: 'I'm here,' he called out, 'if you should want anything. Goodnight,' and he shut his door.

"I went along the passage to my room, undressed, switched on a lamp beside my bed, read a few pages of the *Jungle Book*, and then, more than ready for sleep, switched the light off and went fast asleep.

"THREE HOURS LATER I woke up. There was not a breath of wind outside. It was so silent that my ears found employment in listening for the throbbing of the blood within them. There was not even a flicker of light from the fireplace. As I lay there, an ash tinkled slightly as it cooled, but there was hardly a gleam of the dullest red in the grate. An owl cried among the silent Spanish chestnuts on the slope outside. I idly reviewed the events of the day, hoping that I should fall off to sleep again before I reached dinner. But at the end I seemed as wakeful as ever. There was no help for it. I must read my *Jungle Book* again till I felt ready to go off, so I fumbled for the pear at the end of the cord that hung down inside the bed, and I switched on the bedside lamp. The sudden glory dazzled me for a moment. I felt under my pillow for my book with half-shut eyes. Then, growing used to the light, I happened to look down to the foot of my bed.

"I can never tell you really what happened then. Nothing I could ever confess in the most abject words could even faintly picture to you what I felt. I know that my heart stopped dead, and my throat shut automatically. In one instinctive movement

I crouched back up against the headboards of the bed, staring at the horror. The movement set my heart going again, and the sweat dripped from every pore. I am not a particularly religious man, but I had always believed that God would never allow any supernatural appearance to present itself to man in such a guise and in such circumstances that harm, either bodily or mental, could result to him. I can only tell you that at that moment both my life and my reason rocked unsteadily on their seats."

THE OTHER *OSIRIS* PASSENGERS had gone to bed. Only he and I remained leaning over the starboard railing, which rattled uneasily now and then under the fierce vibration of the over-engined mailboat. Far over, there were the lights of a few fishing-smacks riding out the night, and a great rush of white combing and seething water fell out and away from us overside.

At last Colvin went on:

"Leaning over the foot of my bed, looking at me, was a figure swathed in a rotten and tattered veiling. This shroud passed over the head, but left both eyes and the right side of the face bare. It then followed the line of the arm down to where the hand grasped the bed-end. The face was not that entirely of a skull, though the eyes and the flesh of the face were totally gone. There was a thin, dry skin drawn tightly over the features, and there was some skin left on the hand. One wisp of hair crossed the forehead. It was perfectly still. I looked at it, and it looked at me, and my brains turned dry and hot in my head. I had still got the pear of the electric lamp in my hand, and I played idly with it; only I dared not turn the light out again. I shut my eyes, only to open them in a hideous terror the same second. The thing had not moved. My heart was thumping, and the sweat cooled me as it evaporated. Another cinder tinkled in the grate, and a panel creaked in the wall.

"My reason failed me. For twenty minutes, or twenty seconds, I was able to think of nothing else but this awful figure, till there came, hurtling through the empty channels of my senses, the remembrance that

Broughton and his friends had discussed me furtively at dinner. The dim possibility of it being a hoax stole gratefully into my unhappy mind, and once there, one's pluck came creeping back along a thousand tiny veins. My first sensation was one of blind unreasoning thankfulness that my brain was going to stand the trial. I am not a timid man, but the best of us needs some human handle to steady him in time of extremity, and in this faint but growing hope that after all it might be only a brutal hoax, I found the fulcrum that I needed. At last I moved.

"How I managed to do it, I cannot tell you, but with one spring towards the foot of the bed I got within arm's length and struck out one fearful blow with my fist at the thing. It crumbled under it, and my hand was cut to the bone. With the sickening revulsion after my terror, I dropped half-fainting across the end of the bed. So it was merely a foul trick after all. No doubt the trick had been played many a time before: no doubt Broughton and his friends had had some bet among themselves as to what I should do when I discovered the gruesome thing. From my state of abject terror I found myself transported into an insensate anger. I shouted curses upon Broughton. I dived rather than climbed over the bed-end on to the sofa. I tore at the robed skeleton—how well the whole thing had been carried out, I thought—I broke the skull against the floor, and stamped upon its dry bones. I flung the head away under the bed, and rent the brittle bones of the trunk in pieces. I snapped the thin thighbones across my knee and flung them in different directions. The shinbones I set up against a stool and broke with my heel. I raged like a Berserker against the loathly thing, and stripped the ribs from the backbone and slung the breastbone against the cupboard. My fury increased as the work of destruction went on. I tore the frail rotten veil into twenty pieces, and the dust went up over everything, over the clean blotting-paper and the silver inkstand. At last my work was done. There was but a raffle of broken bones and strips of parchment and crumbling wool. Then, picking up a piece of the skull—it was the cheek and temple bone of the right side, I remember—I opened the door and went down the passage to Broughton's dressing-room. I remember still how my sweat-dripping pajamas clung to me as I walked. At the door I kicked and entered.

"Broughton was in bed. He had already turned the light on and seemed shrunken and horrified. For a moment he could hardly pull himself together. Then I spoke. I don't know what I said. Only I know that from a heart full and over-full with hatred and contempt, spurred on by shame of my own recent cowardice, I let my tongue run on. He answered nothing. I was amazed at my own fluency. My hair still clung lankily to my wet temples, my hand was bleeding profusely, and I must have looked a strange sight. Broughton huddled himself up at the head of the bed just as I had. Still he made no answer, no defense. He seemed preoccupied with something besides my reproaches, and once or twice moistened his lips with his tongue. But he could say nothing, though he moved his hands now and then, just as a baby who cannot speak moves his hands.

"At last the door into Mrs. Broughton's room opened and she came in, white and terrified. 'What is it? What is it? Oh, in God's name! what is it?' she cried again and again, and then she went up to her husband and sat on the bed; and the two faced me in speechless terror. I told her what the matter was. I spared her husband not a word for her presence there. Yet he seemed hardly to understand. I told the pair that I had spoiled their cowardly joke for them. Broughton looked up.

"'I have smashed the foul thing into a hundred pieces,' I said. Broughton licked his lips again and his mouth worked. 'By God!' I shouted, 'it would serve you right if I thrashed you within an inch of your life. I will take care that not a decent man or woman of my acquaintance ever speaks to you again. And there,' I added, throwing the broken piece of the skull upon the floor beside his bed, 'there is a souvenir for you, of your damned work tonight!'

"Broughton saw the bone, and in a moment it was his turn to frighten me. He squealed like a hare caught in a trap. He screamed and screamed till Mrs. Broughton, almost as terrified as I, held on to him and coaxed him like a child to be quiet. But Broughton—and as he moved I thought that ten minutes ago I perhaps looked as terribly ill as he did—thrust her from him, and scrambled out of the bed on to the floor, and still screaming put out his hand to the bone. It had blood on it from my hand. He paid no attention to me whatever. In truth I said nothing. This was a new turn indeed to the horrors of the evening. He rose from the floor with the bone in his hand, and stood silent. He seemed to be listening. 'Time, time, perhaps,' he muttered, and almost at the same moment fell at full length on the carpet, cutting his head against the fender. The bone flew from his hand and came to rest near the door. I picked Broughton up, haggard and broken, with blood over his face. He whispered hoarsely and quickly, 'Listen, listen!' We listened.

"After ten seconds' utter quiet, I seemed to hear something. I could not be sure, but at last there was no doubt. There was a quiet sound as of one moving along the passage. Little regular steps came towards us over the hard oak flooring. Broughton moved to where his wife sat, white and speechless, on the bed, and pressed her face into his shoulder.

"Then, the last thing that I could see as he turned the light out, he fell forward with his own head pressed into the pillow of the bed. Something in their company, something in their cowardice, helped me, and I faced the open doorway of the room, which was outlined fairly clearly against the dimly lighted passage. I put out one hand and touched Mrs. Broughton's shoulder in the darkness. But at the last moment I too failed. I sank on my knees and put my face in the bed. Only, we all heard. The footsteps came to the door, and there they stopped. The piece of bone was lying a yard inside the door. There was a rustle of moving stuff, and the thing was in the room. Mrs. Broughton was silent: I could hear Broughton's voice praying, muffled in the pillow: I was cursing my own cowardice. Then the steps moved out again on the oak boards of the passage, and I heard the sounds dying away. In a flash of remorse, I went to the door and looked out. There at the end of the corridor

was a small, bowed figure in a gray veil— I knew it only too well. But this time there was a pathos in the drooped head that left me standing with my forehead bowed in shame against the jamb of the door.

"'You can turn the light on,' I said, and there was an answering flare. There was no bone at my feet. Mrs. Broughton had fainted. Broughton was almost useless, and it took me ten minutes to bring her to. Broughton only said one thing worth remembering. For the most part he went on muttering prayers. But I was glad afterwards to recollect that he had said that thing. He said in a colorless voice, half as a question, half as a reproach, 'You didn't speak to her.'

"We spent the remainder of the night together. Mrs. Broughton actually fell off into a kind of sleep before dawn, but she suffered so horribly in her dreams that I shook her into consciousness again. Never was dawn so long in coming. Three or four times Broughton spoke to himself. Mrs. Broughton would then just tighten her hold on his arm, but she could say nothing. As for me, I can honestly say that I grew worse as the hours passed and the light strengthened. The two violent reactions had battered down my steadiness of view, and I felt that the foundations of my life had been built upon the sand. I said nothing, and after binding up my hand with a towel, I did not move. It was better so. They helped me and I helped them, and we all three knew that our reason had gone very near to ruin that night. At last, when the light came in pretty strongly, and the birds outside were chattering and singing, we felt that we must do something. Yet we never moved. You might have thought that we should particularly dislike being found as we were by the servants: yet nothing of the kind mattered a straw, and an overpowering listlessness bound us as we sat, until Chapman, Broughton's man, actually knocked and opened the door. None of us moved. Broughton, speaking hardly and stiffly, said: 'Chapman, you can come back in five minutes.' Chapman was a discreet man, but it would have made no difference if he had carried his news to the 'room' at once.

"We looked at each other and I said I

must go back. I meant to wait outside till Chapman returned. I simply dared not re-enter my bedroom alone. Broughton roused himself and said that he would come with me. Mrs. Broughton agreed to remain in her own room for five minutes if the blinds were drawn up and all the doors left open.

"So Broughton and I, leaning stiffly one against the other, went down to my room. By the morning light that filtered past the blinds we could see our way, and I released the blinds. There was nothing wrong in the room from end to end, except smears of my own blood on the bed, on the sofa, and on the carpet where I had torn the thing to pieces."

COLVIN HAD FINISHED his story. There was nothing to say. Seven bells stuttered out from the fo'c'sle, and the answering cry wailed through the darkness. I took him downstairs.

"Of course, I am much better now, but it is a kindness of you to let me sleep in your cabin."

💀 💀 💀

The frequently reprinted ghost story "Thurn-ley Abbey"—which M.R. James described as "almost too horrid"—first appeared in the October 1908 issue of McClure's Magazine. *The author expanded the story for his 1908 collection* Raw Edges, *from which this text is taken.*

British author, war correspondent (cov-ering the South African War for The Times*), world traveler, and lifelong friend of Rudyard Kipling, Perceval Landon (1868–1927) is per-haps best remembered today for a handful of terror tales, including "Mrs Rivers's Journal" (1908) and "Thurnley Abbey," which Ramsey Campbell called "that most terrifying of Eng-lish ghost stories."*

The Kipling Society remembers Landon for "his many travels in the wild places of the world, his uncomplaining endurance of dangers and discomforts, his magical tales, lightly told, and his shrewd criticism of Kipling's own work."

LOST RIVER BOYS

BY
DAVID SURFACE

I DON'T KNOW WHO BROUGHT THE FIRST GIFT DOWN TO THE CAVE. I'd heard about it but didn't want to believe it. One lonely gift-wrapped present sitting on the cold ground outside that deep, dark hole—it was too sad, too terrible to think about. But it was impossible *not* to think about.

That first Christmas was the hardest. No one could bring themselves to put up a tree or lights, except for Mary Davis. Her boy Jordan had loved Christmas. *What if he comes back*, she said, *and there's no tree, no lights? How will he know he's home?* No one had the heart to argue with that.

That's how it started. You spend so many years doing things for your kids, it's hard to stop. Besides, once one of us had done it, how could the rest of us just stand by and *not* do it?

There were a couple of video games that I'd bought for Billy a few months ago and hidden in the closet. I took them down and wrapped them in Christmas paper. Then I put on my winter coat and drove down to the cave.

There were a lot of cars parked along the road when I got there. I climbed down that steep trail and saw candles flickering in the darkness ahead of me. They were all there—Mary and Bill Davis, Betty and Randall Corwin, Elly and Robert Carver, and all the rest of us.

Today we keep the mouth of the cave clear and open as it was ten thousand years ago. No wire fence, no KEEP OUT signs—because there's no one left to keep out. We're a small town, barely a town at all, and when Billy went down into the cave that night, he took every boy in town with him. Every one.

The pile of presents was bigger than I'd expected. They weren't inside the mouth of the cave, but on the wide, flat shelf of limestone rock that led down into it. Big presents and little presents wrapped in bright, colorful wrapping paper covered with candy canes, Christmas trees, laughing Santa faces, and angels blowing long golden trumpets.

My legs felt heavy like I was walking through something thick and unyielding, but I pushed my way through it and walked over to that big, shiny pile and laid my gift down alongside the rest. I was just going to drive home and drink the pint of bourbon I'd bought this morning. Then I noticed that no one else was going anywhere. They were all standing around the presents like people gathered around a bonfire, waiting for something to happen.

Someone handed me a candle, the flame trembling in the cool breeze blowing from the mouth of the cave. We all stood there in the dark with our little candles, not speaking. I thought of pictures I'd seen in the news of men and women doing the same thing in New York City, in Israel, and other places. Always the same faces, always the same candles.

Then Mary Davis started to sing *Silent Night*. That thin, quavering voice stung me like an electrical shock. I could feel the candle in my hand, a drop of hot wax landing on my index finger and turning cool and hard while Mary sang. By the time she got halfway through, a few more voices had joined in. I sang too. How could I not?

When we were done, no one spoke. The air had turned cold, bitter cold, and I could see a few flakes drifting down from the darkness into the weak circle of light we made. Randall Carver put his hand on his wife's arm, turned her around, then they left first. Then the Bakers. Finally, we all turned around and started climbing the steep trail back up the ridge and away from the cave.

I didn't want to look back, but I couldn't help it. I'd thought that a whole pile of Christmas presents somehow wouldn't look as sad as one or two, but I was wrong. It was the saddest thing I'd ever seen in my life.

• • •

BOYS LOVE FORBIDDEN PLACES. Put a sign over the gates of Hell that says KEEP OUT and boys will run right into the fire, every time. A few warning signs and some chicken wire might keep out chickens, but it won't keep out young boys.

The first time Billy came home with that red clay all over his knees and elbows, I knew where he'd been. I was all set to punish him, then he started telling me about the things he'd seen down there. Rooms big as cathedrals. Snow-white fish with no eyes. Crickets big as dogs. I listened and knew he was making it up, but the longer he went on, the more I started to believe it. Not because I thought it was true, but because it made him happy, and that made me happy too.

That first Christmas when we all sang and left our presents at the cave, I went home and had a dream. In my dream I saw snow falling from the sky, each flake so perfect it looked like they were cut out of paper, like that snow you see in a school play. I watched it gather on the presents until they were all buried under a blanket of white.

The next morning I stopped by Johnson's for a cup of coffee and saw Elly Carver and Betty Corwin talking with Bud Johnson in the back of the store. Mary Davis was sitting at the orange formica table, not saying anything.

"What time did it happen?" I heard Bud Johnson ask.

"I don't know," Betty said, "She says she got there around eight o'clock."

"And she didn't see anyone?"

"No. No one."

At first I thought someone's house had been broken into. I walked over and Betty Corwin glared at me.

"They're gone," she whispered fiercely.

"Who?" I said.

"The presents. They're all gone."

Elly and Betty kept talking about how awful it was. *What kind of person would do something like that?* Bud Johnson talked about calling Sheriff Perkins, but in the end we decided that nothing had been stolen because the presents didn't really belong to anyone. The whole time, Mary Davis didn't say anything. She just kept sitting at that orange table, staring straight ahead like she was looking at something the rest of us couldn't see.

BILLY WAS THIRTEEN when we lost him. That's old enough to feel the things a man feels. But boys are slower to grow, slower to understand and realize things.

I'd noticed Kathy watching Billy long before he did. Letting her eyes linger on him a little longer, standing a little closer than she had to. Billy didn't notice, not at first, and when he finally did, I'm not sure he understood. He'd known her all his life which probably made it easier for him to not see her in the way that she was just beginning to see him.

Kathy ran with Billy's crowd, made it *her* crowd so she could be near him. She followed him everywhere, and on that night when Billy led those boys down into the cave, she went with him. They say that when the search parties found her and brought her out, she fought them. I even saw the scratches and bruises on her arms. That's the kind of love you have to admire, the kind that deserves a chance to grow.

One morning not long after that terrible night, I found a note in my mailbox, a piece of loose-leaf paper with two words written in a careful, childish hand. *I'm sorry.* Even though it wasn't signed, I knew who it was.

I found Kathy sitting alone in the lunchroom the way she had every day for the past six months. Her eyes grew wide when she saw me, and I saw her muscles tense like she was about to get up and run. Then she sank back into her seat, head down.

I slipped onto the bench next to her, careful not to sit too close. "Kathy, honey," I said, "You don't have anything to be sorry about."

That's when she started crying. It surprised me; I'd never seen her cry before, not even right after Billy had disappeared. She cried silently, but in that way that's impossible to hide, her mouth twisted and ugly like she was in pain.

My heart hurt for her, and I put my hand on her back and rubbed it in slow, comforting circles, the way I used to do for Billy when he was a baby. "Sweetheart, don't cry," I said. "It's not your fault." I knew how false my words must have felt to her. But in words of consolation, there's a greater truth at work. So I said them anyway.

Sometimes I wonder what would have happened if she and Billy had more time. Maybe it's not a proper thing for a mother to wonder about, but I can't help it. We all want our sons to be happy. Even when it's too late for that.

THAT NEXT CHRISTMAS, we did it all over again. We brought our presents down to the mouth of the cave, lit our candles, and sang. Before we left, there was some talk about last year, about whether or not the same thing might happen. Bill Davis got angry and said he was going to wait up all night with his shotgun and shoot the first son of a bitch who put his hands on those presents. As soon as he said it, Mary Davis grabbed her husband's arm like he was already pointing the shotgun and cried out, *"No!"*

That's when I knew. That's when we all knew what we'd been thinking deep down inside but didn't have the nerve to say. Can you blame us? Even Christ's disciples when they saw his tomb empty didn't realize what it meant at first. We were no different.

I went home and dreamed that we were all standing outside the cave. The snow was falling like bits of lace and we were singing. I couldn't hear the words, and the melody was unclear, but I could feel the sound of it swelling inside my chest and rise in my throat and come pouring from my mouth. It was the most wonderful thing I'd ever felt. I could see a light inside the cave, not from a lantern or a fire, but like the air itself was made of light, the way the sky just before sunrise looks swollen with it. The light inside the cave was pulsing, and I realized it was pulsing in time with our singing, and the louder we sang, the brighter it grew.

The next morning the presents were gone.

At first, there was some talk about going to the authorities and asking them to search the cave, but it never got any farther than that. The authorities had come and gone the year before, the cave had been searched and the search had been called off. What were we supposed to tell them now? What could we say that anyone else would believe? We could pretend it never happened. Or we could just keep going.

And for three more winters, that's what we did. The presents and the candles and the singing. I think it's fair to say that those were the last happy years of my life. And even though I can only speak for myself, I think it was probably true for all of us.

You might wonder how we could just go on like that and never talk about what was happening and what it meant. Once in a while, some of us would start down that road, but never very far. There was no need to. When something is perfect, why question it?

Then, in the fifth year, it stopped. The next day, and the next, and the next, the presents sat there on the cold, hard ground. They stayed there until the bright paper started to wrinkle and sag in the cold and the freezing rain. Mary Davis ignored our warnings and took to sitting up all night on the ridge above the cave until her husband would come and take her home.

For me, it felt like losing Billy all over again. The past four years had been a sort of gift, a period of grace I could never have asked for or imagined. I'd never thought of it stopping, but now it had, and all the grief that was left over from that terrible time five years before came rushing to the surface.

Every morning when I stepped outside, I saw the same houses, the same roads stretching back and forth to the same places. But it had all changed. Everything looked ugly to me now, flat and lifeless like a bad painting of itself. It may be that miracles run their course like a human life, and that it's no one's fault when they end. But that's not how this felt. I felt like I'd been tricked. When I looked at the people I saw on the street or in the stores or at work, I wondered if they felt like I did. How could they all act like nothing had changed?

ONE THURSDAY IN LATE OCTOBER I showed up at Johnston's for my morning cup of coffee and found the door locked. I figured Bud was just late for some reason, but when I dropped by that afternoon on my way home from school, the place was still closed.

Later, Betty told me that Bud Johnson's daughter Courtney had gone missing. Bud had called the sheriff around eight o'clock saying that Courtney had not come home from school. Like her father, Courtney Johnson ran her days and nights like clockwork; up at six thirty, out the door by seven, home by four. Bud had called all her friends, working his way down that list until there was no one left.

Because he had no sons, Bud had not been part of our little town's tragedy five years ago. Those of us who'd lost our boys in that cave had been cut off from our neighbors who had only daughters and had escaped our particular kind of grief. Now, Bud Johnson began to fade away right before our eyes. After a while, people simply no longer knew what to say or how to act around him, so they took to avoiding him. I did too. I'm not proud of it. But I'm no better than anyone else.

Then Rebecca Wallace disappeared in early December. A search party found her shirt in the woods about forty yards from the trail that runs from the back of Bud Johnson's store to the old quarry. All the buttons were missing, indicating that it had been torn off. Broken branches and disturbances on the forest floor were consistent with a struggle. That was the phrase the Maysville paper used—*consistent with a struggle*. One word, cold and scientific. The other, raw and terrible.

Kaitlin Simmons disappeared next. This time, unlike the other two girls before her, someone saw her being taken.

Kaitlin's brother Orin, who was four years old at the time, said he saw it happen. Because he was only four, and because the things he said were so odd, few were inclined to believe him.

Kaitlin had taken her baby brother and their dog for a walk in the woods just after supper like they did every night. Orin said that at one point the dog started baying and howling and took off into the woods after something. When police questioned him, Orin said he saw his sister struggling with someone, though he couldn't identify the figure because its hair was long and covered its face. When asked how he knew the figure was male, the boy said *because it was naked.*

State police combed the woods around Lost River and even entered the cave as far back as they could go, but there was no sign of Kaitlin or the other two girls. A homeless man was found living in a shelter he'd built out of cardboard boxes and tree branches about a half-mile out of town, was brought in for questioning and then taken away. For a while, people felt safer and started letting their girls go out again after dark.

"You know why they didn't find anything in that cave?" Betty Corwin said when I saw her at Johnson's one Friday morning. "They didn't go back far enough."

"You think those girls are down there?" I asked. Betty didn't answer but squinted fiercely out the back window into the green leaves at something beyond them.

That night I spent hours on the computer looking at maps of caves. I knew how large the network of caves under us was, but seeing it laid out in graphs and grids made me feel uneasy. It's strange to think that while we're busy at our jobs or in our kitchens making supper or resting in our beds at night, there's a whole world right below us, one that's been there for a million years and will still be there for another million years after we're dead and gone.

I thought again of the wild stories Billy used to tell about his journeys down into the cave and the things he'd seen there. He used to draw pictures of his explorations and had once shown me a whole roll of wrapping paper that he'd covered with a map and illustrations. I remember how he'd come back from one of his underground journeys with his pants torn and muddy, how he'd spread that big roll of paper out on the floor and lay there gripping a pencil in his hand, adding a new tunnel, a new chamber, a new part of that secret world he loved.

I went into Billy's room and reached up to the back of the closet shelf until my fingers touched something that felt like a scroll. I took it down, feeling like a thief, peeled off the rubber band and started unrolling it.

Seeing Billy's drawings and handwriting again made my heart hurt for a moment, but I shut my eyes, took a deep breath, then made myself look again. I'd forgotten how good his drawings were. Here again was the proof. Scaly, eyeless creatures with fins like dragon's wings, towering waterfalls high as skyscrapers with tiny human figures for scale, and below each drawing, in Billy's careful script, names like *Blind Ghost Fish, Hall of Forgotten Voices,* and *Tunnel of No Turning Back.*

I unrolled the scroll further. In the center

of the map was a drawing of a naked girl with her legs spread far apart. Standing between her thighs and towering above her was some kind of man-like creature, his enormous phallus buried half inside her. The girl's head was thrown back and Billy had drawn her mouth stretched wide open in what could have been a howl of pleasure or agony. The man-creature's teeth were bare and clenched, and rays of light were shooting out of his eyes.

I shoved that scroll as far back as I could into the closet shelf, then sat there at the kitchen table with the blood pounding in my ears, trying to get that picture out of my head. Behind my eyes was an empty space slowly filling with a new thought, one that had been there all along trying to get in.

When Billy was eleven, I'd given him one of those action figures for Christmas, the same ones I'd been giving him since he was four or five. A few weeks later I'd found it sticking out of the trash can in his room. When I asked about it, he said, *I'm too old for that now, Mom.* I'd thought he was just being silly. But when I looked at him and saw how his face was starting to change, grow-ing harder and leaner, I knew he was right. There it was, right in front of me every day, and I'd missed it.

The next morning I met Betty Corwin at Johnson's before heading in to work. We sat at the orange formica table in back with steam rising from our big styrofoam cups.

"How old would the boys be now?" I asked.

Betty's expression was startled, almost angry.

"Fifteen, I guess," she said, her lips tight and her voice flat. "Maybe sixteen."

"Seventeen," I said. "Almost eighteen."

Betty looked at me, waiting for me to go on.

"Betty," I said after a while, "Did Neal... did he ever have a girlfriend? A girl he liked?"

Betty kept looking me in the eye but I could see something inside her flinch. "Rebecca," she finally said in a low, clipped voice, as if saying the names of the missing was disrespectful or unlucky. "Rebecca Wallace."

"Do you think... do you think they ever...?"

"No," she said, shaking her head and glancing away, "He was... he was too young for that."

"What about now?"

Betty looked back at me, her eyes wide and fearful.

"Now?" she whispered.

"Yes."

Betty kept staring at me, her eyes filling with a fear I recognized. For a moment I wasn't sure if she was going to start crying or slap my face. Suddenly she was on her feet, grabbing at her coat. "I have to go," she said, her voice tight and strained.

"Betty, wait..." I said, reaching up to touch her arm. She flailed out and knocked my hand away.

"No!" she hissed, her face angry and terrified. "You're crazy! What the hell is wrong with you? Stay away from me!" She walked away fast and didn't turn around again. A moment later I heard the screen door slam.

I thought about following her and telling her I was sorry. But I wasn't sorry. I hadn't even known what I was going to say until I'd said it. Now it was out there and I couldn't take it back. I wasn't sorry. I was angry. Angry at myself for not understanding. Like Christ's disciples, like young boys, we're all too slow to realize the truth of things.

THAT WAS THE SUMMER when Kathy came back home. I knew her the moment I saw her. Taller now, the same chestnut hair covering that same sad, cautious face. She was eighteen now, and in college, which was hard to get used to, although it was right there in front of my eyes. The legs that seemed longer than possible, the sudden and alarming breasts. And above it all, those same sad eyes. She surprised me by pulling a bottle of wine out of her backpack. Red, which I don't like, but for her sake I brought out two glasses and we sat at my kitchen table and drank it while the light outside turned rosy and dim.

We spoke of the usual things that a young woman and an old woman talk about. Her mother who was ill. College, which I'd heard was not going well for her, and which she did not bother to hide from me. We still had not spoken of Billy. I was waiting for her to be ready.

After our second glass, she finally said his name. "Do you think Billy suffered?"

He's suffering now, is what I wanted to say, but didn't. She wasn't ready for that yet.

So I poured her another glass and told the story I'd prepared, the one about the light in the cave. Children had seen it, I told her, a light hovering in the darkness far back in the mouth of the cave like the glow of a candle that had broken free, drifting on its own. Sometimes motionless, other times moving like a dandelion seed caught in an invisible current of air.

"Have *you* seen it?" she asked. Her face looked thirteen again, the years washed away by the wine and the fading light. I couldn't risk her going away again. I could tell she was almost there. Almost ready.

"Yes."

I saw the word hit her like a blow, but the look in her eyes was more hopeful than fearful. She asked me if I was frightened when I saw the light and I told her no, no I wasn't. I told her that the light was warm and peaceful and comforting and every other good thing I could think of. When she finally said that she wanted to see it too, I thought *Of course. Of course you do.*

I told her we should go right now while the spirit was on us. But first, I asked her if she wanted to wash up a little. She'd driven a long way, hadn't she? Yes, she said, she had, so I led her to the bathroom and gave her a clean washcloth and a hairbrush to use, sweet-smelling lotions for her skin. I stood in the hallway and watched her brushing her long dark hair until it was almost shining.

I told her to stay close to me when we climbed down the steep trail into the gorge, but of course she knew the way in the dark as well as I did. We reached the limestone ledge at the edge of the river. I could feel the cave breathing its wet, cold breath over my skin. I knew she could feel it too because I could see her hair lifting in the breeze that was pouring up from underground.

"Is this where it happens?" she asked.

Yes, I thought, *Yes. This is where it happens.*

My heart was hammering so hard in my chest that I couldn't trust myself to speak, so I raised my arm and pointed into the darkness that yawned in front of us. We were both silent for a long while, and in the silence I could feel her looking, searching. When she spoke again, still in a whisper, I could hear the rasp of heartbreak in it, and it nearly killed me.

"I don't see it."

"Go a little closer," I said. She turned toward me and, even in the dark, I thought I saw a flash of fear in her eyes. "It's okay," I said, smiling as best I could. She looked back toward the cave and I could feel her hesitate. I put my hand on her warm, bare arm. It wasn't a push, not really, but it was enough to make her take a step toward that black opening in front of us, then another.

Just before she stepped inside the mouth of the cavern, she paused one last time. "Go on," I said.

She turned once more and looked back at me. I could see the pale oval of her face, like the face of a young deer or a calf in a dark barn. And that's when I realized that she knew. She knew what this was. She knew and she didn't run.

For a moment, I thought I saw a light glimmering in the darkness behind her where I knew there could be no light. Then the darkness slipped around her like a cloak and she was gone.

I turned my back and walked away, back up that winding trail in the dark. I don't remember how I got back, just branches coming out of the blackness to claw at my face and arms, the moon racing overhead behind the trees, following me. When I finally reached the top and saw my car still there, waiting for me, and that empty passenger seat, I bent over and was sick by the side of the road, vomiting out the wine we'd drunk and whatever else was left inside of me.

And that's how I felt for a few days afterward. Empty. Like I'd emptied myself of the thing that had been killing me and was now just waiting for something new to take its place.

The police came with their questions

and their stern, sad faces. What was her car doing in my driveway? When had I last seen her? I told them that she'd come to visit, that we'd talked for a while, then she'd gone for a walk. All of that was true. A few days later her face started appearing on flyers on the post office bulletin board and in store windows. *Don't waste your time,* I wanted to say. All those empty plans for the future, college, a family and a home far from here, were a mistake, an illusion. Her path led back to this place, toward a greater purpose. In the end, she had seen that. It was what she wanted.

All of our old girls are gone now, the ones who were around in the beginning. They've disappeared or been taken away by their parents to safer places, far from this one. I don't blame them. People protect their own. That too is part of the way things are.

Still, nature provides. More and more new families are moving here, drawn to the mountains, and the wildflowers, and the cool blue-green river that runs through it like a dream. It draws them, and they come. Like the family who just moved here from Maysville. They have three daughters, six, seven, and nine. Strong as heifers, they climb trees, throw rocks, and aren't afraid of anything under the sun. Their mother shakes her head and smiles, "They may not look like much, but they're going to make fine wives and mothers one day."

And I think, *Yes, they will. Oh yes. They will.*

David Surface is the author of the collection Terrible Things *from Black Shuck Books. His stories have appeared in* Shadows & Tall Trees, Supernatural Tales, Nightscript, The Tenth Black Book of Horror, Phantom Drift, Morpheus Tales, Twisted Book of Shadows, Uncertainties III, *and* The Best Horror of the Year, Volume 13. *A YA supernatural suspense novel co-written with Julia Rust,* Angel Falls, *is now available from Haverhill House Publishing's YAP imprint. David is also the author of the newsletter STRANGE LITTLE STORIES. To learn more about David and his writing, visit davidsurface.net*

www.ingramcontent.com/pod-product-compliance
Lightning Source LLC
Chambersburg PA
CBHW080744250626
47162CB00010B/3017